WELCOME TO HOLLYHOCK FARM

GEORGINA TROY

First published in Great Britain in 2024 by Boldwood Books Ltd.

Cover Design by Lizzie Gardiner

Cover Illustration: Shutterstock

A CIP catalogue record for this book is available from the British Library.

Paperback ISBN 978-1-78513-760-0

Large Print ISBN 978-1-78513-756-3

Hardback ISBN 978-1-78513-755-6

Ebook ISBN 978-1-78513-753-2

Kindle ISBN 978-1-78513-754-9

Audio CD ISBN 978-1-78513-761-7

MP3 CD ISBN 978-1-78513-758-7

Digital audio download ISBN 978-1-78513-752-5

Boldwood Books Ltd
23 Bowerdean Street
London SW6 3TN
www.boldwoodbooks.com

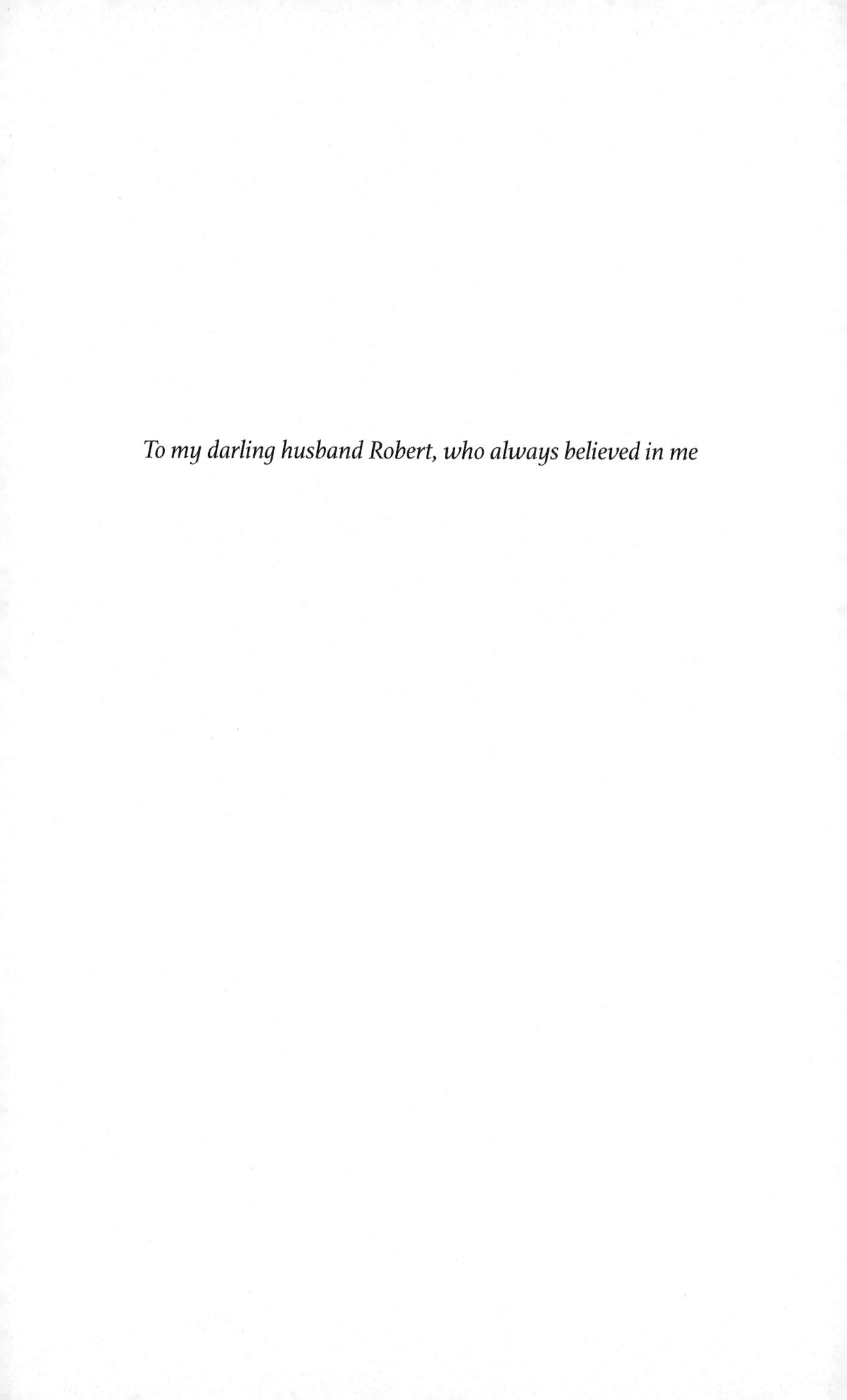

To my darling husband Robert, who always believed in me

1

LETTIE

April

Lettie closed her eyes, relishing the warm early-morning sun on her face as she contemplated what to do next. This was her happy place where she had the time and space to think through all that had happened over the past few weeks, and nothing could beat it. She had missed coming to lie in the long dewy grass among the daisies and buttercups. This was her favourite meadow. She stretched out her right arm until her fingertips were cooled by the water in the stream that ran through several fields in Hollyhock Farm.

Finally, after a long, cold and mostly wet winter, April seemed to have finally arrived in all its blossom-filled glory. This was the first day for months that the weather would have been warm enough for her to lie like this without freezing or getting wet. The nearby fields were humming with voices and engines as workers – some driving tractors – and her father continued to harvest the Jersey Royal potatoes the island was famous for. Lettie knew April to June was the busiest and most vital time of year for her parents' farm as the harvest continued and precious small, buttery potatoes were packed up, the majority taken to the harbour ready to be shipped to the English mainland and sold.

She loved Hollyhock Farm, with its pink granite farmhouse, sunny yard and outbuildings surrounded on three sides by fields. These wild meadows and woodland had been the only home she had known until leaving the island five years before to study fashion at Loughborough University.

It made a pleasant change being back here with the only sound being the occasional seagull or pigeon, and she hadn't realised how much she had needed this week's break back on the island.

Lettie moved her hand above her face and closed her eyes as droplets of water splashed down onto her warm skin. She was single for the first time in two and a half years and although she had initially been delighted when Scott had joined the fashion house in the accounts department, discovering another side to him at work had soured their relationship and slowly his behaviour had worsened towards her, with him becoming jealous and more controlling of her until she had felt she had little choice but to end things with him. She had been surprised to discover that it hadn't been nearly as difficult to get over her first great romance as she had expected. At least during this visit to the farm she didn't have to spend the majority of her time pandering to him so that his rudeness didn't annoy her parents.

'Lettie, where the hell are you?'

She groaned, hearing her brother's voice in the distance. It wasn't like Zac to be up this early or be staying at the farm, but there had been issues with the boiler in his flat and their mother had insisted he come to stay with them for a few days while it was fixed. Lettie loved him but could have done with more time to herself. What did he want? She decided to ignore him for a bit, wanting to enjoy her peace for as long as possible.

'Lettie, will you answer me?' She could hear his footsteps

coming closer to her. 'I know you're lying down in that damp grass again.'

'For goodness' sake.' She gritted her teeth, aware he clearly had no intention of giving up until he had found her. She sat up and looked in the direction his voice had come from but couldn't see him. 'What do you want?'

Zac didn't reply and she let herself hope that he had gone back to the farmhouse. She lay back down and closed her eyes. He probably wanted her to go and eat breakfast but she wasn't very hungry, having got used to missing breakfast since living in the UK. It was something that exasperated her mother, who had always taken pride in the delicious meals she'd cooked them when they lived at home.

A shadow fell over her face and, opening her eyes, Lettie peered up at her brother's scowling face. Lettie groaned. 'What is it?'

'Mum has cooked breakfast.'

'I'm not hungry.' She closed her eyes again suspecting her brother had been given instructions not to return to the kitchen without her.

'You know as well as I do that isn't an acceptable excuse as far as Mum is concerned. Now get up. I'm starving.'

Lettie sighed, aware that she had little choice but to do as her mother asked. 'Fine.' She got up and accompanied him through the long grass, stopping to pick several wildflowers to put into a small vase for her bedroom windowsill. 'You'd think Mum would trust us to eat properly at our age, wouldn't you?'

'I guess. Unlike you though, I'm glad she still likes cooking for us.'

'I suppose I am, too,' she admitted as her stomach growled noisily. Maybe she was hungrier than she'd thought.

They passed the top field where earlier that morning their father had finished ploughing.

Lettie stopped and watched seagulls congregating on the rich, dark soil and was reminded how peaceful life usually was here on the farm.

'Hurry up, sis,' Zac moaned, walking a bit faster. 'I prefer my cooked breakfast hot and anyway I have work to do.'

She followed him across the dusty yard. 'I thought you were on holiday.'

'I'm working remotely this week and—' he checked his watch '—I have a Zoom call in a couple of hours, so please, let's get a move on.'

'Why didn't you say that in the first place.' Her brother's lousy communication skills hadn't improved, she noted, despite being well thought of as a sound engineer. Maybe it was because he spent more time working on a computer than speaking to people.

'Where were you?' their father grumbled before biting into a piece of buttered toast. 'Down by the stream, I suppose.'

'Right – first time.' Zac pulled out his chair and plonked himself down, immediately reaching for some toast.

'It's the first opportunity I've had to spend time there since I was last here,' Lettie said, sitting down. She smiled gratefully at her mother as she placed a plateful of perfectly cooked eggs, bacon, tomato, sausage and mushrooms in front of her. 'This looks and smells delicious, Mum. Thank you.'

Her mother kissed the top of Lettie's head. 'I love having both my chicks back home again.'

Their father gave an amused snort. 'I would if they did more to help around the place.'

'We all know you're just as happy to have them back again, Gareth Torel, so don't waste your time pretending otherwise.'

'I can't get much past you, Lindy. Can I?'

'I hope not.' She narrowed her eyes at him, but Lettie saw the amusement in them. She loved that her parents were still close. So many of her friends' parents had divorced and she couldn't imagine how it must feel to have to split your time between two households, especially if the divorce had been a difficult one.

Lindy winked at Lettie. 'I've got more bread in the toaster, so you can help yourself to the last couple of pieces in the toast rack.'

Before Lettie had a chance to take one, Zac reached out and took the last two pieces, dropping them triumphantly onto his side plate.

It was something he had liked to do when they were growing up, knowing it would irritate her. 'I don't think so.' Lettie snatched one back and began buttering it, ignoring his protests.

'Don't fight with your sister,' their father said. 'We're not used to the pair of you bickering like a couple of teenagers any more.'

Lettie thought back to the old days before she and Zac left home to follow their careers. It must have seemed strange for their parents to go from four of them living in the large farmhouse down to just the pair of them.

Pushing away any guilty feelings, Lettie picked up the large blue-and-white teapot her mother always used and poured the two of them mugs of tea. 'You want another one, Mum?'

Her mother shook her head. 'I'm fine for now thanks, love.'

Lettie watched her mother for a few seconds. She might be in her early fifties, but she was still youthful, probably because she was fit from helping out on the farm in all weathers over the years. She knew her mother had initially found the transition from fashion model to farmer's wife very difficult, especially as the two worlds were poles apart. Lettie recalled asking her mother about it and had been cheered to hear her say it had all been worth it and that she had already grown tired of modelling when she had met and fallen in love with Gareth. Hearing her mother speak of her years in fashion had deterred Lettie from wanting to do the same and instead she'd forged a career brand-building for the fashion house where she ended up finding work.

She realised her father seemed preoccupied. 'Something wrong, Dad?'

He looked at her but didn't reply.

Lettie caught a strange glance being passed between her parents. There was something going on – she was certain of it. But what?

Her mother wasn't eating and Lettie presumed she must have finished hers earlier. At least she hoped that was the case and that nothing was the matter. Studying her mother's face, Lettie couldn't help suspecting that something was amiss. She would ask her about it later when the two of them were alone. Aware her mother was waiting for them to eat their breakfast, and deciding that her parents would tell her and Zac whatever was on their minds when they were ready, Lettie began eating her food.

'This is delicious, as always, Mum.' Her mother's food was always the best. It didn't matter how many cafés or restaurants she had visited in England, she had yet to sample a tastier cooked breakfast or roast dinner than those made by her mother. She supposed it was almost three decades of practice that helped, or maybe it was simply that her mother had the knack of cooking delicious food. 'It's good to be enjoying home-cooked food again,' she said, almost to herself.

'It is,' Zac agreed in between mouthfuls. 'You're the best cook ever, Mum. It's good to be home.'

'Aww, thank you.' Lindy ruffled their hair and sighed happily.

Lettie was glad she had come home after her mother had mentioned it was about time she visited the farm again. She had planned to return to the island a few months before but then her relationship with Scott had deteriorated and she hadn't wanted her parents to see her looking strained and miserable. Instead she had focused on her work as an assistant to one of the upcoming designers, which kept her busy. Anyway, she had told herself, her parents were always on the farm so there was no urgency to rush back to the island. Her mother had never mentioned about her coming home before and Lettie wasn't sure why she was insistent this time. Was it because she simply missed her and Zac? Maybe it was because Lettie usually made plans to return as soon as the weather improved? Either way, she was happy she had listened.

'It doesn't matter how amazing some of the places are that I visit for work, nothing will ever beat Hollyhock Farm for me,' Zac said, a dreamy expression on his face.

'It's true,' Lettie insisted. 'There's something special about being here where everything is familiar.'

Again her father gave her mother a strange look.

Unable to wait a moment longer, Lettie lowered her cutlery and set it neatly on her plate. 'What's up with you both?'

'What do you mean?' her mother said, sounding suspiciously guilty.

'I've seen you giving each other meaningful glances,' Lettie said, shooting a questioning look at Zac in case he had some idea why the atmosphere was so odd this morning. 'And that's why I'm asking you.'

'I hadn't noticed anything.' Zac frowned. 'But now I'm worried there's something wrong.'

'Lindy, I think the time has come,' their father said. 'You'd better take a seat.'

Lettie realised her mouth had gone dry and anxiously took a mouthful of her tea. She wished they would hurry up and let Zac and her in on whatever was going on.

As soon as their mother was seated next to their father, she gave him a nod.

'Your mother and I have been making a few plans.' He paused, seeming at a loss for words, then after exchanging a serious look with their mother, he frowned and continued, 'We've decided to sell most of the land and therefore the business. I've given your Uncle Leonard first refusal and he's considering it.'

Lettie wasn't sure if she had heard him correctly. Surely he couldn't have said what she thought he had. 'Sorry, what?'

Her father repeated what he had just told them. 'Your uncle has always talked about increasing the size of his farm and what better way than to take on mine? He just needs to work out his finances first though.'

'But you've worked so hard for years building the organic side of the farm. How can you just walk away from it?' Zac gasped. 'Dad, you can't do that.'

Their father looked sympathetic. 'I can, Zac. And what's more, I am going to do it. Your mother and I have talked about this for months now and we've made the decision together.'

He wasn't kidding, Lettie realised with shock. 'But why?' Lettie turned her attention to her mother. 'Mum? Surely you're not happy with this – not really? You've always been so happy at the farm. Haven't you?'

'I have loved our time here, Lettie.'

'Letts, I don't think they're serious about this.' Zac puffed out his cheeks. 'Surely this is a joke.'

'We'd hardly joke about our livelihood.' Their father patted their mother's hand before taking another drink from his mug.

How could he talk so calmly about such a monumental decision? 'But, Dad, I thought you loved what you did,' Lettie said.

He shrugged. 'I did, most of the time. But now I'm tired of the early mornings, late evenings and the responsibility I've had all my adult life.' He smiled at their mother before addressing them again. 'I want to relax a bit. *We* want to. We've lost a few friends this past year and it's brought home to your mother and me that we need to make the most of what time we have left.'

Zac dropped his fork. 'You're talking as if you're both old.'

'The trouble is, Zac, that our friends weren't old either and it's made us re-evaluate our lives. We want to be free to take time to do what suits us when it suits us. Travel more.' He took their mother's hand in his. 'Don't you think we deserve this?'

Lettie couldn't miss the undertone of his question. He had worked hard all his life, as had their mother. They had been amazing parents, always giving her and Zac whatever they could afford and had always being there for them. Now their father was waiting to hear whether she and Zac appreciated all that they had done for them. She thought of the long hours and cold and wet winter months when their father had been out in all weathers looking after his fields and the various animals. Their parents' hard work had put her and her brother through school, given them a comfortable home and although they hadn't often been able to take family holidays, they had always eaten well and grown up in a close-knit and happy environment.

'You deserve this more than anyone else I know,' she replied honestly. 'You both do.' She smiled at her mother to include her. 'I suppose I'm just shocked that's all. I never imagined you'd ever be able to part with your livestock, let alone choose to sell them.'

'Yeah, Lettie's right. I think we're both a bit shocked; that's all, Dad.' Zac swapped glances with Lettie and she could see he was as stunned by the news as her.

'And you've definitely made up your minds?' Lettie dared ask, willing her father to say otherwise.

'We have. My brother will always look after the animals, so it's not as if I'll need to worry about them. And as I said before, your mother and I want to travel more.' He sighed. 'I'm not really sure I understand why you both seem so upset.'

'You don't?' Lettie couldn't believe he was taken aback by their reactions.

'Let's face it, it's not as if either of you ever showed any interest in wanting to take over the running of this place, is it?'

Lettie couldn't miss the regret in their father's voice. Neither she nor her brother had returned to the farm after leaving for university, apart from the occasional holiday. Each time her visits had come to an end, she had struggled to leave Jersey. She loved it here and realised that her reasons for not coming home more often weren't because she didn't like it here, but because she found it so upsetting to leave. It was easier not to come back.

'I blame myself for that though, Gareth,' Lindy said stroking his arm. 'Maybe if I hadn't constantly encouraged the children to travel as much as they possibly could, then one of them might have settled here.'

'I'm back living here though, don't forget,' Zac said.

'But not as a farmer.'

Their father was right. Zac was continuing doing what he loved most, being a sound engineer.

A thought occurred to Lettie. Maybe this was a sign for her, an answer to her current situation that had been causing her so much worry.

Her mother gave her a sympathetic smile. 'You mustn't feel badly either of you. You both love your careers and it's not as if Lettie can continue working for one of the bigger fashion houses in London if she's living here.'

Lettie was grateful for her mum's support. 'I can't get over that you want to sell the land though, Dad. I assumed you'd be running Hollyhock Farm for—' she thought for a moment '—I don't know, another ten to fifteen years.'

'Yeah, Dad. Same here. You've never mentioned about wanting to do anything else before now.'

Lettie saw Zac look at her to check he was right.

'It's true, Dad,' she said to back him up. 'This really isn't something either of us could have seen coming.'

'I did enjoy it, for a very long time.'

'But then why are you selling? Why not just get someone in to manage the place while you take a holiday?' She felt like she had tripped and fallen into some sort of strange parallel universe where everything was topsy-turvy.

Their mother groaned. 'I'm sorry, Gareth,' she said. 'I know you didn't want to say anything to the kids about it but they need to understand our reasons behind this decision.'

'No, Lindy.'

'Yes. They deserve to know. They're old enough and have independent lives and it's not as if they rely on us for anything.'

Lettie's stomach churned as anxiety coursed through her. 'What's the matter?' she asked, unsure whether her mother was correct and if she actually was ready to hear what she sensed was bad news. She swapped a worried glance with her brother.

'I knew it,' Zac said. 'You've been hiding something from us, haven't you?'

Lindy nudged her husband. 'Are you going to tell them, or should I?'

He scowled at her. 'You started this off, so you can do it.'

Zac stood. 'I don't care who tells us, but I wish one of you would hurry up and do it.'

'Do sit down, Zac.' Their mother indicated the chair. 'Your father is fine now,' she began. 'But he had a slight heart attack.'

Lettie gasped. 'Is there such a thing?'

'It seems so. He's fine, mostly.'

'What's that supposed to mean?' Lettie felt her own heart race.

'It means,' their father said calmly, 'that I've been advised to change my lifestyle. No more fry-ups, and less stress.'

But hadn't they just had a fry-up? She glanced at his plate and hers.

'Your father only had poached eggs with grilled tomatoes and mushrooms,' their mother said in answer to Lettie's unasked question.

Feeling terrible for having a go at him earlier, Lettie apologised, hurried over to stand behind his chair, slipped her arms around his neck and hugged him. 'Sorry, Dad, I shouldn't have been so quick to criticise you before. I was shocked about you thinking of selling the land – that's all.'

'Me, too,' Zac agreed.

'It's not just that,' Gareth continued. 'You know as well as I do that looking after animals is a full-time thing. Going away always takes a lot of planning and with neither of you around much, well it's not as if I can rely on either of you to step in at short notice.'

She realised guiltily that he was right. 'Oh, Dad.'

'I would never mind coming to stay here if you went away,' Zac said, clearly hurt by his father's accusation.

'But you already work full-time, Zac, so it wouldn't really be viable to expect you to take care of the farm too.' Lindy took Gareth's hand. 'Your father's right. We deserve some time for ourselves now you two are older and before we get too old to enjoy some of the fun things we want to do.'

Lettie felt like her world had turned on its axis. She stared at her parents, amazed they seemed so calm about having made such a monumental decision. She desperately wanted to help them, and unlike Zac she might be in a position to do so.

'But selling the land from Hollyhock Farm?' She heard the catch in her voice as her emotions almost got the better of her. 'It won't really be a farm any more if you do that.'

Her father finished his drink and set his empty mug back down onto the table. 'That can't be helped, I'm afraid.'

'She's right though,' Zac said, his tone flat and his misery obvious.

'All right, Lettie, what do you suggest we do?' her mother replied. 'I can see you've got something on your mind.'

Lettie's mind raced, her thoughts scrambled as she tried desperately to come up with a sensible solution. She had thought life couldn't get more perfect when she had been given her job working on promotions for the fashion house over the past two years – well, at least until things had started to go wrong between her and Scott. And then there was the meeting she had been called into the previous week. She hadn't shared what had happened with her family yet, not wishing to worry them. And now this had happened. She couldn't bear to stand by and watch her beloved fields being sold. The solution came to her unexpectedly and took her by surprise.

'I'll take over farming it.' Yes, she decided, that's what she would do.

No one spoke. Even Zac didn't make a smart comment for once. She looked from one to the other of her family, hurt by their stunned expressions. 'It's not that silly a suggestion.'

Her father stared at her as if she had just announced she had sprouted wings. Closing his mouth, he thought for a moment before speaking. 'Lettie, when was the last time you did anything other than help muck out? And even then, you had to be asked to do it, rather than noticing for yourself that the work needed doing.'

She tried to think. It had been a long time. Last summer, in fact, and she hadn't been thrilled to help clean out the mucky barn, especially during a heatwave. 'That's true. But I've grown up here surrounded by these animals, by these views, knowing the fields, stream and trees are here whenever I want to enjoy them, and I can't bear the thought of them going.'

Her father rested his large hand over hers. 'I know this has come as a big shock, but your mother and I have reached the conclusion that this is the only sensible way forward.'

'It's a generous offer, Lettie,' her mother said, her hand resting on her heart. 'And we love you for making it, but we could never let you give up all you've worked for to leave your wonderful life in London.'

Zac gave her a confused look. 'What are you on about, Letts?' He leant back in his chair and looked at their parents. 'I can't understand why you didn't tell us you were considering doing this.' Zac sighed. 'Or, more importantly, that you'd been ill. We might have been able to help in some way.'

Lettie looked at the remainder of her fried egg congealing slowly on her plate next to the uneaten rasher of bacon. Her appetite had vanished and she wished she had thought to finish her food before pushing her parents to share what was going on.

'But what about my suggestion?' Lettie reminded them.

'We wouldn't hear of it,' her mother said, frowning. 'Your father doesn't want either of you to feel shackled to this place,' she explained. 'Isn't that right, Gareth?'

'It is. You both know Uncle Leonard and I inherited our two farms from our father and his brother, and although we've both loved our lives here, I have to admit that at times I felt restricted by feeling obliged to carrying on the family farm. I never wanted either of you to feel that way. Which is why I decided...' He reached out and took Lindy's hand in his. 'We decided after many very long discussions that your uncle should be given first refusal to buy the land and take on the stock and animals.'

Lettie loved her uncle and thought about his twin sons, Adam and Damon. 'But surely he'll only be in the same position as you at some point?'

Her mother frowned. 'Why do you say that?'

'Because Adam works in finance and Damon has been away

travelling for the best part of two years. Neither of them have shown much interest in farming either, have they?'

Their father shook his head. 'That's for Uncle Len to work out, not me. Anyway he mentioned something about Damon coming back to the island in the next few months, so maybe he's planning on joining his father on their farm.'

Or taking over *their* parents' farm, she mused with irritation.

Now their parents had explained the situation, Lettie understood their reasoning far better, not that it lessened her frustration that they clearly hadn't taken her offer seriously.

Her mother rose and, after checking everyone had finished eating, began clearing the plates.

'It's OK, Mum,' Lettie said. 'Zac and I can do this. You and Dad go and relax. Leave this to us.'

She busied herself clearing the table as her parents left the room. As soon as they'd closed the door behind them, Lettie, irritated to have been dismissed, turned on the taps and squirted washing-up liquid into the large Belfast sink. Were her parents right to ignore her suggestion? Did she really want to take over the running of the farm? She closed her eyes for a moment, trying to focus on her true feelings. Her heart said that yes, she did want to, very much. Practically though, she had grown up seeing her father and uncle working long, exhausting hours. Did she want that for herself?

She thought about the meeting at work where her boss had explained that the business was struggling financially and that she was going to have to let a couple of staff members go, one of them being Lettie. She had been devastated initially, wishing they had given Scott the push instead, but apparently, he was needed more than her as he worked in accounts and she was only working on the fashion side of things. It hadn't seemed fair.

Now though, if her parents did agree to her coming home and

running the place for them, then she wouldn't have to worry about facing him any more or decide whether she really wanted another job in fashion. And at least if she gave it a go on the farm then she would be helping her parents out and might even manage to save her family home. Did she have it in her to run it successfully? She decided she was willing to find out.

2

LETTIE

As Lettie pushed her hands into the warm soapy water it occurred to her that she didn't have the luxury of time. 'Right,' she said turning and leaning against the worktop as she addressed her brother. 'Dad and Mum clearly aren't willing to listen to me, so I need you to speak to Uncle Leonard and persuade him to have a chat with Dad about me taking over the running of the farm.'

Zac looked perplexed by her suggestion, though she couldn't understand why. 'What good do you think that'll do?' Zac asked scraping the remnants off the plates before lowering them into the sink.

'Dad listens to his brother, and Uncle Leonard might listen to you if you suggest the idea to him. It would be awkward for him if I was to ask him direct. You need to try to get him to persuade Dad that he's making a mistake, and if that doesn't work, then try to get him to agree to give me a chance to run Hollyhock Farm and delay his purchase of it. I just need time.'

'He's hardly likely to do that though,' her brother said throwing a clean tea towel at her. 'I'll wash; you can dry.'

Why was no one taking her suggestion seriously? She caught

the tea towel and decided now wasn't the time to argue with him, not when she wanted him to do something for her. It was like old times when they quibbled about who did what every evening after dinner.

'Are you ready for our parents to sell this land?' She folded her arms and waited for him to answer.

He shook his head slowly. 'No, of course I'm not.'

'Then we need to think of a way to stop them. Dad and Mum have obviously given this a lot of thought and their minds are made up. So, the only other option is for you to persuade Uncle Leonard not to buy the farmland and the business, and for him to at least try to get Dad to let me have a go at running the place. At least before he goes to any trouble to raise funds to buy it.'

Zac sighed heavily. 'I wondered why they wanted you to come back rather than wait until we were both here at the same time in the summer.'

He had a point. As she waited for Zac to wash the first plate, Lettie thought how similar they both were with their light brown hair, blue eyes and spattering of freckles over their noses. People had occasionally assumed they were twins when they were children even though Zac was eighteen months younger than her. He was now twenty-four and her twenty-five. He rinsed the plate and put it onto the drainer for her to dry.

'You don't think you'll be taking on too much by doing this though do you, Letts?'

'What do you mean? I grew up here, Zac, like you.'

He turned to face her, unaware that soapy water was dripping from the scrubbing brush in his hand onto the tiled floor. 'Yes, but both of us have only ever helped out during school holidays and the last time we did that must be at least five or six years ago. Dad's done this for years and no doubt makes looking after the farm seem easy. Farming is all he's ever known. Anyway, I thought you were into your career and had ambitions about rising through the ranks. Won't you miss all that if you move back here?'

She understood his concern and explained what had happened the previous week. 'You're making a mess all over the floor.' Lettie pointed at the small pool of water at his feet.

He grabbed a few sheets of kitchen roll and mopped it up, leaving her to consider his question. 'That's rough, Letts. I'm sorry they're talking about letting you go. I know how excited you were to get that job.'

She had been very excited to move to London after graduating from university. It had been a dream come true initially to make friends in the vibrant city, topping it off by landing the job that she had thought of as perfect until Scott's move to the company had turned everything sour, even their relationship.

'I did love it initially,' she admitted, 'but things changed along with mine and Scott's relationship, and to be honest with you I think that subconsciously I've been waiting for something to inspire me.' She saw the look of astonishment on his face and smiled. 'I'm aware it will be a massive life change, but ever since Scott and I broke up last summer, I haven't found life in London quite so much fun, so now I'm beginning to think that it won't be the end of the world leaving.' She noticed him looking at her askance. 'What?'

'It's not like you to let some bloke ruin the way you see things, Letts.'

He was right. 'It wasn't the break-up alone, more that by the time we broke up the magic of the place had faded slightly. I think I was caught up in the glamour of it all.' She sighed. 'Or probably I was working such long hours trying to prove to my boss that I was worthy of a promotion that I didn't have much energy left for going out and socialising any more. I know looking after the farm will take up most of the hours in each day too, but

I'm already used to that and at least I won't have a commute here.'

She could tell he wasn't convinced. 'Maybe not, but you're not used to doing such a manual job.' He looked down at her feet. 'Or working in wellies and overalls.'

Lettie laughed, grateful for the release in the tension. 'True. But I'm sure I can find some glam ones.'

'I wouldn't suggest wearing them though, not if you want to be taken seriously.'

She slapped his shoulder lightly. 'It was a joke, Zac.'

'I know, Lettice.' He laughed enjoying using the name she hated. And it wasn't even her real name. 'I don't want to speak to Uncle Leonard about this,' he moaned.

'You're closer to him than I am,' she said. 'After all, he is your godfather.'

'You're such a pain, do you know that?' He began washing the next plate.

'Will you speak to him for me, or not?'

'Of course I will. If you're willing to deal with all these nutty chickens, goats and whatever else Dad has taken on, and farming his precious crops, then I'm not going to stand in your way. I'll pop round to see him a bit later, if you like. In the meantime, I think you need to tell Mum and Dad about your job, so they don't feel so guilty about your offer to come here.'

Lettie groaned. 'All right.' She hoped she wasn't underestimating what running this place meant. She knew how hectic life was on the farm between April and June when the Jersey Royals were harvested and how imperative it was to ensure no time was wasted taking the potatoes to the harbour to be loaded onto the boat for delivery to be sold on the mainland. There were other harvest periods too for the tomatoes, squash and beetroot her father grew in his large polytunnels.

They would need to be cared for and harvested to then be sold to local shops and that was without having to milk the goats, collect the chicken eggs and look after the few cows they still had and the five alpacas.

'Do you want to come with me?'

Should she? Would she have more chance persuading her uncle if she was there, or if her brother went alone? 'I'm not sure.' After another moment, she added, 'I think you should talk to him first. Give him a heads-up about what I'm planning on doing. Then if you fail, I'll go and see him.'

Zac narrowed his eyes and she could tell he had thought of something. 'Go on,' she said smiling. 'What is it?'

'Uncle Leonard is far less likely to turn down your suggestion if you're there. He's not a confrontational person and will probably feel mean saying no to your face.'

He had a point. 'You could be right.' She dried her hands and hung the towel on the Aga rail. 'Come along then, let's go.' She didn't add that her reason for hurrying was to speak to their uncle before she lost her courage.

'You're such a pain – do you know that?'

She did, but right now Lettie didn't care all that much.

Zac smiled. 'Poor Uncle Leonard – he has no idea what he's about to deal with, does he?'

It didn't take very long to cycle to their uncle's farm as it neighboured their own. Lettie was relieved to find him working quietly and alone in one of his barns.

'Mind if we join you?' she asked as they walked into the cool space.

He looked up and beamed at them. 'Well, this is a treat. When did you get back to the island?' He jerked his head in Zac's direction. 'I thought you were away working somewhere, too.'

'Me – yesterday,' Lettie said feeling a little nervous now that her uncle was standing in front of her. 'Zac had a job on the mainland for a few weeks but got back the day before.'

'It's good to see you both.' He indicated the house. 'Want to come in for a cool drink, or something?'

Lettie suddenly felt the urge to get her question out of the way, needing to find out his thoughts on the matter.

Zac must have noticed her nerves. 'Lettie's had an idea and wanted to ask a favour of you.'

Her heart pounded as her anxiety increased.

Uncle Leonard locked eyes with her. 'I have a feeling I might know what this is about.'

'You do?' Did that mean she might not have any need of persuading him to change his mind?

'You've discovered your father's offered to sell me the farmland. Is that it?'

'Yes.' Lettie held her breath, waiting for him to speak again.

His smile slipped. 'Aren't you happy about it then?'

She looked at Zac for support but he seemed to be purposely not looking her way.

'Go on,' Zac said finally. 'Spit it out.'

Lettie swallowed and cleared her throat. 'I was hoping you'd agree to let me take over from Dad.'

Her uncle didn't speak for over a minute and as she waited for him to say something, Lettie watched his expression change from one of surprise, to thoughtfulness, then something bordering on sadness.

'Uncle Leonard?' She hoped he hadn't been offended by her suggestion. 'I didn't mean to upset you.'

'Sorry, I'm a little taken aback – that's all. Have you told your father you're hoping to do this?'

She nodded. 'Yes. I'm not sure he thinks I can do it though.' There was no point in lying, especially when he would probably only ask her father anyway. 'I suspect he thinks me wanting to is just a knee-jerk reaction to him telling us about wanting to sell.'

He stared at her silently for a moment. 'But you believe you can?'

'I do,' she said not completely convinced she was right. She explained about her job in London, hoping that might help persuade him.

'I don't know what to say.' He went over to a hay bale and sat down. 'Look, Lettie. I would hate you to think I would ever get in the way of you keeping Hollyhock Farm in your family.' It was a relief to hear him say so. 'I understand how much that place means to you both, and to your parents.' He sighed. 'Like this place means to me and my family.'

'Can I sense a but coming?' Zac asked.

He nodded. 'You've put me in a difficult position. I've been talking everything through with Auntie Sue and I know she'll be disappointed if we weren't to go ahead with the purchase.'

Lettie thought of her cousins.

He rubbed his chin. 'If I'm honest I was hoping Damon might want to take on your Dad's land when he comes back to the island. He's the only one who's ever shown any inclination,' her uncle admitted. 'He's slowly working his way home now. I told him about my plans to diversify from our dairy herd and take on your father's organic crops to see how it goes. I was hoping he could look after those, you see.'

'Has he said he wants to do it?' Zac asked, folding his arms. Their uncle shook his head looking sad. Zac sighed. 'I can see how us asking this of you is really messing with your plans. And Dad's. But Lettie is serious about wanting to give it a try. Would you agree to hold back on pressing ahead with plans to buy the land and consider giving her some time to try and prove she can do it?'

Lettie wasn't sure whether she only wanted to be trusted with the work for a few months. She suspected her uncle was less impressed to realise they were hoping their father would make her tenure running the farm a permanent one. 'I know we're asking a lot, Uncle Leonard.'

'You are but I understand why. I'd do the same as you if the circumstances were reversed. I've been trying to raise funds to buy your father's land before Damon gets back, hoping to present him with a fait accompli.'

She swapped glances with her brother and wondered if Zac was thinking the same thing as her. 'Are you certain Damon even wants to do this as his future career?'

Her uncle didn't reply immediately, which told her all she wanted to know. Clearly Uncle Leonard was the one encouraging their cousin.

Zac turned to her. 'We all know that you've never done much farm work before, so you don't even really know whether you'll be any good at this. You'd have a probationary period in any new job, so why not this one? Then, if you feel you love it and you make a good go of it, maybe Uncle Leonard here will be kind enough not to hold Dad to any prior agreement to sell and let you take it on, at least for a while so you can decide if you can or want to continue farming.' He turned his attention to their uncle. 'You've also only ever been a dairy farmer until now, so maybe the crop side of farming won't be right for you.'

Lettie sensed her uncle starting to open up to Zac's suggestion and if it persuaded her father and uncle to give her time to prove she had what it took to run the farm, then it would be worth it. 'Zac's right. How about you give me a chance to prove myself? What's the harm of me trying it out for a while?'

'When you put it like that, I suppose there's no harm in you having a go, Lettie.' He shrugged. 'Fine. I'll speak to Gareth and let him know that I'm happy to give you time to have a try. At least that way he will be able to take time away from the place with Lindy and you can see for yourself just how much hard work is involved.' He stood and picked up the fork he had been using when they entered the barn. 'And I won't need to worry about finding the money just yet.'

'Exactly.' Zac gave Lettie a triumphant look, which she returned.

'Thanks, Uncle Leonard.' Lettie stepped forward and kissed his cheek. 'I really appreciate you agreeing to this for me.'

'Yes, well, I'm not sure I'm doing the right thing.' He grinned. 'I have a feeling I'm doing myself out of a good business deal, but we are family and you might not find this suits you once you try it. And I still have to speak to your father.'

'Rather you than me,' Zac said, his eyes twinkling with mischief. 'He's not going to listen to us about this, so we're going to need you to persuade him that it's a good idea.'

Lettie was astonished. How had she never known her brother was so persuasive before? He had obviously learnt a lot from dealing with stroppy musicians and their managers.

Leonard ruffled Zac's hair like he always had done when he was small. 'You, young Zac, are a force to be reckoned with – do you know that?' He hugged Lettie. 'And I'm proud of you for wanting to do this, Lettie. I know that secretly your dad must be too.'

'Thank you,' Lettie said, taken aback at his reaction.

'Right then, I suppose we'd better break the news to your father that I won't be taking over his business, at least not for the time being.'

3

LETTIE

'Three months, but that's all. One of them working with me, then by yourself for the two months your mother and I are travelling.'

Lettie saw the familiar determined expression on her father's face and didn't waste any of their time by trying to argue. She had explained her situation in London and suspected that her father and uncle felt too guilty about her being out of work and not giving her a chance to turn her idea down completely. 'Thanks, Dad. You won't regret it.'

'I'd better not.' He smiled at her and Lettie suspected her uncle had been right about him being happy that she wanted to give it a go.

Lettie gave her father a hug and turned to her uncle who, she noticed, looked pleased with the outcome. 'Thank you, too, Uncle Leonard. I appreciate this isn't what you had expected to happen.'

'It isn't, my love, but I would want your father to do the same thing should the tables be reversed and one of my boys had voiced his hope of having a go at running my farm.'

'That goes without saying, I hope,' Gareth said. 'After all, being able to hand our farms over to our kids has been both our dreams, as it was for our father and uncle before us.'

'That's right.'

Lettie listened to the brothers' nostalgic chat and wondered if there might be an opening for negotiating a bit longer. 'Maybe I should have a little more time to see how things go,' she suggested quietly.

Both men stopped speaking, their heads snapping in her direction. 'What?'

'No,' her father said shaking his head. 'We've agreed three months. That's more than enough time for you to work out whether this life is for you or not.'

She wasn't certain how she could do very much at all in that period but didn't want to push her luck. 'It was just a suggestion.'

'Yes, well keep the next one to yourself,' her dad said, but his tone was jovial.

She gave her dad a squeeze. 'I will, Dad.'

Zac smiled at her. 'I think this calls for a celebration.'

Their father groaned. 'You think most things are worth celebrating. I have stuff to do, so don't let me hold you back.'

As much as Lettie liked her brother's idea, she wanted to start as she meant to go on. Proving herself to her father was going to take some work she now realised. 'Maybe later, Zac. I'm going to stay here with Dad and pick up as much as I can before he retires.'

She knew she had said the right thing when her father gave a satisfied nod. 'That's what I like to hear. Right, Lettie, you come with me. Leonard, I'll chat to you a bit later.' He walked over to his brother and shook his hand. 'I appreciate you doing this for Lettie, thank you.'

'No need to thank me.' He turned to Lettie. 'If you need anything from your old uncle, just shout.'

Lettie ran over to him and hugged him. 'Thanks so much.'

Zac laughed. 'I just hope you don't end up regretting that offer.'

Lettie nudged him. 'Shut up.'

'No, you shut up.' Zac pulled a face. 'Right, I'm off. I'll be back later though, Letts. Then we can take a stroll to the village and have a celebratory drink in the pub if that suits you.'

'I'd love that.'

Lettie followed her father and uncle outside when Zac left. As she watched her brother go, she mused about how much she had missed his company. He was always the boisterous one out of the two of them, always encouraging her to do things she might not have the confidence to try. It was enjoyable with them both being at home. She was happy that he wasn't away working and was grateful to him for having her back with this situation. She decided she would join him at the pub as soon as she was finished on the farm.

4

BRODIE

Brodie sat nursing his pint at the pub near the veterinary practice he had taken over only a few months before. He was enjoying living back on the island, but having lived in Devon since qualifying as a vet he was still getting used to bumping into people he had known years before. He had left Jersey to go study for his veterinary degree at Bristol University. Following it with two years working for a large veterinary practice in the South West of England before his father tipped him off that the local vet – who everyone referred to as Old Man Winter – was retiring and needed someone to take over his practice.

Brodie leapt at the chance to return home, back to the place where he could settle in a village not far from the sea, closer to his parents and family and, with a loan from his grandfather, took on the lease for the practice and the cottage that went with it, where he now lived.

Brodie listened to Bethan, the practice nurse and receptionist. She had taken over from the elderly lady who had done the job for over four decades before deciding that it was time she retired when Old Man Winter sold up. Bethan was extremely efficient and liked by everyone, probably because she knew most people who came in with their pets. Brodie was also relieved to discover that she was very knowledgeable and it had been she who had persuaded him to join her at the pub for a few drinks.

'You need to get to know the locals again,' she had insisted that lunchtime when he had tried to turn down her suggestion of an after-work drink. 'Learn to relax at the end of a long, tedious day.'

Now he was here, it felt good to be sitting at one of the oak tables listening to the chatter around him.

Bethan seemed to know everyone. She was chatty and confident and couldn't do enough for him, and he decided he was very lucky to have her working for him at the practice. He watched as she said her goodbyes to her friend by the bar before returning to join him at the table.

'My friend was telling me that her mother's cousin's youngest daughter was speaking to someone who had brought their tabby to the surgery a couple of weeks ago.'

'Sorry, what?' Brodie wasn't sure if it was because he was tired, or that Bethan simply talked in riddles.

She didn't explain further, but leant over the table slightly and lowered her voice. 'She only brought the cat to you because she couldn't get an appointment at any other surgery.'

Was telling him this supposed to be inspiring confidence in him? Brodie had no idea, or where the conversation was going. Hoping she might be going somewhere with her thoughts, Brodie kept eye contact with her and concentrated on listening. 'That doesn't sound very complimentary.'

She shook her head. 'No. I mean, it is. Listen, I'm getting to the point.'

He wished she would. 'OK, go on.'

'She said that she was extremely impressed with the new vet.' She pointed at him unnecessarily. 'And will be bringing her cat to us should she need to in future.' He went to reply, but Bethan raised her hand to stop him. 'And, that's not all. She's going to tell all her friends to bring their animals to you, too.' She lowered her hand indicating she had finished. 'That's good, isn't it?'

Brodie nodded enthusiastically, mostly because he presumed that's what Bethan expected of him. 'Very good. Yes. Nice of your friend to tell you all that.'

'I thought so.' Bethan sat back looking satisfied and took a sip of her lager before looking up and catching his eye.

The door opened and a man walked in, closely followed by a woman he thought he vaguely recognised. She followed the man over to the bar, both scanning the room. The bloke spotted Bethan and raised his head before motioning for the girl to go over to their table.

Who was she? Brodie wondered, racking his brains to try and picture where he might know her from.

Bethan clocked him staring and turned in her seat, immediately waving for them to join her and Brodie. 'I'd heard she was on the island again. Lettie, come and sit with us.'

The girl, Lettie, beamed at Bethan and immediately did as she asked. 'Bethan! So good to see you again.'

Bethan stood and hugged her. 'I haven't seen you in such a long time.' She pulled out the chair next to her for Lettie to sit on.

The man she had come in with looked very like her, Brodie noticed. Both had chestnut-coloured hair and dark blue eyes and freckles. He supposed they must be siblings.

'Hi, I'm Zac,' the bloke said carrying two drinks and kissing Bethan on both cheeks before giving Brodie a friendly nod. 'You don't mind if we join you, do you?'

Brodie shook his head, just as Bethan laughed. 'When have you ever worried about anyone minding anything you did, Zac Torel?'

Torel? The name rang a bell. He'd had a crush on a girl with that last name once, but the girl Brodie knew hadn't been called Lettie. Maybe they were related? It was a local name after all.

'True.' Zac placed the two drinks on the table and pulled out a chair next to Brodie.

'This is Zac's sister, Lettie,' Bethan explained smiling briefly at her friend who, Brodie mused, also seemed vaguely familiar to him for some reason. 'We were at school together.'

Brodie said hello but instead of Lettie reacting in a similar way to her brother, she seemed a little subdued. Maybe she was shy. He hoped that was the case and not that they had met at some point in the past and he had inadvertently upset her.

'Good to meet you both,' Brodie said.

'Letts promised to come and meet up with me earlier,' Zac explained, 'but she's been helping Dad out on the farm, so I've been catching up with a few mates in the next parish.'

'You're working on the farm?' Bethan asked.

Brodie wondered why this seemed so surprising to Bethan. 'Is there something odd about that?'

'Only because Lettie here has a fancy job in a fashion business in London. At least you did the last time I bumped into your mum in the village store.'

'You wouldn't think it fancy if you worked the hours I do each day,' Lettie scoffed. 'Although I do love it. Did.'

'I'm intrigued.' Bethan nudged her and smiled.

'Which farm does your father run, if you don't mind me asking?'

'Hollyhock Farm,' Zac replied pointing towards the window. 'It's not one of the bigger farms, only about thirty-two verges.'

Brodie had no idea what that meant. 'Right.'

Lettie must have seen his confusion. 'Just under eighty acres. It's only a mile that way.'

'Yes,' Zac said. 'Close enough to walk here, thankfully.'

Brodie decided he liked the siblings. They were friendly and not at all wary about him being a relative stranger. He decided he wanted to know more about them. 'And what does he farm?'

'Organic produce,' Lettie explained. 'Mostly vegetables, Jersey Royals, of course, and apples, plums and damsons late summer. He also has a few animals, too. Goats, which we sell on to other locals to either use or make cheese, and our chickens. He has a couple of cows left over from his dairy herd when he sold them on over ten years ago. They're useful for grazing on the fallow land during a rest period.'

He was surprised to hear that he didn't still have a dairy herd. 'Really? That sounds interesting.'

He noticed Lettie study his face and hoped he hadn't sounded sarcastic. 'I mean it. I don't know if he's one of the practice's clients but if he is I look forward to visiting the farm.'

He was relieved when Bethan began chatting again, asking Lettie how long she was over for, before Lettie explained she had been given the opportunity of running their father's farm and needed to find a way to prove herself in three months.

'That's not long enough to prove anything much.' Brodie laughed, shocked to think anyone could expect to do much with a farm in that time. Everyone glared at him and, mortified, he realised he had said the words out loud. 'Sorry, I hadn't meant to say that.'

'You did though,' Lettie snapped, clearly offended. 'And you thought it was funny.'

Brodie grimaced as he locked eyes with the pretty girl glaring furiously at him across the pitted bar table. 'I really didn't mean to offend you.'

'I'm not sure I believe you.'

He realised she wasn't joking. Taken aback by her reaction, he took off his glasses and busied himself cleaning each lens before putting them back on. 'We seem to have got off to a bad start. I haven't been back on the island long and the last thing I want to do is upset people.'

'Brodie's taken over the veterinary practice that Old Man Winter used to run,' Bethan explained. 'He's lovely really.' She gave Brodie a pointed look. 'And not always this hopeless with people.' Her expression changed and Brodie suspected she was thinking he liked Lettie. Did he? He pushed the thought away. Now wasn't the time for getting ideas about people.

He had no intention of getting romantically involved with a client, not after what had happened in the last practice he had worked. Brodie shuddered to think about the drama that had ensued when his kindness had been taken as attraction when a farmer's wife assumed there was more between herself and Brodie, and rumours had begun flying, causing the practice to lose several much-needed clients when the husbands lost their trust in him. He needed to make amends and quickly.

'He is?' Lettie asked doubtfully.

Brodie gave what he hoped was an appealing smile in Lettie's direction. 'I like to think so.'

She didn't seem impressed.

He heard a laugh and realised it was Zac. 'Maybe you two should start again?' He held his hand over the table. 'Brodie, meet my older sister Lettie. Letts, this is the new vet you're going to have to get along well with if you expect him to help you out with any animal emergencies.'

Lettie's eyebrows shot up, as if this thought hadn't occurred to her. She glanced at her brother before turning her focus back to Brodie. 'I suppose he's right.' She sighed and held out her hand, waiting for Brodie to shake it. He slipped his hand into hers, grateful to her brother for the chance to smooth things over. 'Hello, Brodie. I'm pleased to meet you.'

For all her niceties, Brodie could tell she still wasn't

convinced about him. He decided that he liked how she had made up her own mind and doubted Lettie Torel would be intimidated by anyone. He had his work cut out if they were to become friends, and for some reason he couldn't understand, he felt compelled to find a way to make sure they did just that.

He shook her hand. 'Very pleased to meet you too, Lettie. If there's anything I can do to help with your father's animals, please call on me.'

'She'll do that,' Zac replied before Lettie had the opportunity to do so.

Lettie glared at her brother. 'Thanks, Zac, I'm perfectly capable of answering for myself.'

'I can see that,' Brodie interrupted. 'I just want to offer my personal services, if you ever need me.' He saw her looking confused and realised he hadn't been very clear. 'That is...'

'I know what you meant,' Lettie said quickly before he could finish. Her expression softened. 'And I am grateful to you for offering. Thank you.' She raised an eyebrow in her brother's direction before focusing on Brodie again. 'I just get a bit defensive when I'm being pushed into something.'

'And, let me guess,' Brodie said with a laugh, 'you then don't want to do whatever it was, whether you had been intending to, or not.'

'He's got you summed up already, Lettie,' Bethan teased.

Lettie threw her head back and laughed. 'Exactly that.' She gave her brother a pointed look. 'You see, Zac? Other people can understand where I'm coming from. I don't know why you find it so difficult to do the same. You're supposed to know me better than anyone.'

Brodie leant slightly forward. 'I think it's a sibling thing.' He turned to his side. 'Am I right, Zac?'

Zac nodded. 'I get more entertainment winding my sister up than I do most things.'

'I have a sister, Maddie, so understand your pain.' He looked across the table at Lettie to see her reaction, relieved when she pulled a face. The mood lifted and he relaxed.

'Why don't you tell us a bit about yourself, Brodie?' Lettie asked.

Bethan grinned, clearly happy that they were all getting along well now. 'Yes, why don't you.'

'I'm from a family of dentists. Apart from my sister. Maddie did qualify as one too, but decided it's not for her and recently finished her training to become an interior designer. She hopes to set up her own business.'

'Were your parents upset when you didn't choose to follow in their footsteps?' Lettie asked.

He nodded. 'They were at first, mostly because my parents and grandfather always assumed I'd join the family practice, but now they're fully behind me being a vet.'

'And a brilliant one you are, too,' Bethan said.

Brodie was grateful to her for saying as much. 'I'm glad you think so, Bethan.'

Bethan's cheeks flushed. She finished the rest of her drink and, placing her palms flat on the table, got to her feet. 'I'm off. I have to get to my mum's early to walk her two dogs before work, so don't want a late night.'

'Is your mum all right?' Lettie asked.

'She's fine, but she's gone to a spa for a few days with a couple of her girlfriends and Dad is on an early shift, so they asked me to take them out instead.' She shrugged. 'I rather like having a reason to get up extra early and always feel more energised when I've walked on the beach before breakfast.'

'I suppose we should be going too,' Lettie said smiling first at Bethan and then at Brodie, causing a strange sensation in his stomach. He reminded himself that she was probably going to be a client and the thought made his mood dip. 'I've got to be up early for a lesson in how to drive Dad's tractor and I'm not looking forward to it.'

'I doubt Dad will be either,' Zac quipped giving Brodie a wink and making him laugh, relieved for the distraction.

5

LETTIE

The following morning, after almost crashing her father's beloved tractor into a copse of trees, Lettie decided to take a walk to calm herself. She began on the farm, intending to familiarise herself once again with the fields, but this time she was looking at everywhere with a view to farming it and the crops either being planted or harvested in each one rather than just enjoying the scenery. If she was to take this place on then she needed to know exactly what she would be dealing with. Her father might have agreed to give her a chance but she knew he was nervous about leaving her to do the work. Rightly so, she reminded herself, picturing his puce face when she finally gained control of the tractor after a lot of trial and error.

She breathed in deeply, enjoying the fresh spring air. As she strode to the top field, she was surprised to notice Zac drive away in their mother's car.

She thought back to the previous evening and her shock at seeing Brodie in the pub with Bethan. She suspected Bethan liked him by the way she watched him intently whenever he spoke. It still smarted that he didn't remember her, or their one and only kiss.

She might have been fifteen and him a couple of years older, but she had given him her number when he had asked for it, promising to text and arrange a date for them to go out to the cinema. Lettie remembered only too well the mortification and heartache she had suffered for weeks afterwards when no text appeared. Had her kiss been that unmemorable to him? It certainly hadn't been for her. Lettie sighed. All those years dreaming that one day he would come and sweep her off her feet, tell her she was the most beautiful girl he had ever laid eyes on, or simply plead with her to go out with him on a date.

'Hah, like that's ever going to happen.' She began walking again. Not that she wanted to date him. No. She had moved on now, thankfully, as had her taste in men. She thought of Scott and his superior attitude and decided that maybe she had moved on in the wrong direction.

She was back on the island for another week before returning to London. She had already emailed her boss to let him know she was happy to be one of those made redundant from the company and was determined to make the most of her time here before leaving. She had no intention of letting someone like Brodie Murray ruin her enjoyment of being back on the island.

Being here was so much nicer than the exhaust-fumed air she was used to in London. She imagined her daily commute changing from forty minutes on packed tubes crammed up against weary travellers, who were wet some days and sweaty during the hotter summer months, and realised there was no comparison to being back at Hollyhock Farm. At least here all she needed to do was dress and walk outside. No more struggling to find the cost of her monthly rent, or resent having to pay excessive amounts for train or tube fees simply to get to a job that paid her far less than she had hoped to receive. Or have to worry about coming face to face with Scott in the staff canteen, or in one of the corridors any longer and have to deal with him whining about her being too hasty to end their relationship and the reasons why he felt she should give him a second chance.

No more fantasising about Brodie either. Not after last night and the realisation that he clearly hadn't given her a second's thought since that school disco and certainly hadn't spent the best part of a decade dreaming what might have been between the two of them. She had her sights set on far more important things now than fantasising about a good-looking vet.

Having opened herself up to potentially moving back home, it dawned on Lettie that she wouldn't miss living in the capital all that much. She could always visit friends there, if she felt the need for a little excitement, or she could invite them over to stay at the farm, if she wasn't able to get away. The thought settled her slightly. Yes, she could move back here and settle in again – she was sure of it.

Each step through the luscious grass towards the five-bar gate reaffirmed her determination that she was doing the right thing. She might be putting herself in a position where she would need to learn an enormous amount, and have to learn it quickly, but surely her dad would teach her all she needed to know. And, she hoped, her parents might agree to delay their holiday plans and stay in Jersey long enough for her to settle in properly and really learn the ropes.

'Hello, girls,' she said reaching the paddock where her father's small herd of older cows he had kept after selling the main herd a decade before were contentedly grazing. She recalled her father saying how Jersey cows lived on average until they were twenty-five, three years longer than most other breeds of cow. The first few cows noticed her and began ambling over to greet her. They really were beautiful, with their huge dark eyes. Lettie smiled fondly at them, stroking their soft faces and ears, trying to recognise some of them.

Warm from her uphill walk, she undid her cotton jacket and

tied it around her waist, wanting to make the most of the sunshine. She wished she still didn't need to return to London to find someone to take over her room in the flat she shared with Nessa and pack everything up to send it back to the island.

She felt a sneeze coming and remembered how it felt to suffer from hay fever. Damn. She had forgotten about this and knew she was going to have to buy some antihistamines to stop it from happening most days. The last thing she wanted was a runny nose and puffy, watery eyes. She had enough to contend with making her plans come to fruition successfully without dealing with that sort of thing.

Was she overestimating her ability to do this? She looked around at the beautiful scenery and down the hill to the granite farmhouse with its wooded area to the back and walled yard to the right-hand side. The driveway curved away through more trees so that Lettie's view was partially obstructed. The village was only a ten-minute walk from the end of their driveway where her mother shopped for small things, preferring to visit the bigger stores in St Helier fifteen minutes' drive away for larger items.

She pictured the village pub where she and Zac had enjoyed Bethan and Brodie's company the previous evening. As well as the pub, the village had a garage and several small businesses including the food store, veterinary practice, a doctor's surgery, a tiny pharmacy, a small café, and a hairdresser; everything she could want.

If she felt like going out for the evening to a restaurant or nightclub with friends all she needed to do was take the bus that conveniently stopped a little way down the road from their driveway into town. Not that Lettie could see herself wanting to do too much of that. She had lost contact with most of her friends since going away to university and decided she'd had her fill of nightclubs during her time living on the mainland. And, she reminded herself, if she was going to be working as hard for as many hours as she had witnessed her father doing, then she doubted she would have any energy to do much at the end of each day other than fall into her bed and sleep.

A while later, as she walked slowly towards the yard, past the purply blue carpet of bluebells, she spotted an old blue Land Rover coming down the drive, its wheels throwing up clouds of dust in its wake. She stopped and peered at the vehicle. It wasn't one she recognised. She didn't recognise the driver either, which was unusual. Not that she could make him out very clearly as the driver appeared to be wearing a peaked cap. The vehicle stopped just inside the yard and her brother got out of the passenger door. What was he doing? she wondered, and where had he left their mother's car?

Picking up her pace, wanting to find out if he had been in an accident, Lettie arrived at the open yard gate in time to see the two men enter the house. She followed them inside and hearing voices coming from the kitchen went to meet their guest.

'Ah, there she is,' Zac said looking suspiciously pleased with himself.

'Here I am,' she said unnecessarily.

The guest turned, and any further quips she had ready to share vanished. He pushed his sandy hair from his forehead and she realised it was Brodie. Lettie stared at him, taking in the tall, well-built man, his neatly trimmed hair and tortoiseshell glasses that seemed to have a habit of slipping down his Roman nose, making her wonder if she really was going to be able to act calmly whenever he was around. Either way he seemed very comfortable in their large farmhouse kitchen.

Lettie realised her brother, mother and Brodie were watching her and it dawned on her they were waiting for her to say something. Had someone asked her something?

'Why don't you three sit down,' their mother suggested giving

Lettie a concerned look. 'I'll put the kettle on. Unless you'd prefer coffee, Brodie?'

'I'd love a coffee if you don't mind, Mrs Torel.'

Damn, she thought, even his voice had an effect on her.

'Letts.' She realised Zac was addressing her.

'Sorry, I was thinking. What is it?' She hoped Brodie hadn't noticed her reaction to him.

'Brodie has been trying to work out where he could have seen you before, Lettie.'

She cringed inwardly wishing their mother wasn't in the same room and hoping her memory wasn't as sharp as usual.

'What's your surname, Brodie,' her mother asked thoughtfully.

'Mum, stop interrogating the poor man,' Lettie said even though her mother had asked a simple question. She was desperate to divert the attention away from him and what he might be about to say.

'It's Murray, Mrs Torel.'

'Please,' her mother said taking mugs from a cupboard and setting them down on the worktop. 'Call me Lindy.'

'Lindy.'

Lettie watched her mother hesitate and stare at the closed cupboard door in front of her for a moment. Anxious in case she worked out where she recognised Brodie's name from, Lettie tried desperately to think of something to distract them all.

'You haven't asked how my driving lesson went,' Lettie said a little too loudly.

Brodie's mouth drew back into a smile. 'I didn't like to ask in case it hadn't gone well. Those things can take a bit of mastering.'

'You're not kidding,' she said, unsure when he might have ever had the need to drive a tractor. 'It went badly,' Lettie admitted going to fetch the two coffees her mother had finished making. 'Let me take those, Mum.'

'Thanks, love.' Her mother carried over the biscuit tin and placed it in the middle of the table. 'Please help yourselves.' She stared at Zac. 'Hold on, didn't you go out in my car earlier?'

Zac cringed. 'Ah, yes.'

'Then why did Brodie bring you home?' She smiled at Brodie. 'Lovely as it is to see you again.'

'That's fine, Mrs, er, Lindy.' Brodie reached to take a biscuit from the tin, his hand brushing against Lettie's as she did the same thing. 'Sorry.' He flinched as if he had been stung.

'No, after you,' Lettie said hurt by his reaction. 'You're the guest.' She wished her voice wasn't squeaky and saw Zac giving her a confused look. She ignored his amusement.

Waiting for Brodie to help himself to the biscuits, she willed her mother to continue questioning Zac.

'So, where's my car then?' Without giving him a chance to answer, Lindy added, 'It's not as if I need to go and do any shopping this morning, is it?'

'Do you, Mrs Torel?' Brodie's hand stopped in front of his mouth as he lowered the biscuit he was holding. 'I'm happy to take you wherever you need to go.' He looked at his wristwatch. 'I don't have to be at my next client's place for another half an hour yet.'

'That's very kind of you, Brodie,' she said standing and going to fetch her beloved blue-and-white teapot and carrying it to the table. 'Zac, my car. Where is it?'

6

BRODIE

After Brodie left the farm, promising to return if any of the family needed him for anything, he dropped Mrs Torel at the garage where Zac had left it, having treated her to four new tyres.

'What a sweet thing for him to do,' she gushed as they drove through the village. 'Zac's grown up to be such a thoughtful young man. I feel a little guilty being suspicious of him earlier but when I think of all the mischievous things he got up to growing up, I have to admit I despaired of him on more than one occasion.'

'I'm sure my mother did about me.' Brodie laughed, certain he had pushed his mother to her limits on many occasions, not just one.

'I can't imagine that for a second.' Lindy frowned. 'She must be incredibly proud of you, especially now you've taken over your own practice.'

'She is.'

'You're from here, are you?'

Brodie supposed Mrs Torel knew most of the people who lived on this side of the island. 'Yes. My family moved here from Devon just before I was born. I must admit it feels good living so close to the sea again after living on the mainland for a few years.'

'I love it here too.' She smiled. 'I was born and raised here on the island and although I long to travel more, I can't imagine ever settling anywhere else. Not for long anyway.'

Was that why she and her husband were wanting to hand the farm over to Lettie? he wondered. He had known many farmers in his time and all of them worked incredibly hard. It was, he supposed, a rewarding life although one that seemed to be filled with continuous struggles of varying kinds.

'Are you planning on travelling soon, then?'

He felt her gaze fall on him and hoped he hadn't offended her by asking too personal a question.

'Yes. But please don't say anything to Lettie or Zac because we haven't broached the subject of exactly when we go away with them yet,' she said, her voice lowered, although he wasn't sure why because it was only the two of them in his car. 'It's also why we've had to come to the difficult decision to part with the business side of the farm. It's something Gareth and I have been building up to doing for a few years now.' She sighed. 'I wasn't certain my husband would be able to do it, but the other week he told me he'd already spoken to his brother, Leonard, about it.'

'That must have taken you by surprise,' he said, certain by what Zac had said earlier that he and his sister had not seen this coming. He knew only too well how difficult life could be when the unexpected happened and couldn't help feeling sorry for them. On the one hand, he hoped Lettie was given permission to take on her family farm long-term, because she seemed determined, but he also knew how difficult it was for farmers to keep everything going and that was when they had experience. He might not know Lettie well at all but he couldn't imagine how she expected to move from working in fashion to running an organic farm with any ease.

'Are you all right, Brodie?'

Embarrassed, Brodie realised she must have noticed him deep in thought. 'Sorry, yes. I, er, was just thinking of something I should have done this morning.'

'Zac mentioned that you were trying to work out where you'd seen Lettie before. Could you have attended the same school?'

He told her which school he attended. 'But I don't recall her name. I mean, there were a few Torels but no one called Lettie.'

When Lindy didn't reply, he glanced at her and noticed she seemed very thoughtful. 'Maybe you just didn't come across each other because you're a few years older.'

'It could be that.'

She tapped the window, pointing to the kerb. 'This will do, right here.'

He wished they had longer to chat about Lettie. Maybe he might have discovered more about her life before she'd left for university and resolve his curiosity about where they might have crossed each other's paths in the past, but clearly it wasn't going to happen today. 'We're only a hundred or so yards from the garage. I can take you all the way there. I'm not in a rush.'

'We both know you have a client to get to.' She retrieved her handbag from between her feet. 'Don't worry about me. Here will be perfectly fine. I'd like to pop into the newsagent's first, anyway.'

Doing as she wished, Brodie steered the car to the pavement and stopped.

She unclipped her seatbelt and picked up her basket from the footwell. 'Thanks for the lift. And don't be a stranger. Please feel free to pop in to Hollyhock Farm whenever you wish.'

'That's very kind of you, Mrs Torel, thank you.'

She opened the door and got out, then closed the door and bent to talk to him through the open window. 'I told you to call me

Lindy. Everyone else does. Mrs Torel makes me sound old and makes me think of my mother-in-law.'

She turned and walked away, leaving Brodie wondering if she had really wanted to go to the newsagent's or if his question about Lettie had been the cause behind her deciding to do so. What a family, he thought as he pulled away from the kerb and drove on to his next client. He was going to enjoy getting to know them better and now he was even more intrigued about why Lettie seemed familiar to him.

7

LETTIE

'Stop tormenting me, Zac,' Lettie said, following her brother outside as soon as Brodie had driven her mother out of the yard.

'I don't know what you mean.'

She could see by the self-satisfied grin on his annoying face that he knew exactly what she was referring to. Why was her brother so good at winding her up? Then again, she mused, he had spent his life finding new ways to goad her and with all that experience she shouldn't be surprised that he did it so well.

'Bringing Brodie Murray here without warning.'

'I didn't. He happened to be passing and offered me a lift, and so I invited him in. He is the new vet, after all, and I thought it a good idea you get to know him.' He slapped her playfully on the back. 'Ah, so you do like him then. I knew it.'

'Get lost. It's not that at all.'

'Yeah, whatever you say.'

She wasn't finished with him yet. 'And what was all that about him trying to work out where he knew me from?' She hated reminding her brother but needed to know so she could prevent Zac from saying the wrong thing going forward.

'Exactly what I said.' He frowned at her. 'What's the big deal? It's not as if you recognise him from anywhere, is it? So he must be confusing you with someone else.' He stilled and narrowed his eyes and Lettie knew she had done the wrong thing questioning her brother. Damn. Why hadn't she left the matter alone?

Zac's mouth opened. 'I don't believe it. You do know him from the past, don't you? That's why you've been so odd around him.'

She pushed Zac hard in his shoulder. 'I do not act strangely.'

'You do and you know it.' He leant closer to her, studying her expression. 'Something happened between you both, didn't it?'

'No.' She pushed him away and turned her back on him. Zac knew her far too well for her to get away with lying to him. Determined to change the subject, Lettie said, 'I thought it was sweet of Uncle Leonard to agree to me running the farm.'

'Don't change the subject,' Zac said grabbing hold of her arm and turning her to face him. 'Please tell me what happened between you. I'm dying to know now.'

'I didn't,' she snapped. 'And it was nothing,' she added before Zac had a chance to argue.

'Come on, Letts. You can at least tell me what you think of Brodie?'

Lettie rolled her eyes, irritated with her brother yet again. She knew she had to give Zac something or he'd never let the matter drop. 'He seems nice enough.'

'Nice enough?' He mimicked her voice. 'Don't think I didn't notice the way you were gawping at him when you first saw him here.' Zac laughed.

Embarrassed to have been caught out, but not surprised that Zac had noticed when he was always on the lookout for ways to tease her, Lettie scowled at him. 'Give it a rest, Zac. I did nothing of the sort.' Had she? She thought back to her reaction on the vet's arrival and realised he might have a point. Sod it.

'If you're not going to confide in me about how you know him, can you at least tell me what you think?'

She had no intention of giving her brother ammunition to tease her further. 'I told you, I thought he was nice.'

'You're no fun at all.'

'And your life must be very dull at the moment if you're so interested in what I'm doing, or not,' she added. Happy to have won this bout with her brother, Lettie stopped walking. 'I think I'll pop in to see how Tina is getting along.' She was aware she hadn't been to visit her best friend since her arrival on the island four days ago. She and Tina had been friends since primary school.

Yes, she thought, that's what she would do. She'd had enough of Zac and his nosiness. Tina and she might not see each other all that often now that Lettie lived in London and Tina had chosen to remain on the island, but she was someone Lettie always felt comfortable confiding in. She would know what to do next, or would at least listen to Lettie without making any judgement and let her brainstorm her next step.

* * *

'You're looking amazing, as always,' Tina said as she led Lettie through to her tiny kitchen. She motioned for her to take a seat at the nook where they had both spent many early mornings chatting and evenings sharing a bottle of wine as they confided in each other.

Lettie pushed her fingers through her wavy brown hair. 'You've always been a rubbish liar. I know I look a mess. I haven't had a chance to do anything with my appearance today.'

'All I care about is that you've come to visit me and I'm really excited to see you.'

Lettie noticed the laptop open on a small desk by the window. 'Have I interrupted you working?'

Tina pulled a face. 'No. In fact I'm grateful.' She blew a strand of hair from her face as she switched off her screen. 'I knew it would be difficult setting up as a virtual assistant but I had expected to have more clients by now – and be making more money.'

Lettie didn't like the sound of how things were going for her friend. 'Not picking up as you hoped?'

'Unfortunately not. People seem to want my services, but aren't so quick to pay for them when they receive the bill. I'm going to have to rethink how I do this financially, I think. Anyway,' she said, lifting the kettle and shaking it before filling it under the tap and switching it on, 'I'm due a break by now.'

Wanting to find something to be positive about, Lettie leant against the wall and folded her arms. She thought about Tina's two-year-old son, Noah. 'But working from home must be easier than going into an office each day. Especially with Noah around?'

'Yes, it's much easier. I love it. It was exhausting having to get Noah ready each day to drop him off at nursery, then sit through the traffic each morning before queuing for parking. It drove me nuts, not to mention having to dress up each day. I much prefer working remotely. At least this way I only have to look smart from the waist up and can keep my trackie bottoms and slippers on for online meetings.'

'I'm glad.' Lettie thought of her lengthy commute that probably took three times as long as Tina's did in Jersey and cost a lot more. She would love to work from home, but that wasn't an option in her line of work. She thought again how different life would be working on the farm and having a commute that simply consisted of a walk from her back door across the yard. Bliss.

'So, what brings you here?' Tina took two mugs from a cupboard and spooned coffee granules into each one. 'I don't mean here to see me because I know you always pop in whenever you're over, but why have you come home now? You don't usually come back unless it's Christmas, summer or a special birthday.' She gasped. 'I haven't missed a special birthday, have I?'

Lettie pulled a face. 'We're the same age and our birthdays are three days apart, so no.'

Tina laughed. 'I've been so busy lately I'm finding I lose track of days sometimes.'

'Nothing's wrong, is it?' Lettie didn't like to think of her friend in a bad place.

'No. I'm fine, just busy.' She finished making their coffees and brought them over to the table. Once seated, she continued. 'Busy but poor.'

Lettie thought of how organised her friend always was and how much she enjoyed looking after the interests of others. 'You'll be fine. You're brilliant at what you do, and I've never seen anyone type faster than you can, or be more organised.'

'Let's hope your faith in me is warranted. I worked out how much I could earn an hour as opposed to the salary I was on and thought it was worth a try. Kyle has been very supportive and assured me that if I don't like it, or can't make it work, then I can always go back to working for someone else.'

Lettie wondered if now was the perfect time to admit her plans to her friend. Tina knew her better than most people and was always honest with her. 'I've been hoping to do the same thing,' Lettie announced, excited to think of the pair of them starting new ventures at the same time.

Tina had been about to take a sip from her coffee but instead lowered the mug back onto the table. 'You're setting up as a virtual assistant, too?'

'What?' Lettie laughed to think that she could ever be good at that job. 'No. I'm hoping to take over running the farm.'

Tina frowned thoughtfully. 'What? Not Hollyhock Farm?'

Why was everyone so surprised to think of her doing just that? Lettie wondered, hurt at the thought. Not wishing to react badly to her, Lettie took a calming breath. 'Yes, my parents' farm.'

'But, I don't understand. You've always had the ambition to make a name for yourself in the fashion industry and I thought you were hoping for a promotion soon.'

'Yes, well that never happened and just before I came away my boss told me that they were probably going to have to let me go.' Lettie saw the concern in her friend's face and as they drank their coffees she carried on explaining about why her father had come to that decision.

'Wow, I never imagined your dad giving up the farm.'

'I still can't quite believe it either.'

'And your uncle has agreed to all this?'

Lettie tilted her head from one side to the other. 'Well, tentatively. I think he's just trying to pacify me, which is understandable, I guess. I know I don't have long to show what I can do, but I'm going to give it my best shot.'

Tina gave her a high five. 'That's my girl. Good for you. If anyone can do this, you will.'

Tina stared at her for a moment, obviously concerned about offending her.

'What are you thinking? Go on,' Lettie urged. 'Tell me. I think we know each other well enough for you to say what you truly think.'

'Look, I don't doubt you could do anything you set your mind do,' Tina began.

'Really?' Lettie couldn't believe how relieved she felt to learn that her friend had such faith in her abilities.

'Of course.'

Lettie heard the change in tone. 'I sense a *but* coming.'

Tina looked shocked. 'Not because I think you can't, or even shouldn't do it, but because I thought you loved living in London.' She sighed. 'No offence, Lettie, but it all sounded very glamorous and exciting, and I can't imagine why you would choose to give all that up to look after a herd of goats, or sheep, or whatever it is your dad farms now.'

'Goats, chickens, the alpacas and the girls.' She smiled as she thought of the beautiful dished faces of the cows. 'And I'm getting more interested in learning about farming organic produce, too,' Lettie said, trying her best to sound confident. 'I see what you mean though.' Was she being silly wanting to make such a drastic change to her lifestyle? 'I'm not even sure why I'm so keen to do this, if I'm honest. But for some reason I feel compelled to.'

Tina stood. 'I think this calls for the hard stuff.'

Lettie laughed, aware what Tina was about to do. She watched her friend fetch a small foldaway step and stand on it before reaching up and taking a huge bar of chocolate from one of the high cupboards.

'I've been so good lately – not letting this tempt me – but I think we both need a few squares.'

Lettie thought she needed at least half the bar to even begin to calm down, but was grateful to Tina for sharing any. 'Thank you. Milk chocolate is exactly what I need.'

Once they had both consumed several of the chunky chocolatey cubes, Tina steepled her fingers. 'I think you need to take a bit more time to think about this. First, you should decide why you want to do it. Is it because you're actually tired of your current job, living in the Big Smoke, or is it because you've had enough of trying to avoid Scott?'

'Probably all of those things.'

'Fine. You grew up on a farm, so do you actually think you can make a good go of running it, with all the long hours, crappy weather, trying to balance the books, and whatever else it includes. Or,' she added thoughtfully, 'are you just reacting to your dad's shocking news?' She pushed the bar towards Lettie. 'Go on, take another couple of chunks. I think you need it.'

'You're sure about this?' Lettie teased knowing how possessive Tina could be about her chocolate stash.

'I am. Only this once though.'

'Thanks,' Lettie said, breaking two off then pushing the bar back to her friend. 'You're right,' she agreed swallowing the first bit of chocolate. 'Unfortunately though, I don't have much time to make up my mind and my gut instinct is to go for it.'

'Well in that case,' Tina said, 'go home and think everything through thoroughly before committing yourself. You'll be giving up a lot in London to come back and take this on.'

Tina was right. 'By not doing it I'll be standing by while the land I've always loved so much is sold to my uncle and I can't bear to let the farm change forever without at least trying to do something to save it.'

'Aw, Lettie.' Tina reached out and took her hand for a moment. 'I'm so sorry this has happened.'

'Me, too.' She realised she should be getting a move on if she was to see her uncle and not keep him waiting too long. 'I'd better go now. Thanks for the coffee, chocolate and sympathy.'

'My pleasure,' Tina said giving her a hug and leading her to the front door. 'And don't forget to let me know how it goes. Call me, or pop in – whatever suits you best.'

Lettie knew she should have mentioned about Brodie being back on the island and thinking he knew her from somewhere. Tina would remember only too well what had happened between them and as much as Lettie liked not being the only one to recall how he had affected her back then, she wasn't quite ready to address it. Not yet.

'You're the best friend I could ask for, do you know that?' Lettie said, grateful as always to have her friend's unwavering support.

'It works both ways, Letts. You've always been there for me, too.' Tina looked at her thoughtfully. 'Is there something else on your mind?'

Lettie shook her head. 'Isn't the farmland being sold enough?' She smiled to soften her question.

'I suppose it is. That's a relief then. But don't forget I'm here whenever you need me.'

'I know, and it works both ways.'

8

BRODIE

'She'll be fine with a few days resting quietly in the barn,' Brodie said, patting the brown fur on the Jersey cow's back lightly before picking up his medical bag.

'That's a relief. Thank you for coming so soon, Brodie.' The farmer accompanied him outside. 'It's good to know we have new blood here. Old Man Winter wanted to retire for a few years but was determined to find someone he trusted to take over his practice first, and I think it got a bit too much for him in the end.'

Brodie hadn't realised that was the case. 'Thank you for the compliment.'

'It's true, lad. He insisted he wouldn't go and leave us with some nitwit who didn't have the same feel for the work as himself. We were all very grateful to him for that.'

'I'm glad to know you're happy that I've taken over the practice.'

'I am, now I've seen you in action.'

Brodie smiled as he accompanied the farmer back to his Land Rover. He liked the man's honesty. Not that it was unexpected. Most farmers he had come across since qualifying three years before were direct and didn't spare his feelings, but he liked that. It meant he always knew where he stood with them. If there was one thing to unnerve him it was having to second-guess someone's feelings. His thoughts went to Lettie.

'Bloody hell, I wonder what's happened now.'

Brodie followed the farmer's gaze and saw someone cycling down the driveway. The person got off the bike, resting it against the wall by the farmhouse and took off their helmet. Seeing the long, wavy chestnut-coloured hair being freed from the confines of the helmet as the cyclist shook her head slowly, he recognised Lettie. Brodie's breath caught in his throat. She was so pretty, in a fresh-faced way.

'Lettie! Over here,' the farmer bellowed. 'Come and meet our new vet.'

Lettie looked up and smiled as she raised her hand in a wave. Then, seeming to notice Brodie, her expression froze for a few seconds.

He wondered why she seemed so surprised to see him there, then it dawned on him that the farmer must be her uncle. Why hadn't he realised it before? Because Bethan's writing was rather messy and he hadn't been able to make out the surname, and the man he had thought of as Len must be Leonard.

Not wishing to interrupt Lettie's conversation with her uncle, he went with him to meet her. 'Good to see you again,' Brodie said, wishing he had thought of something a little less nondescript.

'Hi. I hadn't realised this was the client you were visiting.'

'Ah, so you two already know each other.' Her uncle leant forward and kissed her forehead. 'He's a good lad, this one.' He patted Brodie's back.

'Your uncle is very kind.'

Lettie smiled affectionately at her uncle. 'Uncle Leonard is also honest and wouldn't say anything he didn't mean.'

'That's good to know.' Brodie looked at Leonard. 'I'll leave the two of you. My secretary will get an invoice to you, and I'll come back in a few days to check on the cow. In the meantime, please don't hesitate to call the practice if you have any concerns at all.'

'I won't. Thanks again for coming.'

'Bye, Lettie. Good to see you again.' Brodie wasn't sure if her cheeks had reddened slightly or if they were pink from the exertion of her cycle ride.

'Thanks, likewise.'

Not wishing to outstay his welcome, Brodie left them to their discussion. As he drove, he wondered if Lettie knew what she was letting herself in for by taking over her parents' farm. He had never worked on one himself, but he had visited enough and knew for certain that farmers worked extremely long and tiring hours. He hoped she wasn't acting on impulse. He would hate for someone as lovely as Lettie to regret giving up her life in London and not being able to return to it if her plans for the farm didn't work out. Then again, he mused, if they did work out it meant she would be staying on the island. That idea he loved.

He arrived back at the practice hoping to have a couple of hours to start unpacking the tiny cottage that came with the business. He thought it characterful and pretty when he had first seen it, and it was, from the outside. Inside though it was desperately needing an update. After manoeuvring past his bright blue surfboard propped up against the narrow hall wall, he reached the kitchen. It was an ugly space with little to endear it to anyone, Brodie had often thought, amused. It had two lower cupboards with open shelves above and a porcelain sink with a crack along the bottom that so far hadn't leaked. The fridge barely worked and the lino was worn and a trip hazard. The small living room wasn't much better, or much bigger, but the two-seater sofa and one armchair that just about fitted in there were fine for him. At least the fireplace worked well enough. There was one bedroom upstairs and a bathroom tagged on at the back of the kitchen.

'Nothing a lick of paint can't brighten up,' he had said, unsure whether it would be enough. It would have to do for now though. Brodie knew he was luckier than most to have been given a loan from his grandfather to use as a deposit, which enabled him to take on a large bank loan for his business. It was going to take him years before he managed to break even, let alone be able to treat himself to anything, but he didn't care. This was what he had always dreamed of doing. Maybe not coming back to Jersey, but when he hadn't found a practice near his adopted home in Devon, and a friend had pointed out the advert for this place, everything had somehow fallen into place.

It was meant to be. At least that's what he told himself. Brodie went upstairs to unpack another box of books. It would have been nicer to know more people on the island, but a lot of his friends from school had moved away or were now settled down, or travelling. Having his own group of friends like he had built up while living in Devon, or back when he was at university was what he missed now. Someone to meet up with at the pub at the end of a long day. He thought of his surfboard, taking up too much space in the narrow hallway, and thought how good it would be to meet other surfers. That's what he would do the next free evening when the tide was right. He would take his board down to the beach at St Ouen's and spend a few happy hours ridding himself of all his worries and stresses in the surf.

He hadn't surfed since his arrival. There hadn't been time. But he would have to make time going forward. Anyway, Brodie decided, it would be good to meet other like-minded people. And there were several places along the five-mile stretch of bay where he could treat himself to a meal afterwards. He had driven that way a few times on his way to or from visiting clients and often saw the car parks at least half filled with cars. He needed to settle in as soon as possible. He thought of Zac and Lettie and wondered if maybe meeting them earlier had reminded him how much he missed having familiar faces around him.

'Brodie! Are you there?'

Bethan called to him from the front door.

'Yes,' he said leaving his room and going to the top of the stairs to see what was wrong. 'Do you need me for something?' It was a stupid question. Why else would she come to the cottage and call for him?

She stared at him without speaking for a moment. 'Oh yes, sorry. There's a lady on the phone with a dog she thinks might be in labour. She's in a bit of a panic and asked that you go to her house immediately and check that everything is all right.'

Happy to have something to keep him busy, Brodie nodded. 'Tell her I'll be there in...' He realised he didn't know where he was going or how long it would take. 'Where does she live?'

'Not far,' Bethan said waiting for him to join her. 'Her place is only about ten minutes from here. I'll give you the instructions before you go.'

9

BRODIE

May

It had been almost a month since Lettie's departure and Brodie wondered how soon she would return. He had tried and failed to stop thinking about her, but for some reason she kept popping into his mind. He wasn't sure if it was because she was beautiful, clever and good company, or simply that he was impressed by her determination to completely change her life to save her family farm. He admired her. Maybe that was it?

He reminded himself about his vow not to become involved with a client, which had been cemented more firmly in his mind after his vile break-up from his toxic ex. And anyway, Lettie was soon to be a client of his and he had no intention of mixing business with pleasure. As the farm's vet, he would need to keep any contact between them as professional as possible. The thought lowered his mood until he reminded himself he had far too much going on to even consider hooking up with anyone and needed all his energy for building the practice and gaining his clients' trust after the decades most of them had spent dealing with his predecessor.

Hearing a commotion outside in the reception area, Brodie hurried to the door to see what was going on. 'What's happened?' he asked, finding Bethan comforting a small child of about seven or eight clutching a plastic animal carrier to her chest as an anxious-looking elderly lady stood next to her looking as if she was trying not to cry.

'It's my rabbit. Granny rolled over his foot with her trolley.' She looked up at her grandmother. 'It wasn't on purpose.'

'No, it wasn't,' her grandmother said taking a tissue from her handbag and blowing her nose.

Hating to see the two people in obvious distress, Brodie bent slightly to address the child. 'Do you mind if I take a look at him?'

'Her,' the little girl said lifting the carrier holding her rabbit with a little difficulty. 'She's called Daphne.'

Daphne the rabbit. He smiled. 'That's a beautiful name for a pretty bunny,' he said taking the carrier from the child's arms. 'If you both follow me, we can go and have a proper look at her foot.'

'Thank you.' He noticed the little girl take her grandmother's hand, clearly trying to comfort her. It reminded him of his close relationship with his own much missed late grandmother, who had looked after him from when he was a few weeks old until he started school, when his parents had been at work and couldn't do so themselves. They had formed a very close bond and he had many happy memories of his first time riding upstairs on a double-decker bus when she took him to town, their many visits to the local park near her bungalow, and her teaching him to cook scrambled eggs before the two of them enjoyed a plateful each in front of the television watching one of his favourite programmes. Having her in his life had made his childhood all the more special, and he could see that it was a similar relationship to the one the two people who had brought Daphne into the surgery also enjoyed.

He closed the door behind them and placed the carrier onto the table. Then after opening the mesh door he carefully lifted the rabbit out, cuddling her for a few minutes to calm her racing heart. He saw instantly that her foot had been cut slightly but although the small animal was trembling badly, she seemed to be reasonably all right.

'Do you want to hold her, while I have a proper look?' he asked, lowering Daphne gently to the table. 'I'm Brodie, by the way. Do you mind telling me your name?'

'I'm Betsy and this is Granny.'

The grandmother gave a shaky smile. 'Jean Blanchard,' she said. 'Thank you for seeing us so promptly, Brodie. I really am very grateful.'

'Not at all.' He checked the rabbit was being held before reaching to pick up his stethoscope. 'We're having a quiet morning, which is lucky.'

After examining the little girl's pet, Brodie explained that he was going to have to keep Daphne in overnight. 'She needs a scan to check that there's nothing broken and I'll give her some antibiotics and dress this wound on her foot.'

'Will she be all right?' Jean asked, her voice quaking anxiously.

'We'll do everything we can to make her well. You should be able to take her home first thing tomorrow.'

The little girl brightened considerably when he told her the good news. 'Thank you, Brodie,' she said. 'Can I give her a cuddle before I go?'

'Of course. Sit for a bit with her. She'll be calmer after a cuddle with you.'

After they had left he saw two more patients, then had to drive to a nearby stable to check on a foal and its mother. 'I shouldn't be too long, Bethan,' he said, as he was leaving.

'No worries.' She glanced at her computer screen. 'You have three more appointments after lunch at the moment, so no need to rush back if you want to stop off and grab a bite to eat.'

He picked up his bag and Land Rover keys and left through the back door of the surgery.

10

LETTIE

End of May

As Lettie walked along the narrow country lane on her way to the village she breathed in the sweet country air and felt the tension in her neck go and her shoulders relax.

She wondered when she would next see Brodie. She was bound to bump into him at some point now that he was working in the village. She remembered his younger reputation as a fun-loving, friendly guy. Not that she had known him well, only having a secret crush on him back then. Apart from that solitary kiss after a school Halloween disco when they were teenagers, he hadn't paid her any attention and she had to accept that he wasn't interested in her. She had her pride. She might have done her best in the intervening years to keep her attraction for him a secret, embarrassed to think her kiss wasn't exciting enough to make him want to see her again. It had stung for a long time that to know she hadn't made enough of an impression on Brodie for him to ask her out on a date, like he had said he would do when he had taken her number that night. And now it seemed that he didn't even remember her.

'I'm clearly more forgettable than even I thought.' She sighed and picked a long strand of grass growing from the granite wall she was passing. 'I'm not here to find a boyfriend though, am I? No, Lettie Torel, you're here to prove to your parents you have what it takes to run the farm.'

She wasn't sure why she was talking to herself, but reminded of her ambitions, Lettie strode on breathing in the fresh air, sweet with wildflowers. It really was refreshing to be back home again and exciting to embark on a new chapter in her life.

Lettie neared the post office. She had received an email earlier asking her to collect a parcel and hoped it was the new overalls (two pairs) and wellies she had ordered for herself weeks before, ready to start work. She wasn't sure if her sense of excitement matched her nerves, but hoped that being dressed correctly might help reassure her a little that she did have what it took do this job. The days had passed far more quickly than she had expected and it was intimidating to think that she would be starting work on the farm first thing tomorrow.

As Lettie rounded the corner to the post office, she spotted Uncle Leonard and increased her pace, hoping to catch up with him before he reached his car.

'Uncle Leonard, wait up a sec.'

He turned and seeing her beamed. 'You're back then?'

'I am.'

'I bet your father hasn't wasted any time getting you out working these past few weeks.' He laughed and walked over to her, giving her one of his big bear hugs. 'It's good to have you here again full-time, little one.' He wrapped his arms around her.

She was hardly little at five feet seven inches, but he was around six feet three, so she supposed to him she was still relatively small.

'I'm a bit anxious about how much I've taken on,' she admitted as his arms dropped from around her.

'Don't be. Your dad will still be around to help you for the next week or so until he and your mum leave for their much-needed holiday, and I'll be here to answer any questions you might have. I'm sure you can do this, Lettie. You just need confidence in yourself. You were born and raised on that farm and whether you think so or not, you've probably absorbed far more about the running of it than you assume.'

'I suppose you're right,' she said, praying he was. 'I feel better for speaking to you anyway.'

'Good, I'm glad.'

'How are the twins?' she asked picturing her twin cousins who were a year younger than her and had grown up spending all the school holidays and weekends mucking about with her and Zac.

Leonard smiled, a twinkle in his eyes belying a nonchalant shrug. 'The same. Adam seems to be doing well in his finance job. He was promoted to assistant manager at the accountancy firm where he works and recently passed another exam.'

'Good for him. He must be happy about that,' she said, always amazed that her once tearaway cousin had settled anywhere long enough to start making his way up the career ladder. 'Any news on Damon?'

Her uncle gave her a knowing smile. 'Only that he's now in Japan for a few weeks. Other than that, no fixed return date yet.'

Damon had always been the more introverted of the brothers, and it never failed to astound Lettie how he was the one to go off travelling by himself, whereas Adam had settled contentedly on the island. 'I see.'

'I'm glad he's seeing some of the world and having experiences I never got to enjoy, but I miss him and can't help hoping he chooses to settle down here when he gets back.' He smiled at her. 'I know your dad is secretly delighted you've come back to live on the island too.'

Lettie knew he was but it was warming to hear his brother say as much. 'That makes me very happy.'

'Why? Didn't you think so?'

She recalled her father's reaction to her wanting to take over the running of the family farm and shook her head. 'I know he never understood me and Zac moving away from Jersey, unlike Mum who always insisted travel was the best education anyone could have, but I wasn't sure how he felt about my decision to work on the farm. I think it makes him a bit anxious to leave me in charge.' She gave her uncle an apologetic smile. 'And how my decision has messed up your plans.'

'Don't worry about Gareth and me. We're tough farmers and we're used to plans going awry. I'm sure I speak for both of us when I say we're happy that you're wanting to give things a go. You just enjoy the farm as much as you can.'

Did she sense doubt in his voice? 'And if I fail?'

He frowned. 'There's no such thing as failing in this regard,' he said his voice gruff. 'The fact that you're giving it a try is good enough for me. And for your dad. If you decide this life isn't for you, then at least you know that for a fact and can take your future in a different direction. If you decide you want to carry on with it, then we'll have to figure that out when the time comes.' He puffed out his cheeks. 'This isn't an easy life, as well you know, but it's a satisfying one and I wouldn't change my life for anything. I could never have survived having to sitting behind a desk every day like Adam does.'

'Hmm, doing that didn't suit me much either,' she admitted.

'I'd better get going, but don't forget to call in and see us sometime. And—' he raised his eyebrows '—don't hesitate to ask for help whenever you need it, you hear?'

'I do. Thanks, Uncle Leonard. I feel much better having spoken to you.'

'Good. I'm glad.'

She watched him getting into his car and went into the post office. Being the only one out of her cousins and brother to make a point of wanting to work on the farm made her feel proud, whatever happened in the end. Lettie gave a satisfied sigh. She was bringing her father and uncle's ideas into the twenty-first century and that could only be a good thing. It felt good to surprise them. Now all she needed to do was prove she had what it took to do the job.

Back at the farm, Lettie tried on a pair of overalls just as her mother knocked on her bedroom door.

'Can I come in?'

'Sure.' She waited for her mother to open the door and see what she was wearing.

'You're all kitted out then?' she said proudly. Her mother tilted her head to one side, taking in her look. 'We're very proud of you for wanting to do this, you know.'

'I do,' Lettie said happy to hear her mother say so and reaffirm her uncle's comment. 'Thanks, Mum.' Her mother went to leave. 'Did you want me for something?' Lettie asked.

'I've made a batch of rock cakes downstairs, if you want to join me for one with a cuppa.' Lindy Torel turned back to her again. 'I almost forgot. Your dad asked me to arrange for that nice vet to come over later and help check over some of the goats.'

'What for?' She hoped nothing was wrong with them and didn't have to deal with problems on her first day.

'Nothing to worry about – just their immunisations.' Her mother pushed her hands into the pockets of the pinny she always wore when she was baking. 'You need to develop a good relationship with the vet, Lettie. He's going to be one of your most important contacts, if not the most important one.' She stared at Lettie looking as if she was considering her next words carefully.

'What is it, Mum? I can tell you've got something on your mind.'

'It's been playing on my mind about Zac mentioning that Brodie thought he recognised you.'

Lettie cringed inwardly and hoped her mother didn't recall her teenage angst after Brodie hadn't asked her out after their kiss.

Lindy stepped into the bedroom and pushed the door almost closed. She lowered her voice. 'Isn't he the boy you liked after that school party? The one you kissed and who never called you?'

Lettie cringed. Feeling her face reddening, she wanted to deny it, but her mum was no fool and they always joked about her having the memory of an elephant. It was one of the things her father didn't like about his wife, mostly because she never missed anything he did wrong.

'Yes, Mum,' Lettie whispered, unsure why she was keeping quiet when her father was either out somewhere on the farm or downstairs reading his newspaper. 'But I don't feel that way about him now, so can we forget that ever happened?'

'You were very upset though, Lettie.'

Lettie took a calming breath. 'Mum, I was fifteen and he wasn't much older. These things happen. Anyway, I got over my crush years ago,' she fibbed. 'Can we agree not to mention it again please?'

Lindy stared at her thoughtfully for a few seconds before giving a firm nod. 'Whatever you say.' She opened the bedroom door again. 'Shall I pop the kettle on then?'

'Yes, please.'

Not wanting to dwell on her humiliation, Lettie picked up her hairbrush and scooped her hair back into a ponytail, securing it with a band and tucking any stray bits behind her ears. There, that was better. She studied her reflection in the mirror and sighed. She looked exactly like what she was: a wannabe farmer wearing brand-new, immaculate dungarees and trying to be something she wasn't.

She pushed her shoulders back. She might not be yet, she told herself, but she had every intention of proving herself.

She walked into the kitchen just as her father looked away from his newspaper and stared at her. 'I see you're dressed for the part,' he said thoughtfully. 'Don't you have anything less, er, smart?'

'Smart?' She realised he was only saying what she had just surmised upstairs in her bedroom. 'Ah, I see what you mean.'

'Take no notice of the fashion police,' her mother said with a wave of her hand. 'He's just so used to being scruffy that he assumes that's the way to look. Sit down and I'll bring you over a drink. You'll soon have those clothes all messy and creased and will look like you've been working on the farm for years.'

'I suppose I should make the most of being this tidy while I can.'

Her father shook his newspaper and focused on it again. 'You probably should. Hurry and drink up, then we'll get outside and you can start work.'

11

BRODIE

As Brodie neared Hollyhock Farm he felt his spirits lift at the thought of seeing Lettie again. Bethan had reminded him about visiting the farm and mentioned Lettie had been working there for almost a month. He was disappointed not to have bumped into her at the pub or in the village since her return but supposed she would be working very long hours helping her father, especially now that it was the busiest time of year with the harvesting of the Jersey Royals.

She really had got to him despite his determination not to let her. She was nothing like his ex, Tiffany. Then again few people were, he thought with relief. He pushed away all thoughts of Tiffany and focused on the lane, its long strands of grass slapping against his vehicle as he glided past the banks of wildflowers. It was a glorious afternoon, enriching his sense of happiness to be living back on this pretty island.

Turning into the farm driveway, Brodie saw farming machinery and workers busily collecting the precious buttery potatoes in a large field to his left, then spotted movement ahead. Someone was pushing a wheelbarrow out of the larger barn to the right of the yard. They disappeared past another smaller barn. He slowed slightly and, after parking, went to find Gareth Torel.

Brodie reached the entrance to the barn and looked around, but unable to see the farmer, called out to him. 'Mr Torel, it's Brodie Murray. I've come to give your goats their vaccination.'

'Brodie.' Gareth stepped out from behind one of the metal barriers holding a wide broom. 'I'll not be a moment.'

'No rush,' Brodie said, happy to wait. It was his final call of the day and he was in no rush to return to the practice.

Hearing footsteps and grumbling, he turned coming face to face with Lettie.

'Oh, hi.' She pushed the wheelbarrow, catching it on the side of the open door, and said something under her breath.

'Hello.' She didn't seem very happy to see him, Brodie realised. She had a puce face and messy hair, which looked as if it had previously been held back in some sort of elastic band, and her dungarees were mucky especially around the knees where she must have knelt in cow manure. He doubted he would be very happy to be found in that state and wished he hadn't arrived until a bit later.

'There you are,' Gareth bellowed. 'I've cleared up the rest of it, so if you just give the flooring a go with the power wash then we'll leave it at that.'

Gareth saw Lettie give a brief nod before passing him.

Aware he had arrived at an awkward time, Brodie tried to think of a way to remove himself briefly. He realised he hadn't thought to bring his bag from the car and pointed over his shoulder. 'I'll just fetch my things,' he said to anyone who was listening. As he walked back to his car, he wondered how long Lettie was going to keep working at the farm if she was to get in a state like this each day. She looked exhausted and had obviously taken a tumble into some of the manure. Would she start having second thoughts about what she had taken on? He hoped not. Even if there wasn't anything romantic between them, he couldn't help liking her. There was something about her that made him think of her even when she wasn't around.

He retrieved his bag and went to go with Gareth to start the immunisation process. He hoped none of them had any unexpected issues. As much as he loved his work, he still struggled when people had to part with their beloved animals and, as much as he knew farming was a business, he had yet to meet a farmer who wasn't devastated when they lost an animal.

'They're this way,' Gareth said, striding out of the barn and pointing to the smaller barn nearby.

Brodie hurried to catch up with him.

They reached the pen where the goats were stabled and he waited for Gareth to fetch the first one for him. Brodie stroked the animal's back. 'Hello there,' he soothed. 'This won't hurt at all.'

'What's the vaccine for?'

He heard the concern in Lettie's voice. She must have followed them into the barn. He wasn't surprised to know she was there, wanting to find out how their goats got on. 'They need this for tetanus and Clostridium. It won't hurt them. Only a slight pinch.'

'That's what doctors say when they're about to inject you. You'll only feel a little scratch, but it never really feels like that at all.'

'Will you let Brodie get on with what he's doing please, Letts?'

'Sorry, Dad.'

Brodie quickly examined the first animal. She seemed perfectly healthy. He took hold of a small area of the goat's skin from its neck between his thumb and forefinger and administered the injection. 'There.' He patted the little goat for it to move away. 'Right, next one.'

He soon finished injecting them and once done heard Lettie give a grateful sigh. 'That's an enormous relief, isn't it, Dad?'

Her father gave her a bemused look. 'This is all perfectly normal and nothing to worry about, Lettie lovey.'

Brodie was happy there hadn't been any drama. He waited for Lettie to move the animals into another pen and followed her and Gareth back outside to the yard.

'Do you want to come in for a cuppa, Brodie?' Gareth asked.

Brodie would have loved to but he hadn't missed the look of, what – Shock? Disappointment? – on Lottie's face at her father's question. He wasn't sure but it hurt to think that she didn't want him to hang around now that his work was done. He also had no intention of outstaying his welcome.

'No thanks. Not today. Maybe another time.'

Lettie gave a tight smile. 'Thanks for looking after the goats so well.'

'It was simple enough, I'm glad to say.' He took his keys from his trouser pocket. 'Right, I'd better be going. I'll see you soon.'

As he drove away, Brodie couldn't help wondering what he might have done to cause the almost unfriendly reaction from Lettie. As far as he was aware he hadn't said or done anything to offend her. Had he?

12

LETTIE

Lettie stood under the warm shower, her eyes squeezed shut in mortification that anyone, let alone their gorgeous vet, had seen her in such a disgusting state. What must he think of her? She cringed. She would rather he didn't recognise her than see her looking and no doubt smelling so disgusting. If only she hadn't fallen over shortly before his arrival, and in goat dung too. The horror of it all.

She soaped her aching body and shampooed her hair for a second time, just to make sure there was no mess left anywhere on her. Brodie must think her such an oddball. So far all she had managed to achieve in the past three and a half weeks was pull a few muscles, wear herself out and not be very helpful to her dad at all. Was she making a fool of herself by trying to do this work? Was she out of her depth? Yes, was probably the answer to both questions.

She reached out and grabbed a towel, drying her face before wrapping it around her hair. Then, stepping carefully out of the shower, wrapped a larger towel around her body before leaning forward and wiping away condensation from the bathroom mirror with her hand. There she was, she thought, staring at her pink-faced reflection, obviously exhausted but at least clean at last.

'You've got this,' she told her miserable reflection. She wasn't going to give up without a much better fight than the one she had given so far. She could do this.

'There will be good days and crappy days. Today is simply one of the crappier ones.' Literally, she thought grumpily.

Resolving to be more positive, Lettie brushed her hair deciding to allow it to dry naturally. She didn't mind her curls, not any more. When she was younger and first going out to nightclubs she had spent hours trying to straighten it, but she no longer bothered. It was far easier this way.

Dried and dressed in a pair of baggy jeans and a fresh black and white striped T-shirt, Lettie went downstairs. It was such a beautiful day and she had a lot to learn about the farm, so she decided it was the perfect time to go for a walk around the fields. She took a notepad and biro from by the phone to make notes about any jobs she thought might need doing, like the stone walls she had already noticed that needing fixing.

'We're just popping out to do some shopping,' her mother said, stepping out from the walk-in pantry.

Startled, Lettie dropped the pen and bent to retrieve it.

'Sorry, I didn't mean to give you a fright.' Her mother seemed very happy. Lettie wondered if it was because she was doing her best to learn all she could about the farm. 'Do you need anything?'

'No thanks, Mum.'

Lettie knew her father would have given her mother some sort of update on how she was coping. Or, if he hadn't, he probably would do when they were out.

Her father arrived in the kitchen wearing chinos and a pale blue shirt. 'You look smart, Dad.' She hadn't meant to sound so surprised but it was unusual to see him out of his usual farming gear. They must be going somewhere special. 'Doing something nice?'

'Mostly shopping.' He sounded evasive and Lettie decided to drop the matter.

'Well, I hope you have fun.'

She watched her parents leave the house and soon after drive away. Happy to be alone, Lettie walked outside looking forward to spending a few hours alone.

* * *

That evening she made the most of her parents before they left for their holiday. She was sitting outside in the beer garden at the back of the pub with Tina, and Lettie couldn't help wishing Brodie had never returned to the island. Despite her best intentions, her emotions clearly had no plan to do what was best for her, and she still had a massive crush on him.

'You're very thoughtful,' Tina said narrowing her eyes. 'Are you going to tell me what's happened, or am I going to have to guess?'

Lettie knew Tina would keep something to herself if she shared it with her. They had been best friends for years and she had to confide in someone. 'The new vet.'

'He's gorgeous, isn't he? I bumped into him at the store earlier and he has the bluest eyes. He looks extra cute wearing those glasses too, I thought.'

Lettie nodded her agreement. A bit too cute for her liking, she decided.

'When he looked at me I briefly forgot why I had gone into the shop. Embarrassing it was, I can tell you.'

'Only if he noticed.' Lettie saw disappointment in Tina's face and realised she had said the wrong thing. She knew only too well how it felt not to be noticed by him. 'Remember that school Halloween disco when we were about fifteen?'

'The one I missed because my dad had grounded me for staying out too late the previous weekend?' Tina gasped. 'Not the one where you had your first kiss?'

Tina knew her too well. 'That's the one.'

Tina gazed at her silently, tapping her finger against her lips thoughtfully before her eyes widened. 'Don't tell me he's the guy who kissed you?'

Lettie closed her eyes, recalling the humiliation of that night when so much had seemed possible, but only for a very brief time. His rejection of her still stung. 'That's the one.'

Tina's mouth dropped open. 'No,' she whispered.

'I wish he wasn't, but he is.'

Tina sat back in silence. She waited for Tina to think things through, then, seeing her friend's expression change, she could tell Tina had worked out exactly why this was such a bad thing.

'So, he's not only gorgeous, and has already kissed you, but he doesn't remember either you or that kiss? Is that it?'

Lettie let out a long, miserable sigh. 'It is.'

Tina touched her arm sympathetically. 'Oh Lettie, that's horrible.'

'Exactly. If that isn't bad enough, imagine how mortified I'm going to be when he works out where he knows me from.'

Her friend shook her head. 'Why would he do that?' She took a sip of her drink. 'If he hasn't remembered you yet, then maybe it won't ever come to him?'

If only life was as simple as that, Lettie thought wistfully. 'Because when we first met, he was convinced he knew me from somewhere, that's why.'

'Ah, I see. Tricky.'

'Yes.' She covered her face with her hands. 'Why does he have to be the farm's new flippin' vet?'

'Maybe when you're in sole charge of the farm you could move to another veterinary practice?'

'If only it was that easy,' Lettie groaned. 'I couldn't do that.'

'Why not?'

Lettie tried to picture Brodie's reaction if she did go to another vet. It wouldn't be fair, not when he was trying to build his reputation here and hadn't actually done anything wrong. Anything he was aware of. 'Because he would surely want to know why. And, even if he didn't ask, I know my father would be angry. He already likes him and thinks he's good at what he does, so it isn't really an option.'

'I'd never think of you as forgettable though,' Tina said thoughtfully. 'It's very odd.'

'Embarrassing, is what it is.'

Tina gasped. 'I bet I know what's caused his confusion.'

Lettie shrugged. 'Go on then, enlighten me.'

'It's your name. He's trying to think where he knows Lettie Torel from, not Violet Torel.' Lettie winced at the name she hated so much. Why had her mother let her father persuade her to call Lettie after her paternal grandmother? 'Don't pull that face. Those older names are becoming more popular now.'

'Well this particular one wasn't when I was at school.' Lettie shuddered. 'Maybe it was the thought of going out with someone called Violet that put him off me.' Could it be that? she wondered.

Tina picked up her drink and raised her glass. 'Whatever his reasons, maybe his memory is so lousy he'll never work out where he knows you from. And if he does, so what? We all kissed people in high school. You two can just have a laugh about it and move on, right?'

If only it was that easy, Lettie thought, but raised her glass anyway. 'Cheers to that.'

13

BRODIE

End of May

It had been a long, exhausting day and despite the sea being perfect for surfing, all Brodie had the energy for was a shower, popping something into the microwave for his supper and collapsing in front of the television for a few hours before going to bed.

Running his own practice had proven considerably more labour-intensive and stressful than he had expected. He wasn't sure why he hadn't realised before. Probably, he thought, because before taking over The Village Practice all he'd had to do was focus on his patients and making sure the paperwork for them was completed correctly. Now, he also needed to stay on top of the accounts, and ensure all the stock was up to date and that they didn't run out of anything. Bethan was excellent at her job but she was doing the work of two members of staff, which wasn't fair. If he didn't find someone to look after reception soon, she might be tempted to go elsewhere and he didn't want to risk that happening.

This morning he had missed an urgent message to call one of the practice's most long-standing clients because he'd had to deal with an emergency when someone's cat had been injured in a fight with another cat. Bethan had been helping him with the animal, then calming the panic-stricken owner and the wind had blown the note from his desk where Bethan had placed it. It wasn't until later when he had bent to retrieve what he thought was a scrap of paper from the wrapping of a dressing that he had seen it.

'It's not your fault, Bethan,' he had assured her before hurriedly phoning the client and apologising profusely. He'd had no choice but to make amends by racing out to the woman's home and examining her pet pot-bellied pig causing him to be home later than usual.

'We need to find someone to come and cover reception, and soon,' he'd said to Bethan earlier that day.

'We do, but who can we ask? I suppose we could advertise for someone.' Bethan had thought for a moment. 'So many people like working from home since the pandemic and this isn't the sort of job you can do remotely. Last Christmas my parents were hoping to book their Christmas lunch out somewhere nice, but most restaurants were closed over the holidays because they couldn't risk letting people down through lack of staff.'

He had agreed and thought of the store in town where a large sign saying *Staff Wanted* had been stuck onto the window since his arrival on the island.

'We must know someone between the pair of us who might want the job.'

He wished he could think of someone. He had been away from the island for so long and most of the people he knew had either settled into full-time careers or had moved to the mainland or even further afield. He couldn't think of anyone who might want a job working for his tiny practice.

* * *

'How about Tina Thornton?' Zac suggested a couple of days later when he had stopped to chat with Brodie on the slipway while Brodie had been fastening his surfboard to the roof of his car after an hour's surfing.

'She's busy with her little boy though, isn't she?' Brodie asked.

'Yes, but if she is considering finding work, maybe she could ask her mother to take care of Noah for a few hours each week. I know she's spoken to Lettie about needing to earn some money and she only lives down the road from the surgery on the other side of the village, so it would probably suit her well.'

Brodie liked the idea. 'I suppose I could ask her if she has a few hours free each week?'

'No harm in asking,' Zac said. 'Do you want me to ask Lettie to give her a call? Or she could give you Tina's number and you could phone her yourself?'

'Either suggestion is fine by me.'

He liked the thought of Lettie having his number. He thanked Zac and left to drive the short distance home. The mention of Lettie made him try once again to work out where he had seen her before. She seemed so familiar, but he couldn't work out where he knew her from. She was probably a couple of years younger than him. He'd been heavily into his sports at school and didn't mix much with younger pupils. Why couldn't he shift that nagging feeling that something happened between them. Something he would rather forget?

14

LETTIE

'I'm sure Tina would jump at the chance to earn a bit of money,' Lettie assured Zac.

'Great. Give me your phone and I'll put Brodie's number into your contacts so you can message him and pass on Tina's details.'

She ignored her brother's amused look and decided there was no harm in her having Brodie's number; after all, she might need to speak to him urgently if there was an emergency with one of the animals after her parents were gone. Lettie handed her phone to Zac. 'I'm sure they can work out her hourly rate and times so Tina will be able to work at the practice.'

Zac tapped in the number and saved it, but instead of passing it to her simply gave her a knowing smile.

'I don't know what you're thinking but you can stop it right now.' Lettie held out her hand. 'Let me have my phone back now. I've promised Dad I'll go and help him fix the dry-stone wall and he wants to talk to me about the alpacas in the top field before we have lunch,' she said determined to distract her brother. She loved the alpacas and suspected that it had been her mother who had persuaded him to keep them so that they could sell the wool. 'I have a feeling he and Mum have something they want to get off their chests for some reason.'

'Do you?' Zac frowned, her tactic clearly working. 'What do you think they could have to tell us this time?' He groaned. 'I don't think I want to hear any more unwelcome news from them.'

'Me neither,' Lettie agreed. 'But I'd rather know than try to guess.' She looked at the time on her phone. 'Damn, I'm late. Dad will go mad.'

She ran off without waiting for her brother to reply. Thankfully she was already dressed in her oldest jeans and a T-shirt and only had to push her feet into her wellies when she reached the back door. Grabbing her sunglasses, Lettie ran out of the yard and up the first field, hating the incline as she ran out of steam. This farming business was either going to help her become very fit or kill her off entirely. She was certain she used to be much fitter, but those years standing around while models were fitted and taking notes, then sitting in restaurants and bars with friends had obviously taken their toll.

She saw her father standing next to the damaged dry-stone wall, arms crossed and a scowl on his face. He noticed her and tapped his wristwatch. 'What time do you call this, young lady? You'll have to up your game with your timekeeping if you're going to do this work.'

'Sorry, Dad. Zac was talking to me about something important.'

She reached her dad and bent over, resting her palms on her knees as she tried to catch her breath. 'That's some hill.'

'It isn't all that bad. I'm twice your age and it doesn't bother me to walk up it.'

Lettie didn't point out that she had run up the hill not walked it; there was little point in antagonising her father any more than she had already done.

She realised he was looking her up and down but couldn't think why. 'Is something the matter?'

'Have you brought any gloves up with you?'

Bugger. 'I forgot them,' she admitted, irritated with herself for being unprepared. 'Sorry.'

He tossed his old pair to her. 'Take these.' When she went to argue, he said, 'My hands are toughened from years of this work. Yours—' he peered at them before closing his eyes and shaking his head '—are not.'

She pulled on the gloves and they turned to study the wall. Her father kept his farm pristine, and this wall had only been damaged recently when she had accidentally reversed into it, knocking part of it down with the tow bar on the back of the tractor. She wasn't sure what had upset her father more, the damage to his otherwise spotless wall, or the scratches on his immaculate tractor. She hadn't liked to ask.

'Right watch me and then try to do the same thing.'

After removing the loose stones, Lettie watched her father select a stone with a flat front and place it neatly on the top one, then moving it slightly until it sat flush at the front and neatly on the top. He then searched for another stone to fit the next place.

'It's rather like a jigsaw puzzle, isn't it?' she said, wondering when the last time might be that she had completed one of those.

'Not quite,' he said sounding weary. 'Are you concentrating, Lettie? I won't be here to help you soon and I don't want you bothering your uncle too much while I'm away.'

He motioned for her to continue working. 'Your mother and I were going to tell you and Zac over lunch.'

'Tell us what?' she asked nervously. 'Nothing's wrong is it?' She thought of his previous heart attack. 'You haven't had another...'

'No. Nothing like that.' He picked up and put down several other stones.

'Then what is it?'

He stopped what he was doing and frowned at her. 'Will you keep working?'

'Please tell me.'

'For pity's sake, Lettie. I need to go away for a few health checks, but what we're wanting to tell you is that we've booked a cruise. Quite a long one, in fact. Now will you hurry up and get on please?'

'Yes, sorry.' Relieved, she did as he asked. So her parents had booked their trip now? They wouldn't have done that if he was ill. She relaxed slightly.

'I don't think there'll be many times in the next few months when you'll need to do this, unless you drive other machinery into different areas. Although I'm hoping you don't make a habit of doing that.'

'I certainly don't intend to.'

Why was everything so much harder than her father made it look? Lettie wondered after they had finished building the wall and she had watched her father redo most of her lousy effort. Years of practice, she supposed.

'And I need you to make a note in that book of yours to contact the bloke who shears the alpacas. They'll need to be done just before the summer. The beginning of June should be fine. I'll give you his details before we leave, so don't worry about that. He knows what he's doing.'

'Dad, I don't think three months is nearly enough time for me to prove myself here,' she said as they walked together back down the field on their way to the farmhouse.

'It depends on how you look at it.'

What was that supposed to mean? 'I don't understand.'

Her father stopped and turned to her. 'I don't expect you to be proficient in anything here, but I want to give you the opportunity to see for yourself that this isn't the life for you.'

So that was it. Hurt by his lack of support, she struggled to think of a reply. Her father seemed to assume she had not wanted to answer and carried on walking home.

Lettie hurried to catch up with him. 'You don't think I'll stick it out, is that it?'

He shook his head. 'Not at all. In fact, I know you're determined and believe you'll do as you've said and show us all that you're far better at farming than any of us expect.'

'If that's the case then why don't you think this is something I might wish to continue doing?'

He didn't speak for a few steps then stopped again. Taking her by the elbows, he smiled. 'Sweetheart, I believe you can do whatever you set your mind to. I just don't want you to feel obliged to stick with it because you've taken on this challenge. I want you to have a go, see what you really think, and how much pressure it is to run a farm of this size, and I don't just mean the day-to-day stuff but finding workers to help during the busier times and whatever admin is required too.'

A thought occurred to her. 'Would you be having this same conversation if I was Zac?'

He seemed affronted by her question. 'Do you mean because he's a boy, or for some other reason?'

'Because he's male and I'm not.'

Her father surprised her by laughing. 'Lettie, I've been married to your mother for twenty-six years and lived in the same house as you for most of your life and I know without doubt that both you women are more than capable of running this place as well as or even better than me. Therefore, in answer to your question, no, I'm not saying this because you're a girl. I'm saying this because I want you to have the freedom to be exactly what you imagined yourself being. I want you to live a good life and not have to struggle daily and be at the mercy of the unreliable British weather.' He smiled at her. 'Look, if running this place is that life, then we'll have to figure something out with Leonard I want you to see for yourself exactly what it entails. All the nitty-gritty, greasy, hot and sweaty bits of it. Then, if you still feel that you want this, we'll extend your—' he thought for a moment '—probationary period and take it from there.'

Feeling much better to hear her father's assurances, Lettie hugged him. 'Thanks, Dad. I'm going to prove to you and Uncle Leonard that I do have what it takes.'

'That's fine. Just remember, if you change your mind no one will think any the less of you. You need to be honest with yourself about all this, Lettie. Promise me you'll do that.'

'I promise.'

They arrived back at the house and after removing their boots and washing their hands and faces both were seated at the scrubbed pine kitchen table that held so many memories of countless meals, and evenings when she and Zac struggled to do homework. Lettie ran her finger over an indent in the wood in front of where she sat, recalling getting into trouble with her mother when she had been caught pressing the nib of her blue biro into the grain several times to make an L. Now it was a familiar reminder of her happy childhood growing up in this place.

Whatever promises she had made to her father, she wasn't nearly ready to give up on this farm yet.

* * *

'You're going on a cruise?' Zac asked, his fork halfway to his mouth. 'Since when did you two like cruising?'

'There's always a first time for everything,' their mother replied, ruffling his hair and annoying him. 'Anyway, we don't need any smart comments from you. What we do need is your reassurance that you're not going to be away working on the mainland most of the time we're away. We need to feel reassured that you'll be around to help your sister if she needs you to.' She looked at Lettie. 'Although I'm fairly confident that she'll manage perfectly well.'

'I'll do my best to, Mum,' Lettie reassured her. 'But thanks all the same.' Wanting to take the attention off herself, Lettie asked, 'Where have you booked to go?'

'All over,' their mother said, her eyes sparkling with excitement. Their parents had taken short holidays each year, at least one, but had never gone on a cruise before. 'We're starting off in the Mediterranean, then instead of returning to Southampton we decided to change ships and go to Norway and up the fjords.' She beamed at their father. 'Your father and I have always wanted see that part of the world, haven't we, Gareth?'

'We have.'

He didn't seem as certain as their mother, Lettie noticed. 'They do look lovely,' she said. 'I was watching a documentary a few months ago on that area and it looked spectacular. I'm sure you'll both love it.'

'You see, Gareth,' their mother said. 'Even Lettie thinks it's a perfect place to visit.'

Lettie ate a mouthful of her roast lunch. She wasn't sure why her mother said 'even Lettie' or what that meant, but she let it go. Now wasn't the time to cause any friction. Despite being anxious about them leaving her to run the farm alone, all she wanted was for her parents to be happy, go away and to enjoy themselves. It was the only way she would be able to prove to everyone that she could do it.

It occurred to her that they hadn't mentioned a departure date. 'When will you be going?'

'When is it again, Lindy?' her father asked.

Her mother gave him a meaningful glare. 'Anyone would think

you weren't excited about going away with me on this trip,' she said before eating a mouthful of food. 'We've only got another week before we go away.'

How had the weeks flown by so quickly? Then again, she mused, one day seemed to merge into the next now she was completely shattered.

'I know isn't it exciting?' her mother said, opening the fridge to take out the milk.

'So that's why you needed to go shopping for clothes for your trip?'

Her mother grinned and Lettie couldn't miss the excitement on her face. 'Did I tell you there are several gala evenings while we're on board?'

Lettie was too busy panicking to answer for a moment. 'But next week?'

Zac nudged Lettie. 'Don't worry, sis, I'll be around to help you if you need me to.'

'That's kind of you, Zac,' their mother said. 'Now, let's all calm down and eat our food.'

Lettie listened while her mother told them all about the different galas and how she needed a black dress for one. 'It's a black and white ball and I'm going to wear my mother's pearls and a white chiffon shawl for the white bit. There's also a masked ball but I'm told we can buy masks on board. It's so exciting, don't you think?'

Lettie smiled. 'Yes, Mum, it sounds amazing.'

Her father looked at her and wiped his mouth on a piece of kitchen roll. 'I'm aware you don't feel quite ready to take everything on for herself just yet, Lettie.'

Not wishing to ruin their excitement, Lettie forced a smile. 'I'll be fine,' she assured him. 'And we all know Uncle Leonard will be at the end of the phone.'

'He will be. He's agreed to ensure you have enough farm workers to come and help with the harvesting and two of them will take the potatoes to the harbour each day, so you don't need to concern yourself about that. I mostly need you to care for the animals, milk the goats and ensure that their milk is delivered to everyone we supply on time. Then I've written out a list of the vegetables needing to be planted and harvested in the polytunnels and when to do it all. Mostly you need to keep an eye on them and keep them watered.' He picked up his cutlery again. 'It's all written down. Just pace yourself.'

It was easy for him to say that, she thought. Her father had done this job for decades and she'd only been working here a month, not even that. 'I'll do my best, Dad.'

'I know you will, lovey.'

'And,' Zac said, 'Brodie Murray has offered any help she needs.' He grinned at Lettie. 'Hasn't he, Letts?'

'He has?' It was the first she had heard of it and she wasn't sure how it made her feel.

Lettie ignored her mother's obvious delight at the thought.

'I said he was a lovely young man. Didn't I say that to you only yesterday, Gareth?'

Their father glared at Zac. 'Stop stirring.' He looked at Lettie. 'He is a good chap though and I'm glad he's offered his help while we're away.'

Lettie relaxed slightly. If she was completely honest with herself, she was also a little relieved to know she could call on him if necessary. She just hoped his help wasn't needed but if it meant that her parents could go away and completely relax and enjoy their trip, then she wasn't going to say anything that might worry them. 'So you see, Dad, there's no need for you to concern yourself with me or this place while you're away. Zac and I want you to make the most of your dream holiday.' She looked to her mother. 'You both deserve this.'

'Thanks, love,' her mother said tilting her head to one side. 'We've talked about this for such a long time that I was beginning to think it might never happen.'

'And I'm only in town and can be here in fifteen minutes if there's any emergency.' Zac grinned. 'You see? Everything will be fine.'

The three of them looked at Zac and Lettie couldn't hide her amusement at her father's confused expression.

'I'm not sure how that will help her,' he said shaking his head. 'You'd probably be more of a hindrance than a help now I think of it.'

Lettie threw her head back and laughed. 'You see, Zac, I'm not the only one who thinks that.'

Zac stuck his tongue out at her and turned his attention back to his meal. 'Fine, then I won't bother to rush over if I'm such a nuisance.'

Feeling bad for hurting his feelings, Lettie smiled at him. 'Don't be silly. You know I'm always happy to see you. Anyway, you've promised Mum you'll be there for me, so you have to now.'

'Yes, you do,' their mother said. 'Now, eat.'

15

BRODIE

Deciding to wait and see if he spotted Tina out and about instead of troubling Lettie for her number, Brodie was delighted to see her a couple of days later at the small supermarket in the village.

As luck would have it, he was about to enter the shop when he noticed Tina pushing her son out of the shop door in his buggy. Not wanting to miss the opportunity, he rushed over to speak to her.

'Hi, Tina.' He noticed four heavy-looking bags, two hanging from her elbows and another two hooked onto the sides of the buggy handle. 'That lot looks cumbersome. If you don't mind me walking with you, I'll carry them for you.'

She considered his offer and for a moment she seemed to be about to refuse.

'Or I could give you a lift home, if you'd rather?' he added.

'Thanks, but I don't have Noah's car seat. It's only down the lane there, so it won't take me long. Honestly.'

'Then I'll carry the bags for you.' He didn't think the buggy could cope with the weight although he assumed Tina had done this many times before.

Her face lit up. 'Really? You don't mind?'

He took the bags from her, careful not to let the buggy tip up. 'I'm happy to.'

They began walking and Brodie was about to bring up the subject of a job, when Tina spoke. 'I feel badly that I'm taking you away from whatever it was you were about to do.'

'I was only popping into the store to buy something for my supper later. I like to get down to the beach as soon as I can after finishing work on days when the tide is just right, which I noticed it was when I drove along the Five Mile Road earlier.'

She frowned. 'And now I've taken you from your shopping.' She stopped walking. 'Give those back to me and go and buy your food.'

'Really, it's fine.'

'No, I insist. I can manage from here.'

Brodie realised he needed to let her know the real reason he had stopped to help her. Although, he would have offered to help, having seen her struggling with the bags anyway.

'I was hoping to catch you at some point,' he admitted.

Tina frowned suspiciously, then raised her eyebrows and smiled. 'Is this about Lettie?'

Lettie? Why would he be stopping Tina to talk about her? 'No, er, I was wanting to ask you if you might be interested in working a few hours each week. At the practice.'

Tina stared at him for a moment, clearly taken aback. 'Me? But I haven't worked for a vet before.'

'Shall we walk on again?' he suggested as the circulation in his fingers threatened to be cut off by the heavy bags.

Tina glanced down at his hands then grimaced. 'Yes, good idea.'

'I don't need a veterinary nurse, but someone to do a bit of admin, answer phone calls, file records, that sort of thing.'

'Like a receptionist, you mean?'

'Yes. Bethan Davies, my practice nurse, has been covering reception as well as her other work, and I've been doing it too, but it's unsustainable if I want to keep my clients happy and especially if I'm hoping to grow the practice.'

They walked on in silence for a little while. 'I'm this way.' Tina pushed open a wooden gate and led the way to the door. 'You can leave those on the path. I'll settle Noah and fetch them in a bit.' She opened the door and turned to him. 'I would ask you in for a coffee, but I suspect you'd rather go back to the store and do your shopping.'

Unsure whether she was looking for an excuse not to invite him in, Brodie relented. 'Thanks, I would.' Not wishing to leave until he had some sort of answer, Brodie slowly lowered the bags onto the pathway. 'I'll leave you to have a think about the work. If you have any questions, you can call me at the practice, or leave a message with Bethan and I'll get back to you.'

'Sorry, I should have said, I'd be very interested in working for you.'

He was lost for words for a few seconds. 'That is brilliant news. I'm delighted.'

'I'd need to know what days you'll want me and the hours, of course. And, um...'

'The pay. Yes, well, if you like I can email a few details to you.' She gave him her email address and Brodie typed it into his phone. 'Regarding hours, I'll be happy to fit in with you. I'm aware you'll probably need to arrange childcare. You could let me know what suits you and we can take it from there.'

'And you'd want me to start when?'

'As soon as you possibly can, but no pressure. I presume you'll want to discuss this with your husband and have a think about whether this does suit you, which of course I hope it will. But I'm aware this is a bit of an unexpected request so I'm happy to wait for you to get back to me.'

'I'll do that first thing tomorrow,' she said sounding very determined he was relieved to note. 'And thank you so much for thinking of me, Brodie. I really appreciate it.'

'Don't thank me,' he said. 'Zac was the one to put your name forward when I told him I was hoping to employ someone.'

'Then I'll have to buy him a drink when I next see him at the pub.'

Brodie laughed. 'I'd wait and see if you like the work first.'

He heard Tina's laughter as he turned and walked down the pathway back to the lane. He liked Tina and felt sure she and Bethan would get along. The day was turning out very well.

16

LETTIE

June

'You'll never guess who I saw coming out of the veterinary practice this morning when I went to collect your father's suit from the dry cleaner's,' Lindy Torel said as she carried it and two bags of shopping past Lettie towards the house.

'Who?' Lettie asked immediately wishing she hadn't sounded quite so interested when her mother raised an eyebrow and gave her a knowing smile. 'And you can stop that nonsense. I'm only interested because I still haven't got round to speaking to someone about working there.'

'I've no idea what you're on about. Anyway, I was talking about that teacher of yours. You know the one, she taught you French in Year 2, or was it Year 3?'

'Mum, please get to the point, I have animals to look after.'

'Fine. Well, she was saying that they have a new receptionist in there. And you'll never guess who it is?'

Lettie wished her mother would stop with all the intrigue. 'Are you going to tell me, or is this a twenty questions kind of conversation? Because if it is, I really don't have time to indulge you.'

'Hark at you?'

'Mum!'

'Oh, all right then, it's Tina.'

'Tina?' How had that happened? she wondered, feeling guilty for not having passed on Tina's details as she had offered to do. 'She has a job there?'

'That's what your old teacher said.' Her mother pushed open the front door and hung the hanger over one of the coat hooks in the hallway before turning back to Lettie. 'What was her name now? I know, it was Miss Bastian. That's right, isn't it?'

'Yes, Mum, that is right. But please can you tell me what she said about Tina?'

'Nothing much. She said she was very good and helped her settle the invoice for her little terrier dog she had taken to be checked with the vet. She was mostly excited about passing on a little news more than anything, I think.'

'I'm pleased. I know Tina's been wanting to do something a little different since Noah turned two, but the virtual assistant work hadn't taken off as she hoped it would, and she and Kyle could definitely do with the money. I'm glad Brodie asked her.'

'You knew about this?'

'Sort of. Right, can I get on with my work now? I don't want Dad getting upset because I haven't finished all the jobs he wants me to do.'

'Sorry. I'll leave you be.'

She watched her mother disappear into the house and turned to go to the barn. Brodie must have taken it upon himself to track Tina down, she mused. Although he could have always sought her out to ask for Tina's number. It would have been the perfect excuse to do so if he was interested in her. Clearly he couldn't be, she decided.

Lettie was disappointed for a while, but focused all her attention onto her work. She had far more important things to be focusing on now than to let a man distract her attention from the farm, especially one who had already shown that he couldn't be relied upon.

Later, as she finished packing that day's collection of eggs, it occurred to Lettie that it was probably just as well that Brodie wasn't interested in her. If he had been then he might kiss her at some point and be reminded of that first kiss they'd shared and how dreadful it must have been for him not to bother even talking to her again. She shuddered at the thought.

Later, having fed the livestock, Lettie sat down in the shade, leaning back against the wall with a cool glass of water when she felt her phone vibrating in her jeans pocket. She took it out and looked at the screen, answering immediately when she saw Tina's name.

'Hi, Tina, how's the new job going?' she asked, excited to hear how her friend was getting on working away from home for the first time in over two years.

'Sorry, Lettie,' she said her voice tense.

'What's the matter?' Lettie sat upright.

'I'm at work and there's an emergency. I need to fetch Noah but can't get hold of Kyle to collect him. I hate to ask you when you're so busy, but would you be able to get him today?'

'No problem at all. Shall I take him home, or to your mum's?'

'She's out shopping somewhere. Could you bring him to the practice please. Hopefully I'll be able to leave by then, but they're going to need me for a bit longer and I can't leave Noah waiting for me.'

'Don't be silly. That's no problem at all.'

'Thank you, that's such a relief. I'll message the nursery now and let them know to expect you.'

Lettie ended the call, wondering what could have happened at the practice to cause such alarm. She noticed how grubby her clothes were and ran into the house for a speedy shower. Tying her hair back and without wasting time to dry herself properly, she pulled on a clean pair of shorts and a T-shirt and ran out to her mother's car.

She was relieved to notice that there were two other children waiting with Noah and his teacher at the nursery school. They knew her there mostly because she had attended the same school as several of the teachers, or had been taught by others, so most of the staff knew she and Tina had been best friends since they had started school.

'Hello.' She smiled at the teacher as she ruffled Noah's thick hair. 'Tina's been delayed at work and was going to message you to say she had asked me to pick up Noah today. Is that all right?'

'We received her message, so it's fine.' Miss Collier had been in the year above Lettie and Tina, and neither of them had been surprised when she had trained to be a teacher. The children loved her – well, Noah and the two other pupils standing with her seemed very calm in her presence and not at all fazed that their parents hadn't arrived at the school yet.

'Thank you.' She smiled at Noah. 'Shall we go and see how Mummy's getting on at her new job?'

Noah's smile widened. 'Yeth pleath, Auntie Letts.'

She reached out her hand, a warm feeling sweeping through her when his little hand took it. 'Let's go then, shall we?'

'Yay. We're going to my mummy's work,' he bellowed over his shoulder to the other two children and Mrs Collier.

The short walk to the practice was filled with Noah's excited chatter, which didn't stop until they reached the entrance. Lettie led him up to the door, hoping there weren't going to be any shocks to greet him but trusting that if that had been the case then Tina would be looking out for them to arrive and would no doubt come outside to warn her.

'Mummy!' he shrieked, running into her open arms.

'Shush, Noah,' Tina whispered. 'There are sick animals waiting to see the vet.'

He covered his mouth with his hand and gazed around the room at the three clients waiting, one with a dog on a lead and two with cats in pet carriers.

'Do you want to come and say hello to Monty?' the lady with a Labrador puppy asked. 'He's very friendly.'

'Can I, Mummy?'

'Yes, but be gentle with him. You don't want to frighten him just before he has his injections.'

'No, I don't.'

Lettie and Tina watched Noah, and Lettie couldn't help asking what the drama was about.

'A mare at the stables down the road has given birth.'

'Was it all right?' Lettie asked.

'Yes, but the owner discovered there was another still to be born.'

'Twins?'

The people all looked up at Lettie and Tina motioned for her to lower her voice. 'Yes. Brodie had to rush off and called after him for Bethan to follow. He didn't like to let the other patients or their owners down by rescheduling their appointments, so asked me to stay behind and keep them updated until they returned and he could see them.' She lowered her voice further. 'I gather Brodie had offered to do a scan but the woman didn't think it necessary because none of her mares had ever given birth to twins before.'

'I bet she wished she had listened to him now.'

Tina nodded. 'Bethan suspects it's because he's new here and so much younger than the previous vet, so some clients are finding it difficult to trust his diagnoses and think they know better.'

Lettie couldn't help thinking how silly that was. Much as she found being in Brodie's company a little disconcerting, as far as she was concerned the fact that he had only a few of years before qualified as a vet meant to her that he had been trained with the latest equipment and knowledge. Surely that was something to inspire confidence, rather than the opposite?

'He raced off and Bethan followed as soon as I arrived and she had handed over to me. He's incredibly dedicated.' She smiled. 'But I sense you've already noticed that about him. I can see that Bethan clearly has.'

What was that supposed to mean? Lettie wondered, not missing her friend's innuendo. 'I've noticed he's a trustworthy vet, if that's what you're insinuating.'

She wasn't surprised though. She might not know him very well but everything she had discovered about Brodie since meeting him again had shown her how caring he was to others, especially the animals he looked after. How could she not have a soft spot for someone who loved animals?

'Hey.'

She realised Tina was trying to get her attention.

'Sorry, I was thinking.'

'About my dishy boss, no doubt.' Tina raised an eyebrow, lowering it when Lettie glowered at her.

Tina knew her far too well to be fobbed off with a fib. 'Maybe.'

Tina sighed as another client entered the reception. 'I'd better get on. Thanks for collecting Noah.'

'I can take him with me back to the farm if you're going to be a while. You or Kyle could always fetch him on your way home from work.'

'He'll be fine. He loves animals and we have snacks here he can eat if I'm longer than I expect.'

'Well, if you're sure. Do call me if you change your mind. I'm only five minutes away.'

'Thanks, Lettie.' Tina kissed her on the cheek. 'Noah, say goodbye to Lettie.'

Lettie bent to give the little boy a hug and left Tina to attend to the new client who had just arrived, relieved her friend's attention had been distracted just when things were getting tricky. As she walked to the car, Lettie mused about Tina's notion that Bethan seemed to like him confirmed what she had thought seeing Bethan's reaction to Brodie that night in the pub. Lettie knew it shouldn't bother her, but the pang in her heart told her otherwise. It was no business of hers if Bethan and Brodie became close. They worked together for long hours and were both single, so it shouldn't be too surprising that they might become close. It wasn't as if she was looking for a relationship with him, not when she had so much responsibility weighing on her for at least the next three months.

She pushed thoughts of Brodie aside, irritated with herself for daydreaming about him and silly what-might-have-beens. She needed to focus on the task ahead of her if she was going to succeed in looking after the farm while her parents were away, and the only way to do that was to ensure she had no distractions, real or fantasy, to take her attention from her farm work.

17

BRODIE

Brodie stopped to let a vehicle out of the car park and spotted Lettie walking along the pavement away from the practice. If only he hadn't been stuck behind two tractors on the way back from the stables he might have been back in time to speak to her.

He parked the car and wondered why she had called in. Remembering Tina was working on reception, he grabbed his case and hurried inside. He opened his mouth to apologise to the waiting people who had brought in their pets when something slammed into his legs. Reaching down to catch whatever it was, Brodie laughed when he recognised the little boy of about two years old with a mop of dark wavy hair who had been in the pushchair when he helped Tina with her shopping.

'Noah, be careful. I'm so sorry,' Tina said hurrying out from behind the reception desk. 'He can be a little whirlwind sometimes.'

'It's fine. I hope he hasn't been waiting too long.' He looked at the other people and gave an apologetic smile. 'I hope none of you have been here for too long and I'm sorry to have kept you waiting. I'll just go through to my surgery and then Tina can start sending you in. If any of you would rather come back another day, we can arrange an alternative appointment with you.'

He turned to her and lowered his voice. 'Bethan is on her way back now too, so shouldn't be very long.'

'That's fine,' she said glancing at Noah. 'Come and sit with Mummy please.'

'Don't worry about him,' Brodie soothed, wanting to calm her. 'He's been very good to have to spend time here when I'm sure both of you would have rather be at home by now.'

'It's fine,' Tina said.

Brodie couldn't imagine that was the case but thought it kind of her to try and reassure him. 'Give me two minutes then send in the first person, please.'

'Will do.'

Half an hour later, the second client was shown in by Bethan. 'Ah, you're back. Has Tina left yet?'

'She has. I thanked her for both of us. She did a great job today.'

'I thought so too.' He smiled at the elderly man holding a pet carrier and went to take it from him. 'Good afternoon, Mr Billings. How's Smudge this week?'

* * *

By the end of the day, Brodie was tired and looking forward to an hour's surfing but when he got down to the beach he was disappointed to see there was little surf. Instead of returning to his cottage behind the surgery he decided to leave his board and go for a quick swim instead.

This is the life, he thought, as he waded out in the shallow waters before reaching waist-deep and submersing himself into the chilly but calm sea. Once completely wet, he lay on his back and floated on the small rolling waves, staring up at the azure blue sky with only the hint of the odd wispy cloud. He thought back to when he was eighteen and desperate to leave the island for some excitement. Now, here he was years later ecstatic to be home again. He had loved the nightlife in England and being able to take a train to the next town to concerts or the theatre if nothing much was happening where he lived. Taking flights direct to holiday destinations without having to take one first from the island to connect to Heathrow or Gatwick was another plus, but the novelty had worn off and, after the end of his relationship with Tiffany, all he had wanted to do was get back to the relative peace of island life.

He was glad he had made the decision, grateful his change in lifestyle had come at the same time as Old Man Winter's retirement. Fate had stepped in and been very generous to him.

He had hoped to enjoy running the practice but even he was surprised at how perfect his life seemed now. Well, almost perfect. He missed having a group of friends to meet up with for meals or a few drinks but was slowly getting to know others. This was a new stage in his life and realising his ambition of having his own business made everything worthwhile. Hopefully things could carry on this way and maybe then in a few years he might be able to afford to refurnish the cottage and buy it outright. The lease was for twenty-five years but ideally he was hoping to find a way to own the place himself.

Slow down, he thought, turning over and starting to swim. There was enough time for all these ambitions to happen. He needed to take things one stage at a time and not overdo it and end up losing everything, which was what Tiffany had insinuated might happen when she decided that living on an island must be the most boring thing in the world. Not that he had ever asked her to join him. Typical Tiffany to offer an unwelcome opinion the one time he bumped into her after their split.

Back at his Land Rover, Brodie shook water from his hair and checked his phone. A message from his mother.

> You've avoided us long enough. Supper at home tonight if you can make it, which I truly hope you can. Mum x

Not wishing to offend his lovely mum and aware he had been neglectful of his family since taking over the practice and being so busy, Brodie texted her back confirming he looked forward to seeing them all later and enjoying some of her delicious cooking.

He drove back to his cottage feeling revitalised and relaxed. He would certainly sleep well tonight. He realised that despite worrying about taking on this new business his sleep had been much better since returning to Jersey. He thought back to what one of his uni friends had always said, 'You can take the boy from the island but not the island from the boy.' Or something like that.

He realised for the first time how very truthful that sentiment was and it certainly suited him. Maybe that had something to do with why Lettie Torel was so insistent on working back here. Her brother had told him about her fun and exciting life in London and although he'd barely seen her in much other than jeans or messy dungarees, Brodie could imagine her in a smart outfit looking glamorous. Lettie. She really was an enigma to him and very different to any other woman he had ever been attracted to before.

Brodie thought of his ex, Tiffany, and how much in love with her he had thought himself to be. She was intense and a brilliant lawyer. At the time he had thought their relationship passionate, and it hadn't occurred to him that maybe they weren't as suited to each other as he had imagined. He recalled how much she loved to debate. Although those debates, as she called them, seemed more like arguments to him and often left him feeling attacked and hurt.

Lettie seemed independent and determined but he doubted she could be unkind simply to make a point.

His relationship with Tiffany wasn't all bad though, Brodie mused. He had enjoyed their lengthy chats planning their futures, thinking they had much to look forward to, when in fact all it had taken for their relationship to fall apart was him mentioning his wish to take over The Village Practice. He still felt betrayed when Greg, a close friend of theirs, had suggested that Brodie valued his career more than her. Tiffany had believed him, despite Brodie's assurances to the contrary, and ended their relationship abruptly, which made him wonder if she had been looking for a way out that she could blame on him.

Thinking about how much he loved being back on the island and how difficult it probably would have been for Tiffany to settle somewhere this small, he now realised that it had all worked out for the best. Brodie pictured the last time he had seen Tiffany when he had gone back to their flat to return his key and how it had stung to find Greg looking very much at home there. He wondered briefly if the two of them were still an item, then pushed the thought away. Tiffany was none of his business any longer.

18

LETTIE

Lettie waved at Brodie and a tug of disappointment pulled at her as she wished she had delayed her departure by a couple of minutes. What for? she thought, aware she was being silly. Anyway, what would it have achieved? Only her feeling awkward and him completely unaware that she liked him. Which, she reminded herself, was just as well. She noticed a tractor further ahead. It had pulled over and, not wishing to leave a fellow farmer in distress, she stopped and wound down her window, seeing someone leaning over the engine.

'Is anything the matter?'

The man straightened up and turned to her, wiping his hands on what looked like an old piece of rag. 'It's all in hand,' he said staring at her momentarily before adding his thanks.

Lettie had no idea who he might be but was a little taken aback to see this dark, shaggy-haired, handsome man who looked to be in his late twenties. He must farm somewhere nearby. Why didn't she know him?

He walked over to her car and raised his hands. 'I would offer to shake your hand but I doubt you'll be happy to touch these oily things.' He cocked his head to one side. 'That one is being more temperamental than usual.'

She looked past him to the tractor that she guessed must be at least twenty years old. 'Can I give you a lift somewhere?'

'No, but thanks for the offer. I'm Joe, by the way.'

'I'm Lettie.'

'You from around here then?'

'Yes, I run Hollyhock Farm.'

He frowned. 'I thought that was Gareth Torel's place.'

'It was.' She corrected herself. 'It is. He's my father. I've taken over the place while he goes away for a few months with my mum.'

'I see. I haven't seen you around here before. Have you been away?'

She wasn't used to sharing so much information with a stranger, but Jersey was a small place and there were fewer farmers than there used to be when she was growing up, so decided there was no harm in being friendly.

'That's right. So where do you work then? Are you new here?'

'I was born here but my parents moved to France when I was fourteen. My uncle needed someone to help him out for a while when I returned and was looking for something different to do for a bit. He offered me a job.'

'Which farm would that be for?' she wondered.

His mouth drew back into a smile. 'Tell you what, why don't you agree to join me tonight for a few drinks and I can tell you all about it. We should be friends if we're both in the same line of work, don't you think?'

She wasn't sure.

He must have sensed her hesitation. 'We can go anywhere you choose but I've discovered that the local pub in the village has a good atmosphere and the lager is pretty tasty. Shall we meet there at seven?'

Lettie was surprised someone in farming would suggest meeting that early. There was no way she would be finished by that time. 'Um,' Lettie said, taken aback. 'I could make it for nine, maybe.' It wasn't as if she had anything else to do that evening, even if she was drained from the physical work she did each day. Recalling her parents were flying to Heathrow the following morning and then to Barcelona for the first leg of their cruise, she reconsidered. 'I'll probably only have time for one drink though. I need to start work earlier than usual in the morning so I can be ready to drive my parents to the airport as soon as I've finished with the goats and chickens.'

'No problem at all.' He raised an eyebrow. 'Would you like me to pick you up or would you rather I meet you there?'

He really did seem rather nice, Lettie thought, amused. 'I'll meet you there, just in case I'm a little late. Now, if you're sure you don't need me to help you with anything, I'd better be off.'

'You know a lot about tractor engines then?'

She was tempted to fib, but didn't put it past him to ask her to fix something just to test her skills. 'No, nothing.'

Joe laughed. 'I like your style, Lettie Torel, and look forward to finding out more about you later.'

She gave him a wave and drove off. She was looking forward to getting to know him too, she decided.

19

BRODIE

'You made it,' his father said greeting Brodie in the driveway. 'Your mother will be happy. She's cooked enough for ten.'

'Who's she invited?' he asked hoping it was just family.

'Just you, your sister and a friend of hers.'

Brodie recognised the look of amusement on his father's face. 'Please tell me she hasn't been invited because Mum wants to introduce her to me?'

His father slipped an arm around Brodie's shoulders. He was the same height as him at six feet one and his years working as a dentist had given him a calming way with anxious people. It was something Brodie appreciated.

'Sorry, son. I'm afraid you taking on the lease for the veterinary practice hasn't reassured your mother enough that you're intending to stay on the island for the foreseeable future. I don't think she has any intention of giving up on trying to find a partner for you until she believes you have no plans to pack up any time soon.'

Brodie stifled a groan. His mother had always found it difficult when he lived away from the island despite his sister never going.

Poor Maddie, how did it all make her feel to have their mother behave in this way?

He had no sooner entered the hallway than his mother appeared from the kitchen and enveloped him in a hug. 'You came!'

Biting back a retort he hugged her back. 'Of course I did. Your meals are always the tastiest and I was looking forward to spending time with you all.'

'I'm not sure I believe you.' She kissed his cheek, then took hold of his wrist. 'But that's OK, I know you mean well.' She began leading him through to the large kitchen–dining area. 'Maddie is here already. Oh, and she's brought a friend with her.'

Brodie fixed a smile onto his face. Even if his father hadn't tipped him off he would have known his mother was up to something by the higher pitch to her voice. Anyway it wasn't the poor girl's fault; she had probably been set up. They entered the room and a pretty girl of about his age with a short, black bob stood by the sliding doors, a glass of wine in her hand. 'This is Cathy.'

'Hi,' Cathy said raising her glass slightly to him and giving a friendly nod.

'Nice to meet you,' Brodie said automatically. 'Hi, sis.' He walked over to his sister and gave her a hug. 'I haven't seen you at the surgery yet. You should pop round and I can show you the place.'

'I'd much rather have a look around your cottage.'

Brodie wished he had somewhere else to be so that he could make an excuse not to have to navigate his family. He loved them dearly but needed more energy than he had right now to cope with them all when they were together. 'I'm not ready to redecorate it yet,' he said, hoping but not expecting his newly qualified interior designer sister to be put off by that nugget of information.

'Rubbish. I've heard on the grapevine that it's in a terribly neglected state. Old Man Winter apparently invested any money he made back into the practice and didn't bother updating his home. It must be horribly outdated.'

It was, and damp, but Brodie had no intention of admitting anything of the sort to Maddie. She was just as determined about things as their mother when she put her mind to it and he wanted to have a chance to get fully settled before even thinking about changing any decor. 'I really don't have the time to focus on it just yet.'

'There's no need for you to do anything,' Maddie answered in her usual enthusiastic way. 'You just leave everything to me.'

He couldn't think of many worse things. 'I'm not sure our tastes are that similar though,' he said trying to be tactful since he knew Maddie's style tended to veer towards busy floral wallpapers and heavily framed paintings, if the look of her recently decorated home was anything to go by. He doubted she would care about that, but it was worth a try.

'I'm qualified to show you what's best for your property.' Their mother walked into the room carrying her own glass of wine. 'Isn't that right, Mum.'

He caught Cathy trying hide a smile as she took a drink from her glass before turning to stare at something out of the window.

'It's very kind of you to offer, Maddie,' he said. 'But I don't have any spare cash to pay for your work.'

'That's fine,' Maddie argued. 'You can settle up whenever you do have some money. Anyway I can use the before and after photos for my portfolio.'

'I think it's very sweet of your sister to offer to do this for you, Brodie,' their mother said proudly.

Brodie gave his father a pleading look.

'Let's leave Brodie alone, shall we?' their father said, resting a hand on his shoulder. 'The poor devil only recently took over the practice and must be exhausted from working all day.'

'It has been a tiring week,' Brodie agreed.

'But I said you could leave the cottage to me,' Maddie argued. 'You won't need to do anything.'

'Madison,' their father barked. 'That's enough. I'm sure your brother will let you know when and, more importantly, if he wants you to do any decoration.'

'I will,' Brodie said, relieved to see his sister press her lips together and end the subject. 'But I appreciate your offer, Maddie.'

Soothed by his thanks, she shrugged. 'I know you do.'

Their mother waved for their attention. 'The food is just about ready, so we may as well be seated.'

* * *

After finishing their roast chicken supper, Brodie began to relax and started to enjoy the evening with his family and Cathy.

'So tell us a bit about yourself, Cathy. How long have you known this one, for example?' Brodie cocked his head in his sister's direction and grinned.

'I've known Maddie since we met at a mutual friend's engagement party a couple of years ago.'

'I see.' He couldn't recall his sister mentioning her before, but then again, when was the last time they had sat and had a catch-up? 'And do you mind me asking what you do, workwise?'

He was intrigued to find out more about the pleasant girl who didn't seem remotely fazed by his sister's enthusiasm towards most things. She was clearly very fond of Maddie and he liked her even more for that. Maddie wasn't everyone's cup of tea and as much as his older sister's bossiness drove him nuts on occasion, he loved her deeply and hated to think that anyone might dislike her.

'I'm a radiographer.'

'Yes, another medical person,' Maddie said smiling. 'I'm surrounded by them.'

'I'm not a medical person,' their mother said.

'Mum, you were a dentist, like Dad.' She looked at Cathy. 'My parents met at dentistry school and Mum fell pregnant with me so didn't end up qualifying but married Dad instead.'

'Er, thank you, Madison,' her mother snapped. 'I'll thank you not to share my, um...'

'Past?' Maddie offered blowing a kiss at their mother.

'Well, yes.' Their mother looked at Cathy. 'Not that I'd change anything about it you understand.'

'No, of course not.'

'I'm a retired dentist,' their father said, Brodie suspected to divert attention away from their angry mother. 'And you know that Brodie's a vet. My father was a dentist too, but retired now of course.'

'I think she gets the message.' Maddie laughed. 'Honestly, I wish I hadn't said anything now.'

'So do I,' their mother said pointedly.

'This food is delicious.' Brodie indicated his almost clean plate. He grinned at Cathy. 'I'm sure you can't wait until you're invited to join us for another meal.'

Cathy laughed. 'I've had a wonderful time, and,' she added turning to their mother, 'Maddie told me you were an excellent cook, Mrs Murray, and she wasn't kidding. Thank you again for inviting me.'

Clever woman, Brodie thought, seeing his mother's expression lighten up immediately at the compliment. 'You're very welcome, Cathy. If only my daughter's manners matched yours.'

'Is there any pudding, Jane?'

Another diversion from their father, Brodie noted, eating the last mouthful of his meal. Poor Dad has probably spent most of his married life finding ways to divert their mother's attention from things that might upset or offend her.

Brodie helped Maddie with the washing up before joining the others for coffee.

'That was delicious, Mum,' Maddie said. 'I know, why don't we all go to the pub for a quick drink?'

'I won't, thank you,' Jane said. 'But you four go.'

'I'll stay here,' their father said pretending to yawn.

'I'm tired too,' Brodie said looking forward to an early night.

'No chance.' Maddie stood and collected Brodie and Cathy's empty coffee cups. 'You two are coming with me. We only have to have one, but it'll be fun and a perfect way to spend the rest of our evening.'

He wasn't sure he wanted to go but not wishing to have another argument with his sister, especially when the evening had been going so well, he agreed. 'Just the one though.'

20

LETTIE

Lettie was late but not by too much. One of the hedge cutters had broken down on the farm and her father had spent a long time showing her how to fix it, concerned she might not remember when it happened again. He had then explained about the farm workers who lived in accommodation on her uncle's farm.

'Remember, if you have any issues with staff just speak to Uncle Leonard. He'll make sure you have enough people each day to cover any harvesting or packing, but as we've pretty much finished with the potato season for now, things should be a lot quieter for you while I'm away.'

Lettie wasn't sure how happy she was about this. 'How am I supposed to prove myself then, if most of the work has been done?'

He laughed. 'Don't worry, there's plenty with the livestock and planting to keep you on your toes until I'm back and there'll be fruit to harvest around the time I'm due back here.'

Satisfied with this information, Lettie went to help her mother who was struggling to make final choices between three evening dresses so that she could finish her packing.

Finally, showered and dressed in jeans and a smarter T-shirt,

Lettie walked into the pub. She smiled a hello to the landlord before scanning the room and seeing Joe sitting at a table, his hand raised to indicate where he was.

She gave a nod and passing two girls she didn't know on the nearest table, sat down. 'Sorry I've kept you waiting.'

'It's fine. There's so much going on in here that I'm happy to people-watch.'

She spotted one of the girls with a neat, dark bob giving Joe the occasional look and wasn't surprised. He was hot, although in a different way to Brodie. Where Joe was dark-haired with a mischievous glint in his eyes, giving a sense that he might do something unexpected any moment, Brodie's hair had a sun-kissed lightness about it. He was muscular in a sporty way and had a calmer vibe about him, giving the impression that you could trust him with anything.

Pushing the thought aside, she looked at Joe and saw he was amused about something. 'What is it?'

'You seemed lost in thought then.'

'Not really,' she lied. 'How's the tractor?'

He thought for a moment. 'It was fine when I dropped it off.' He shook his head. 'I don't work there, if that's what you were thinking. I just help occasionally in my spare time if my uncle needs me.'

Lettie was confused. 'But I thought he had given you a job there.' She tried to recall what he had told her. 'Then you're not a farmer?'

He shook his head. 'Sorry, I meant he gave me work years ago when I first returned to the island. I haven't worked there properly for years.'

'You haven't?'

'No. I'm a firefighter.'

The image of Joe dressed up in his firefighting kit sprang into her mind. 'Wow.'

He frowned. 'Sorry?'

Mortified to have reacted without thinking, she laughed. 'I was just, er, thinking.'

'What about?'

Wanting to change the subject, Lettie said, 'Isn't it a dangerous job?'

He shrugged. 'It can be, but we're extremely well trained and don't forget we have all the protective gear.'

'Of course, you do.' She felt her cheeks heating up and was relieved when just at that moment a door leading to the lavatories opened, until she realised it was Brodie who had stepped out. She was taken aback for a moment.

'You all right?' Joe asked, glancing in Brodie's direction. 'Someone I should be concerned about?'

Unsure what he meant by the question, Lettie frowned. 'In what way?'

'I caught him looking over. He's not a jealous ex, or anything, is he?'

'No, nothing like that,' she insisted, unable to keep the amusement from her voice. Not that she would have minded Brodie having been her boyfriend at some time in the past. Brodie caught her eye as he passed their table and seemed hurt. She hoped he hadn't realised she was talking about him.

'Hi, Lettie,' he said giving Joe a nod.

Joe smiled. 'Hey, aren't you the new vet?'

'That's right.'

'How are you finding it around here?'

Lettie busied herself finding her lip salve in her small handbag as she listened to the small talk before realising Brodie must have sat at the table where the girl who had been looking at Joe was seated. She turned slightly to have a look and found the girl watching her.

Embarrassed to have been caught out, Lettie reached out to shake the girl's hand. 'Hi, I'm Lettie from Hollyhock Farm.' She couldn't help feeling envious that Brodie was out for a drink with someone else, albeit clearly not a date as they weren't alone.

'I'm Cathy.'

When the girl didn't elaborate, Lettie gave her a smile before turning back to Joe who was watching her, an amused look on his face.

'Shall we get out of here?' he whispered. 'It's still light outside and we could go for a walk if you want.'

The place was filling up quickly but then it was the only pub in the village, so she knew she shouldn't be surprised. She picked up her drink and finished before replying. 'I'd like that.'

Joe smiled and drank his lager before standing and turning to Brodie, Cathy and their friend. 'Nice to meet you. Hopefully we'll see you again soon.'

She was unsure whether she liked the use of 'we', as if they were some sort of couple. But she reasoned that at least then Brodie might put any hint of jealousy she had shown in her face down to something else.

'Yes, nice to see you, Brodie. Good to meet you all.'

As soon as they were outside, Lettie gave a sigh of relief.

'Are you still thirsty?' Joe asked.

'I am a bit. It's a warm evening.' Lettie fanned her face with her hand and wondered what he was going to suggest. She was very tired but it was a beautiful summer evening and she was happy to agree to stay out for a bit before heading home.

'So am I. I think we should pop to the shop and buy a couple of bottles of lager, or local cider if you prefer?'

She hadn't had a cider in months. 'Cider for me.' She loved the local brew and now that he mentioned it, she decided that it would be a perfect way to spend part of the warm evening with its gentle breeze.

Shortly afterwards they walked back to her farm, deciding that the top field with its views of the sea on three sides would be the perfect place to watch the sunset while they sat quietly and drank the bottle each had chosen and ate the slightly stale French sticks and slab of Brie Joe had added to their basket.

'This is perfect,' he said once they were seated and had each fashioned a sandwich of sorts and opened their drinks.

'I was thinking the same thing,' she admitted.

They sat in silence for a while and Lettie tried to work out exactly how she felt about each of these new men who had both unexpectedly entered her life. Joe was gorgeous, but so was Brodie, although he seemed relaxed with Cathy. Joe was also fun to be with and she liked the spur-of-the-moment way he came up with fun ideas. It was refreshing how he simply came up with something new, like this walk and this evening snack.

He took a mouthful of his lager and swallowed. 'I'm glad you chose to drive along the lane where I'd broken down,' he said thoughtfully. 'Today has turned out far better than it began.'

'It has for me, too.' Not the bit where Brodie was out with a beautiful woman, her thoughts nagged before she pushed them away. 'I much prefer it out here to in the stuffy pub.'

'You're not the only one.' He pointed out to the sea. 'Look at the way the setting sun changes the colour of the water. I don't think I'll ever get bored of scenes like that.'

'Nor me.' She thought back to living on the mainland. 'I loved my time in England, but being in a city where although there are beautiful sunsets high on some hills, it's not quite the same as when it happens over the Channel.'

'I agree. I lived in France. We were near the sea and often went to the beach to sit quietly and watch the sun going down.'

Lettie was intrigued to know more. She had a dentist when she was a child who commuted weekly from France to work on the island and several of her friends had lived there at one time or another. 'Where did you live when you were there?' she asked suddenly curious.

He nudged her with his shoulder. 'So, you are interested in me. Good. I was beginning to think you might not be.'

Taken aback by his directness, Lettie narrowed her eyes. 'I was only asking about your life in France.'

He turned to her, amusement in his dark eyes. 'I'm only teasing. I lived near Biarritz. Have you heard of it?'

'I have. My brother, Zac, went there on a trip to surf with some friends a few years ago.'

'It's well known for its surfing, although to be honest I never did much of that. I'd rather swim than surf.'

'You said we. Were you there with a girlfriend?' She hoped not. The last thing she wanted to do was inadvertently have drinks with someone's boyfriend.

He nodded. 'There was a significant other, but it didn't work out.'

'No?'

He shook his head and for a fleeting moment she saw pain cross his face. 'We met when she came here to work at one of the hotels for the summer season a few years ago and I went back and moved in with her.'

He sighed. 'We should have left it as a summer romance, but it's easy in hindsight to know these things.'

'I know that only too well,' Lettie said not meaning to voice her thoughts out loud.

'Same thing happened to you then?'

'What? Oh, no. I met my ex, Scott, when I moved to London after university. We worked in the same company, but where I was in fashion, he worked in the finance part.' She thought back to those exciting days when everything seemed so straightforward. 'We lived together for a while until...' She wished she hadn't begun sharing about her relationship with Scott now that she had started.

'Until?' Joe leant forward looking concerned.

Lettie shrugged. 'Basically, until I discovered that he wasn't as placid as he had led me to believe. In fact, he became quite nasty when I tried to address how controlling I was finding his behaviour.'

She saw the muscle working in Joe's jaw and sensed his anger on her behalf. 'And how did it end? If you don't mind me asking.'

'Well, another colleague, Nessa, persuaded me to leave him and move into her flat. She and her boyfriend came to help me pack and she threatened Scott when he kicked off that if he didn't let me go nicely then she would report him to HR and get him fired.'

'And that worked?'

Lettie nodded. 'It did, thankfully. He loved his work there and wouldn't have dared let anything mess it up.'

'It sounds like you've had a rough time of it.'

'It was a little odd knowing I could bump into him at work each day. So when I discovered that my parents were wanting to travel and they needed someone to run the farm for them, and the firm was also offering redundancies, it seemed like the universe was trying to tell me something and I jumped at the opportunity to come home and leave London for good.'

He reached out and took her hand briefly before letting go. 'I'm glad it all worked out for you in the end, Lettie.'

'So am I.' She picked up her drink, wanting to change the subject but unsure what to say.

Joe took a mouthful of drink and swallowed, staring down at the grass briefly. 'Man, this is good stuff.'

Lettie gazed at the setting sun, happy to be single and not

having to consider a partner when she was busy trying to learn all that she needed to on the farm.

'Do you mind telling me what the story is between you and the vet guy?'

She had been enjoying the silence, but it was his turn to find out more about her, she supposed. 'There isn't a story.'

'Really?' Joe clearly found that hard to believe. 'What, nothing? I thought I sensed chemistry between the two of you.'

'Nope.' She wasn't lying she decided, wondering why the thought saddened her. She forced a smile and turned to look at Joe. 'Why? Did you think there was?'

He knitted his eyebrows together thoughtfully. 'I could have sworn there was something between you two.' He sighed. 'Maybe I'm losing my touch. I'm usually great at sensing these things.'

'Well, you haven't been this time.' She smiled to show she was teasing.

'I know, why don't you invite me back here during the day?'

'Sorry?' She hadn't expected him to say that.

'You can show me around and then I can reciprocate.'

'Invite me to your uncle's place you mean?'

'Exactly that.' He lowered his voice as if there was anyone around to overhear their conversation. 'They are very different places, so it's not as if either one of us can pinch farming secrets.'

Lettie laughed. 'Anyone would think we worked for Interpol, or different countries, or something.' He was being ridiculous, but she was enjoying his company. She looked at his deep blue eyes ringed with long black lashes and his wavy black hair and wondered why she wasn't desperate to kiss him. He was incredibly handsome and funny and certainly charismatic, but as much as he was all those things she suspected that if Brodie – quiet, unassuming, slightly serious Brodie – was here that she would be yearning to kiss him.

'Well?'

Lettie frowned. 'Well, what?'

'When are you going to show me some of the things you've been doing on the farm?'

She pulled a face. 'I wasn't intending to, but if you insist on it, I suppose you could pop round next week sometime?'

He looked disappointed.

'What's wrong?'

He sighed deeply and looked forlorn. 'I was hoping to come round tomorrow.'

So that was it. 'Tomorrow isn't a good day.' She held up her bottle before taking a mouthful. 'My parents leave to go on their cruise tomorrow and there's bound to be all the last-minute panicking about passports, times to leave for the airport, check-in, and all that stuff, and I know my dad will be wanting to go over everything he thinks I need to know about, for the hundredth time.'

'I can imagine there'll be a lot to go through then. Well, I wouldn't want to interrupt all that fun. OK then, the following day. I'll wait for you to tell me what a good time will be.'

Lettie thought about her first day working alone. 'I'm going to be working from early morning until the evening I imagine, so I'd better not commit to anything just yet. Let's leave it for now and maybe catch up in a week or so, if that's OK?'

He beamed at her. 'No problem at all.'

'I just wish I had more of a clue about what I was doing and don't want to mess everything up.'

Joe put his arm around her shoulder and pulled her gently to him. 'Good luck tomorrow. I'm sure you'll be fine and will soon get the hang of running the farm.' He put a finger under her chin and lifted it slightly so she caught his eye. 'You might discover that it isn't for you after all.' He smiled. 'Your bags could be packed and the car revving to take you away on the day your parents return for all you know.'

Lettie doubted it but he could have a point. She playfully pushed him away. 'That won't happen.'

'Can you be certain of that?'

She knew she couldn't but had no intention of entertaining the notion. She had made a promise to herself to make this work and that's what she intended to do.

21

BRODIE

'Brodie?' He heard his name being called somewhere in the distance, then realised it was Cathy who was speaking to him from across the pub table. He hadn't meant to drift off again, but couldn't seem to help it. Lettie Torel had got right under his skin somehow without even trying.

He finished his soft drink. 'Sorry, I was miles away then.'

She gave him an amused grin. 'I didn't need to be a genius to work that out.'

'I'm sorry, I didn't mean to be rude.'

She leant back in her chair. 'Look, if you'd rather go I won't be offended.'

Embarrassed to think he had given that impression, Brodie shook his head. 'No. Why don't I fetch us another drink and you can tell me whatever it was I've just missed.'

Cathy reached out and rested her hand on his. 'I know we're only here because your sister engineered it. We don't have to stay until the end of the evening, if you'd rather call it a night now.'

He would like nothing better, he decided, still shaken to have seen Lettie out on a date with someone. He hated making people feel bad and suspected that was what he had done here. His sister had made her excuses to leave soon after Lettie's departure, leaving him and Cathy together. Cathy seemed like a lovely woman. She was polite and charming and, actually, he thought looking at her properly for the first time, very attractive. Was Lettie playing on his mind because he was jealous seeing her out with that guy? Probably. He didn't recognise him. What was his name again? Ah, yes, Joe. Another farmer, he imagined. Brodie sighed inwardly. The two of them seemed to have a lot to talk about and clearly enjoyed each other's company.

Cathy lowered her drink and the movement snapped him back to the present. Aware he was being rude again, Brodie apologised.

'It's fine. You didn't ask to have me dumped on you.'

He winced at her comment. 'You make it sound as if I was forced into coming out with you tonight.'

'You weren't?' she asked, eyebrows raised. 'Not even a little bit.'

Brodie realised she was trying to make light of their situation. 'No, I wasn't.' He shrugged. 'But if I'm honest it's been a long day and I'm happy to go home, if that's what you'd prefer.'

'It is.'

* * *

'I'm disappointed in you,' Maddie grumbled later when she arrived at his cottage and interrupted the film he was dozing through. 'Cathy's lovely and enormous fun. I expected the two of you to be well suited. I can't believe you left soon after I did. That's so disappointing.'

Irritated with her interfering, Brodie glared at her. 'Maddie, I love you, but right now not very much. I felt dreadful when you engineered the drink at the pub. Poor woman would have far rather been doing anything else than spending time with me.'

Maddie folded her arms and glowered at him. 'And she said that, did she?'

He wished she would go home and leave him alone. 'No, of course she didn't but I'm sure she was only being polite staying at the pub after you'd done a runner.' He pushed his glasses further up the bridge of his nose.

'Brodie, I don't know why you underestimate yourself, but girls seem to like you.'

This was news to him. 'And you'd know this how?'

'You've clearly never noticed the way they react to you.'

His sister was really getting on his nerves now. 'I'm too tired to carry on with whatever game this is you're hoping to play. Please get off my doorstep and leave me in peace. I've had a long day and I need to get to bed.'

She pulled a face. 'You're such a pain sometimes, little brother, do you know that?'

Why could his sister never get the message?

'I'm the pain? I'm not the one standing on your doorstep in the middle of the night being annoying.'

'Fine, I'll go. But it'll serve you right if Cathy meets someone else and falls for him.'

He doubted she was right. 'Good luck to her – I hope she does.'

'When did you become so antisocial?'

'I'm not,' he argued before stepping back from the door. 'Maddie, please go home.'

Without waiting for her to reply, he closed the door and locked it. Honestly, his sister could be a right pain in the butt sometimes.

Brodie decided to turn off all the lights just in case she came up with another reason to speak to him, and he went to bed. He lay in his bed, his head resting on his hands, arms folded behind his head, and wondered if Lettie had made plans to see Joe again.

He decided he wouldn't be at all surprised if she had. 'Too late to worry about it now,' he mumbled, wishing he hadn't let his promise to not become involved with clients get in the way of his feelings towards Lettie.

22

LETTIE

Departure Day

By the time Lettie reached the spare room where her mother had laid out both her and Gareth's suitcases the following morning, she was exhausted. It had been an earlier start than usual because her father wanted to observe her working and go over everything around the farm one last time. Lettie's tatty notebook was filling up fast and her head ached with all the information she was trying to take in.

The shower she'd just had did little to restore her energy and she supposed it might have something to do with the thought that she wouldn't be seeing her parents again for the next two months. It wasn't that unusual not to spend time with them for that period because she had been away studying and then working. This time though she would be living in their home and taking care of everything on their behalf and the responsibility not to let them down weighed heavily on her. It was also the first time she would have spent time living alone in the house.

'How's it going, Mum?' she asked as she entered the room and saw her mother struggling to close her overfull case. 'Can I help at all?'

Her mother looked up and pushed strands of wavy hair from her flushed face. 'Yes, you can come and sit on this thing while I attempt to zip it up.'

Lettie hoped the case was strong enough for her to sit on. 'Hang on a sec.' She kicked off her slippers and climbed onto the bed before sitting carefully on top of the case. 'How's this?'

'Let me see.' Her mother groaned and slowly pulled the zipper around the case until it closed. 'Done it!'

'Can I get down now then?'

'Yes, then you can help me finish packing your father's case.'

Lettie resisted asking why this job had fallen to her mother when her father was perfectly capable of doing it for himself. She was used to her mother taking on most of the jobs in the house, happily leaving the garden and farm work to her husband.

'He seems to have a lot less in here than you did in yours. Could you have forgotten something?'

'No.' Her mother held up a list with everything ticked off. 'My list,' she said and then turned it to show the other side. 'Your father's. Everything he wanted to take is in here. I think it could be because I need to take more pairs of shoes to go with my evening wear than he does.'

'If you're sure, then we can close this case too and I can take them downstairs while you shower and change.' She glanced at her mother's bedside clock. 'Dad said he wants me to take you to the airport at ten thirty and it's almost ten now.'

'It can't be.' Her mother looked at the time and covered her mouth. 'I'm never going to be ready in time.'

'You will be,' Lettie assured her, indicating the hand luggage standing by the bedroom door. 'You've triple-checked your passports and boarding information, so all you need to do is shower and apply your make-up. I'll go and make you a cup of tea while you do that.'

Her mother took a deep breath. 'You're right.' She hugged Lettie. 'Sorry, I'm nervous as well as excited for this trip.'

'Just think, tonight you'll be asleep in a comfortable hotel bed near the airport, refreshed for your early morning flight to Barcelona.' She smiled. 'This time tomorrow you'll be on the ship, cocktail in hand ready to enjoy your two-month holiday.'

'I am excited. I've wanted this for so long. I think I never expected it to truly happen.'

Gareth entered the room. 'And it's not going to if we arrive at the airport too late to catch today's flight.'

'I'll go and make that tea,' Lettie said without waiting for her mother to answer.

'Thanks, and while you're downstairs you may as well phone the bloke and arrange for him to come and shear the alpacas.'

* * *

Lettie dropped her parents at the airport. She had left a message on the shearer's phone and hoped the person called back soon. She was on her way back to the farm. She was struggling not to cry although wasn't sure why she felt so emotional watching her parents pulling their cases into the Departures Hall. Maybe it was the thought of not seeing them for a couple of months, or simply because she was anxious about what might happen in that time while she was looking after the farm. Lettie attempted to push away the overwhelming fear she might end up failing to prove she had what it took to step in for her father. She decided she needed to pull herself together and focus on her new role, starting with going home and checking on the animals. Start as she meant to go on.

After an exhausting day on the farm, Lettie was hungry but

couldn't be bothered cooking much and decided to go to the village to buy something to pop in the microwave.

On her return, she was nearing the farm when she spotted movement in a bush. She wasn't sure what it was, but it seemed to be the size of a lamb. It was black and she estimated to be only about a foot or two tall. Slowing down to try and get a better look, Lettie peered at the bush to see if she could work out what it might be and hoped that none of their animals had escaped. There were no other vehicles in the quiet lane. Lettie stopped the car and got out, moving quietly and slowly. She held her breath when something moved, and she stopped to see if it came out of its own accord. She didn't fancy whatever it was biting her, but also couldn't leave until she was certain that the animal wasn't hurt in any way.

Lettie waited for a few minutes before turning and pretending not to be interested and walking slowly towards the car as if she intended leaving. When she reached the driver's door Lettie peered in the wing mirror and saw it was a dog. A strange-looking dog at that. The poor thing was trembling and watched her nervously, its front right leg raised. It was clearly hurt but thankfully not too badly.

Turning very slowly, she crouched down and reached out her hand. 'Are you lost, little one?'

The dog stared at her without moving.

Wondering if it was hungry, Lettie recalled having put a couple of gravy bone treats into her jacket pocket a few days before to try and persuade her father's farm dog, Spud, to improve his recall to her. She slowly put her hand into her pocket and withdrew them, holding out her palm towards the injured animal and waiting for it to give in to temptation and take the treats.

Lettie's leg muscles were aching and she was beginning to think she was wasting her time given how slowly the animal took its first tentative steps towards her. It was a sweet little thing with a short snout and legs that looked too long and skinny for its body, which was the shape of a collie's or something similar.

'You're a sweet little chap, aren't you?'

The dog stared at her then, deciding she could be trusted, stepped forward, lunged at her hand and snatched one of the gravy bones before scurrying a safe distance away to eat it.

By the time Lettie had fed it the second treat, her legs were almost numb but the dog seemed calmer. 'Will you come with me?'

She gradually reached forward and stroked the dog's head, then when it didn't seem to mind, stroked its back a few times. She couldn't take it back to the farm with her – she knew that much. This timid creature would probably be terrified of the noise from the other animals, and as for Spud with his territorial ways, she didn't think it would be fair to expect the stray to have to deal with him. She had little choice but to take it to Brodie so that he could check it was all right.

It took a little while longer before Lettie was able to pick the dog up and place it in the car. As she began driving to The Village Practice, she realised her shoulders ached with tension. The dog was sweet and seemed interested in everything they passed. Slowly its fluffy black tail rose and even wagged at one point.

She arrived at Brodie's practice and, finding a length of blue baler twine in the footwell in front of the passenger seat, she reached down and picked it up to tie it loosely around the dog's neck. She couldn't get this far with it, only for it to be spooked and run away.

She carefully got out of the car and encouraged the dog to go with her. It didn't seem to mind the makeshift collar and lead but when they reached the front door of the surgery, she realised it was locked.

'Damn. Now what are we going to do?' she asked the dog who didn't seem in the least bit concerned.

Lettie went to return to her car, stopping before she reached it when she recalled her mother once mentioning something about Old Man Winter living behind the practice in a cottage. Could Brodie live there now? It was worth a try. She noticed it was almost dusk and had little time to find an alternative. Hoping he didn't have company and that she wasn't interrupting a romantic evening with Cathy, she braced herself for his reaction and walked around the side of the building to the back where a sweet, but rather run-down cottage stood. It wasn't very big and she wondered how someone with Brodie's height coped with living in such a little place. Aware she couldn't delay knocking on his door any longer, Lettie stepped forward and, seeing an anchor door knocker, lifted it and knocked twice, surprising the dog and causing it to pull back from her.

'It's all right,' she said, wishing she had thought things through a little better. She held on tightly to the twine and crouched down, willing the dog to come to her so she could comfort it.

When there was no answer at the door, Lettie realised that there were no lights on inside either. Her heart raced as she tried not to panic while she worked out what to do next. For the first time she felt very alone on the island.

Maybe Bethan might have an idea, she thought hopefully as she led the dog back to her car.

23

BRODIE

Brodie pushed a hand through his salty, damp hair. He had lost track of time, the surf had been so perfect. It was the best surfing he had enjoyed since his return to live on the island. Exhilarated, Brodie wondered what he should do for the rest of his evening. He had some bills to sort through but that could wait until his lunch break the following day as nothing was urgent. He indicated and turned into his parking area behind the practice noticing a car parked there.

Unsure why anyone would park at the surgery after hours, he pulled in to park his car by the cottage and spotted someone with a dog on a lead. He turned off the ignition and got out of his car, seeing that it was in fact Lettie and she had a dog that he didn't think was hers on the end of what looked like blue baler twine.

His heart raced. 'Are you waiting to see me?'

He listened while she explained what had happened and why she couldn't take the dog home with her to the farm. 'I'm not sure what to do next but now you're here I'm hoping you'll be able to give him a quick examination just to check he's OK.'

He was happy to. 'Let me just get my keys and I'll meet you at the front door. I won't be long.'

He saw her looking him up and down before smiling. 'You've been for a swim.' He wasn't sure if it was a statement or question, then remembering Lettie was from the island and no doubt used to seeing people who've just come out of the sea assumed it was a statement. 'It was brilliant down there tonight. Do you surf?'

'No, I've never learnt. I prefer swimming.' She bent to stroke the dog.

'Sorry. You go ahead and I'll catch up with you. I need to fetch my keys.'

He realised it was the second time he had mentioned his keys and hoped she didn't pick up how awkward he felt finding her there so unexpectedly.

Shortly after, Brodie unlocked the front door and switched on the lights before holding the door open for Lettie and the dog to come inside.

'If you follow me through to the surgery, we can have a good look at this sweet little guy.'

Lettie smiled and he could see that she had already fallen for the stray. 'He is adorable. I'm not sure if it's because of the odd way he looks, or despite it.'

Brodie wasn't sure either but as soon as he picked up the dog and it nuzzled him, he felt his heart melting. He put a hand on either side of the dog's head and stroked his ears between his thumbs and forefingers. 'Where have you come from then?'

'I don't think he's chipped,' she said frowning. 'I tried to feel for a chip as I stroked him, but didn't come across one.'

Brodie lifted the dog onto the examination table and after a bit of snarling and comforting, the dog calmed down and let him check his paws.

Carefully checking each pad on the paw, then in between each one, Brodie spotted something thornlike sticking into the area between two of the paw pads. 'Ah, this looks like what could be upsetting him.' He selected a pair of tweezers while Lettie soothed the dog. 'If you keep hold of him in case he decides to jump off that'll be great.' He carefully parted the two pads and extracted the offending piece of material. 'I think it's from a thistle or something. Poor little guy. No wonder he couldn't stand on it.' He put antiseptic onto the paw and tidied up while Lettie cuddled the dog.

Relieved that it hadn't been too difficult to resolve the poor dog's issue, Brodie placed the tweezers into a basin and pushed his glasses further up the bridge of his nose.

'What will we do with him now?'

He couldn't miss the concern on Lettie's face and not wanting her to worry said, 'I'll keep him with me.'

'You will?' She gave a relieved sigh. 'That's wonderful.'

'I'm happy to take care of him until we can trace his owners.' It occurred to him he wasn't sure how best to do that. 'I'll quickly scan him to check if he's been microchipped but if we don't have any luck with that we'll have to place an advert about him being loose somewhere.' He picked up the scanner and tested it was working. 'This shouldn't take longer than ten to twenty seconds.' Brodie positioned the scanner above the dog's shoulder blades, then moved it slowly over the dog's sides. 'I'm going to check again to make sure I haven't missed it,' he said, disappointed. 'It doesn't look like he has one though.'

'What are we going to do now?' Lettie asked.

'Is there a parish or village paper or magazine or something?'

'There is but it's quarterly and only came out last week. Leave it with me. I'll take a photo of him now, if you want to hold him still.' She took her phone from her pocket and took a few photos and checked them. 'This one will do don't you think?' She turned the screen to face him and Brodie bent forward to have a look.

'Yes, that's a good one.'

'Great. Now I'll ask Tina where best to post it. I'm a bit out of the loop with local groups and there's bound to be a couple on social media. We can take it from there.'

'Good thinking.' She really was lovely, Brodie thought, his pulse racing when she caught his eye and stared at him.

She frowned after a few seconds. 'Is everything all right?'

Brodie realised they hadn't been having a moment, but that she had been wondering why he was staring at her. He nodded and turned away. 'Yes, I was just, um, wondering what his name might be.'

He turned back to her with an antiseptic wipe ready to clean down the examination table.

Lettie was whispering something to the dog then looked up. 'I know, we could call him Thistle, just until we discover his actual name. What do you think?'

'It's as good a name as any.' Brodie narrowed his eyes. 'I have an inkling that you're getting a little too attached to Thistle already.'

Lettie harrumphed. 'I could say the same about you. You're the one who's offered to keep him.'

She was right. 'I was only being professional.' He laughed when he saw she didn't believe him. 'Never mind me,' he said pulling a face. 'I suppose I should let you get back to the farm.'

Was that a disappointed look? No, but it was wishful thinking on his part. When she didn't move, he wondered if maybe she might want to join him for something to eat. 'If you're not in a rush and haven't had supper I've got a lasagne and salad I'll be happy to share.'

'I, oh.'

Damn, he had misjudged her reaction. 'No, you've probably got something to eat already. Or maybe you're meeting someone for supper?' Why had he said that? Fool.

'Um, no. None of those. I was just wondering how much I owed you for checking Thistle.'

Hurt that she expected him to charge her for examining the dog, Brodie had to bite back a retort. 'There's no charge.'

'Are you sure?'

He bent to stroke Thistle's head, not wanting her to see how offended he was by her question. 'Yes. You've been good enough to bring this little guy in to me and I'm happy to take care of him for now. Why would I charge you for that?'

She frowned. 'Because you've given your professional time when I've asked you to.'

He decided he needed to get to know this girl better so she would read him better in future. 'I tell you what. I won't charge you if you'll keep me company and help me eat the food I bought earlier. Agreed?'

Lettie's expression softened.

He suspected she was feeling as awkward as him. 'Well?'

'Only if you have something for Thistle. I only had two gravy bones to give him, so he's probably very hungry.'

'We can grab a bag of dog food from reception and I'll settle up with Bethan in the morning.'

'Good idea.' She lifted Thistle down from the steel examining table, giving him a cuddle before placing him on the floor. 'In that case, Thistle and I are happy to accept your invitation to supper in your cottage.'

He led the way out of the surgery and opened his cottage door and held it back for Lettie to lead Thistle inside. She stopped and looked around the tiny hallway, 'I was wondering what this place was like inside.'

'Run-down.'

'It is a little, isn't it? This way?' She pointed to the door on the left.

'Yes, unless you want to go to the kitchen and start the cooking.'

Lettie shook her head. 'I'll leave that to the host. I'll make Thistle's supper though, if you can find me a bowl for him.'

Thistle fed and drinking water from the second bowl, Brodie stabbed the film on the top of the lasagne and popped it into the microwave before he set to work washing the salad. 'It's not exactly the sort of fare you're used to.'

'How do you know that?' Lettie asked leaning against the opposite worktop to where he stood at the sink.

'I've been in your mother's kitchen, don't forget. I've seen the cakes she made and tasted one. I can imagine how well she feeds her family.'

'Ah, but I haven't been living at home for several years,' Lettie reminded him. 'When I was in my flat in London I tried to cook proper meals but most of the time I was too hungry after work to be bothered. This sort of meal is very much what I've been used to.'

'So you don't consider this a proper meal then?'

She laughed, clearly embarrassed. 'Sorry, that did sound a little insulting.'

'It's fine. I'll have to make sure to show you just how well I can cook another time, won't I?' He expected Lettie to continue the banter that had been flowing between them but when his only answer was silence, Brodie turned to face her to see what was wrong. 'Sorry, did I say something I shouldn't?'

'No, it's just that...'

She was embarrassed and he had inadvertently put her in an awkward position. 'Sorry. I didn't mean to make things awkward between us. I know you're seeing someone, so I understand that you coming here for a meal probably isn't appropriate.'

'Seeing someone?' She thought for a moment. 'Oh, you mean Joe.'

Who else could he mean? Brodie wondered. 'I just assumed. That is, seeing you in the pub with him last night.'

She stared at him thoughtfully and he couldn't work out whether she was trying to decide if she was seeing Joe on a romantic level, or if she was trying to work out how to let Brodie down gently. Either would be a disappointment. Then he remembered his promise to himself not to get involved with clients. Was she a client though? He thought of her farm and supposed she was as she was now running things for her father.

'Brodie, are you all right?'

Brodie's stomach growled in reply, making them both laugh. 'I think that answers your question.'

'It does.'

'Lettie,' he said just as she was leaving the kitchen. She turned an expectant look on her face. 'I just wanted to say that I know you've got a lot on your plate with the farm, but I hope you know I'm here if you ever need me for anything.'

'Um, thank you, Brodie. That's very kind of you.'

There was an awkward silence, which he felt the need to fill. 'I was thinking about Spud.'

'Spud?'

'Yes. If you have a sheepdog, does that mean you used to have sheep on the farm?' he asked feeling foolish for the random question. He could see he was making things more uncomfortable between them and wished he had the charm he had witnessed Joe exuding.

Lettie smiled. 'We used to,' she said clearly happy to talk about familiar things. 'Dad bought a flock after he sold the dairy herd to my uncle, but only kept them for about six years before selling them on too and deciding to go completely into organic farming. I've learnt so much more in the past few weeks working here than I ever did before my interest was piqued about farming this land.'

He took a couple of plates from the cupboard and some cutlery. 'Don't you miss your life in London at all then?'

She looked thoughtful as she considered her answer. 'I had expected to but I've been far too busy to think about anything much other than the work I need to do each day.'

'I'm not surprised.' He realised he should be getting on with serving their food. 'Why don't you go and sit in the living room and I'll bring it through.'

'Yes, of course. Shall I take the cutlery and the salad?'

'Yes, please.'

Left alone for a moment in the small kitchen Brodie gathered himself. He really was useless sometimes. He grabbed a tea towel to take the hot carton from the microwave and accidentally kicked the water bowl he had put down for Thistle, causing the dog to jump out of the way and knock into him. Shocked, Brodie almost dropped the lasagne but caught it at the last minute, saving it but burning his fingers in the process.

'Damn.' He dropped the carton on the worktop and blew on his fingertips.

'What's happened?' Lettie asked, appearing in the kitchen. She took in the scene and, seeing his raised hand, grabbed his wrist and led him to the sink, turning on the tap and holding his burnt fingers under the cold running water.

'Are you always this clumsy in the kitchen?' she asked after a moment.

Brodie went to try and explain what had happened when she looked up at him, an amused expression on her face. 'They might be sore but I think you'll live.'

Amused by her banter, he tried to look serious. 'I'll have you know I'm suffering, a lot.'

She took them from the water and then studied them. 'I think they'll be fine in a little while.' She lifted them to her lips and kissed them. Brodie stilled. The touch of her soft lips on the tips of his burnt fingers was a salve in more ways than one.

Lettie gasped before lowering his hand, avoiding his gaze. She cleared her throat. 'I, er, I'm not sure why I did that. Sorry.'

Brodie had to swallow to find his voice. 'It's fine. Please don't apologise.' Why were they being so formal all of a sudden? Wanting to take away her embarrassment, he added, 'Actually that felt nice.'

She looked up at him then and his insides felt like they were dissolving. 'You don't mind?' she whispered.

He couldn't speak but shook his head. 'No,' he managed to say his voice strained. 'I didn't mind at all.'

As she stared up at him silently, Brodie reached out to her with his good hand and, sliding his fingers down her messy hair, only vaguely aware of his other hand stinging, he gently pulled her head towards him, leant forward and kissed her.

For a second Lettie didn't react. He wondered if he had, yet again, read the situation wrong. But just as he was about to stop, she slipped her arms around his neck and kissed him back.

Brodie had been kissed before, many times, and lots of those times he had really enjoyed himself, but this was on another level and he never wanted it to stop.

Thistle barked and Lettie jumped away from him. 'What's the matter?' she said bending down to check the dog was all right. She looked up. 'I think he's OK.'

Brodie hoped Thistle wouldn't make a habit of ruining kisses with Lettie, if indeed he was lucky enough to have any more. 'I think he just didn't like the attention being taken from him.'

Lettie stood again. 'You could be right.' She stared at him for a moment, then indicated the living room. 'Should we eat something before it gets cold?'

Brodie nodded. He had lost his appetite and would much rather stay in the kitchen with her and kiss her again, but sharing his supper and spending the evening with Lettie was still a very welcome option compared to sitting alone in front of the television, watching something he'd already seen many times.

They ate in silence for a little while until Thistle came through to the living room and made himself comfortable on the rug in front of the unlit fireplace. Brodie saw Lettie shiver and realised it was cooler now that the sun had gone down. Not wishing to give her any reason to want to leave too soon, he stood.

'Is something the matter?' Lettie asked her fork halfway to her mouth.

'I thought I'd light the fire.'

'Please don't worry on my account.'

Brodie had to think quickly. 'I don't want you to be cold but when you just shivered then it made me think that maybe Thistle could do with a bit of warming up. It won't take a moment anyway and I love having a fire going, don't you?'

'I do. It's so rom—' She glanced at her plate, and without looking up again, said, 'So calming.'

'It is.'

Could she possibly like him as much as he liked her?

Her mobile rang interrupting his thoughts.

Lettie took it from her pocket, then seeing the name on the screen gave Brodie an apologetic smile. 'Sorry, I'm going to have to get this.'

'Hi. Joe?' Lettie laughed, clearly surprised by something. 'Sorry, I had no idea you were the one who does the shearing. Talk about a man of many talents.'

Not wanting to appear to be listening to her conversation, Brodie busied himself by taking the kindling and began setting the fire, then lighting it. He wondered what exactly there might be between Lettie and Joe. Handsome, charismatic, confident Joe. So different-seeming to himself. His joy in their evening so far dissipated when it occurred to him that maybe she had only reacted to his kiss so that he didn't humiliate himself yet again. She was such a kind-hearted girl, he knew that much about her. He thought about how she had rescued Thistle and taken him to the surgery and then his cottage so Brodie could check the dog was unhurt. Maybe it was the sort of thing she would do. His mood dropped but not wishing to make her feel uncomfortable, he finished lighting the fire.

'Yes, come up whenever you're free. The alpacas will be waiting.'

He wondered if she would be too and immediately pushed the thought away, annoyed with himself for being jealous. 'There we are,' Brodie said going to wash his hands, wincing as he dried his burnt fingers with too much vigour. He returned to the living room and sat back down at the small table.

'You're right,' Lettie said finishing her food and sitting back in her chair. 'It is lovely with a fire burning.'

'It helps the room look more welcoming too.'

She cocked her head in Thistle's direction. 'Someone is making full use of it.'

Brodie saw her look down at the dog stretched out in front of the fire on the rug.

'He does appear very at home already,' she said. 'He doesn't seem much like a street dog.'

He hadn't come across any of those on the island. 'I didn't realise there were stray dogs here. I've not seen any.'

Lettie considered the question. 'Nor have I, actually, but I know there are some feral cats because the supermarket down the road collects tins of food from shoppers and someone goes out to feed them.'

He was relieved to hear it. 'Then Thistle must belong to someone. We just need to find out who he needs to be reacquainted with.'

'I'll be sad to say goodbye to him.' Lettie pulled a face and leant forward to stroke the snoozing dog.

'So will I,' Brodie admitted.

He wasn't sure if it was having company in the cottage for once or having a dog snoring by the fire but the place felt like a home to him for the first time since he had arrived, and he rather liked it. 'I think that when I've found Thistle's owners I might look into rehoming a rescue. I'd like the company.'

'That's such a lovely idea. There are always dogs needing homes and who better to take one in than a qualified vet?'

He was glad she thought so. 'It might take a while though. I'll have to find out who to contact to find this new housemate.'

Lettie laughed. 'I'm sure there will be many people offering to help you.'

'Maybe you could help me choose one?' He wasn't sure why he had said that but knew he didn't want their connection to end too soon. Regardless of his promise to himself he now knew that he liked having Lettie around and even if she was seeing someone else and they could only be friends it would have to be enough. 'What do you think?'

'I'd like that.'

He was delighted to hear her say so. 'Great, then we can start looking into it soon.' He thought of Bethan and how she seemed to know everyone on the island, or at least a lot of them. 'Maybe Bethan can help lead us in the right direction.'

'We'll have to ask her.'

Thistle yawned and took a long, slow languorous stretch before falling back to sleep. 'I have to admit I'm already enjoying having Thistle in the house,' he said not meaning to voice his thoughts.

'You are?'

Hearing Lettie's surprise, he turned to her. 'I shouldn't let myself get attached to him.' He said it mostly to remind himself.

'No, I suppose you shouldn't.' Lettie looked at Thistle and smiled. 'Then again, I can see why you would. He's a character, isn't he?'

'He is.' Brodie saw she had finished eating and stood to take her plate, waking Thistle. 'Sorry, boy, you go back to sleep.'

The dog did as he suggested and, surprised to have been listened to, Brodie looked at Lettie and they both laughed, keeping their voices quiet. 'Listen to us trying not to disturb the dog who neither of us knew existed before this evening.'

'He's a prince among strays though and assumes we know our place.'

Brodie agreed. He stood and took her plate through to the kitchen, laughing to himself. This evening was turning out far better than he could ever have dared imagine. He turned on the tap to fill the sink and recalled his promise not to become involved with a client. What had he been thinking kissing her like that? What had he started? It was a stupid mistake and he couldn't help feeling it was a shame that tonight and their kiss could only be a one-off.

24

LETTIE

As she drove back to the farm Lettie recalled how wonderful it had been to be in Brodie's arms and finally kiss him again. Thinking about it now made her go all tingly inside. She sighed. She was sure she wasn't imagining things but his demeanour seemed to have changed in between Brodie carrying their plates to the kitchen and returning to the living room.

She hoped she was imagining things and pushed her concerns aside as being caused by her tiredness. Lettie couldn't help wondering how different things might have been if Brodie had texted her back and they had struck up a relationship all those years before. She sensed that having Brodie as a boyfriend would be completely different to being with someone controlling like her ex – Scott. She remembered only too well how difficult her last relationship had been. He was only her second real boyfriend and it still surprised her how someone as initially thoughtful and seemingly kind as Scott could end up making her feel uncomfortable and causing her to have to secretly plan to move out of the flat they shared.

Growing up with her quiet, hard-working father who although

strict was gentle, and her noisy, slightly annoyingly chaotic brother, it had never occurred to her that she would end up being in a relationship with someone underhanded like Scott.

She thought of Nessa, her flatmate in London, and felt guilty for moving out especially after she had gone with Lettie to help her pack her things and moved her from Scott's flat where she had only been living for a few weeks. If it wasn't for Nessa and her boyfriend, where would she be now? Lettie shuddered, slamming on the brakes in fright when something flew at her windscreen.

It was only a barn owl, she realised. She drew up the lane and saw her uncle wave at her as his car turned onto the road, grateful to him for looking after the place while she was out for most of the morning. As she made her way down the long driveway to the farm Lettie was still spooked by the thought of Scott and the shock of the owl flying towards her so unexpectedly. Suddenly being alone in the large farmhouse wasn't such a welcome one. Spending time with Brodie in his cosy little cottage made her yearn for something similar. Somewhere she knew there were only a few doors and windows that needed checking.

The lights pinged on around the yard as she approached, making her feel a bit safer. At least her father had ensured there was little chance of someone, or something, creeping up on the house without bright lights flashing on and scaring them half witless.

She stepped out of the car and locked it, reminding herself that she might be alone at the farmhouse but she had Spud with her and he was a pretty good guard dog. She was also in Jersey and doubted that even Scott would chance coming here. He had only visited once with her and her father had taken an instant dislike to him, as had Zac. She wished she had listened to them now when they and her mother had tried to warn her.

'That's all in the past now,' she said unlocking the front door and going into the house. She switched on the hall lights and locked the door behind her. She really had scared herself, she thought, irritated that her ex still had such an effect on her even a year after they had parted. Someone, probably Nessa had told her he had found a new girlfriend very soon after they had split, so hopefully he had long forgotten about her anyway. The thought relaxed her slightly.

She thought about making a drink of something hot but seeing that it was now almost eleven, decided to take a shower and go straight to bed.

Joe had said he would come to the farm to shear the alpacas as soon as his shift was over the following day. He was so kind and also, she mused, different to Brodie in so many ways, yet both were attractive and keen to be helpful, which she appreciated.

An hour later as she lay in her bed staring at the ceiling, a familiar anxiety about the farm filled her stomach and throat, and she wondered if maybe she should give up trying to get any sleep and get up instead.

Lettie must have fallen asleep because the next thing she knew the cockerel was crowing and she was sitting bolt upright in bed. It took her a moment to figure out where she was and that she was alone in the house. She hoped her parents would enjoy their time on the ship and that the cruise would turn out to be everything they hoped.

She rubbed her eyes lightly and kicked off her duvet.

Showered, dressed and having fed Spud, she carried her second cup of tea and a half-eaten piece of toast to the hall. Lettie pushed her feet into her boots and went outside to start work, wondering what the day might bring and hoping it was going to be a good one.

Having fed the animals and checked that the final potatoes were being harvested and packed ready to be driven to the harbour, she decided to pack up the eggs she had collected that morning. Lettie thought about Brodie and their kissing the previous evening. She had too much responsibility to contend with over the next two months while her father was away to be able to give much time to anything other than her duties to the farm and animals.

Lettie had a neat stack of moulded wood pulp filler trays, filled with the fresh organic eggs, when she heard Spud barking. Her thoughts interrupted, she then heard tyres pulling into the yard and turned to go and find out who had arrived. Her elbow knocked the corner of the stack and, shrieking in shock, Lettie lurched forward to try and catch the trays before they fell to the cement floor of the barn.

'Noooo!' They slipped through her fingers and she watched in horror as the eggs smashed, splattering their yolky goodness over the floor. Lettie clenched her teeth.

'What's wrong?'

Hearing Joe's voice, Lettie looked at him in despair. 'I've just knocked all these eggs onto the floor. Argh, I'm such an idiot. Now I'll have to clean up this mess and call the village shop to let them know I won't have their full order today.'

He walked over to join her and sighed. 'I suppose my arrival interrupted you, didn't it?'

She nodded. 'I'm not sure why though. It's not as if I wasn't expecting you.' She groaned. She already had too many jobs to try and get through without needing additional things to do taking up her time. She rubbed her eyes. 'I'm going to have to clean this up straight away.'

'Are those to be packed too?' he asked indicating the baskets of eggs to the side of her.

'Yes.'

'I can help with this before shearing the alpacas. Why don't I clean up this mess and you carry on packing those.'

She was tempted to agree but didn't think it right to let a visitor do the mucky job. 'No, it's fine. I'll clean up. I made the mess after all, not you.'

Joe grimaced. 'But I was the one who surprised you, causing this mess. No, you tell me where to find the stuff to sort this lot out then I'll get on with it while you pack the rest of those eggs. Then maybe you can take ten minutes' break and sit with me outside.'

Not having the energy to argue, Lettie agreed. Having told him where to find the bucket, water, soap and other items he needed, she turned back to finish her packing while he cleared up for her.

Twenty minutes later they were sitting on the low wall in the warmth of the sunny yard, drinking cups of tea. Lettie leant back against the side of the barn behind the wall and closed her eyes. 'I needed this.'

'I'm sorry I interrupted your morning, and so messily too.'

She smiled. 'It's fine. You cleaned everything up and anyway it's good to see you again.'

'I'm glad you think so.'

She looked at the bag on the side she realised he must have brought in with him. 'Are those the shears?'

'They are. I thought that once I've shorn the alpacas I can help you here with some of your jobs.'

Lettie was touched by his thoughtfulness. 'That's so kind of you. The alpacas are in the smaller barn. I put them in the stalls in there earlier to keep them quiet. I'll take you to them now.'

He picked up his bag and walked with her. 'Having worked for my uncle on his farm I'm aware how much work there is. I have a few spare hours and would love to muck in and help you with anything I can.'

Touched by his thoughtfulness Lettie's right hand flew to her chest. 'Oh, Joe, that's so sweet of you.'

He gave her a beatific smile. 'We'll my granny Sybil always said I was an angel.'

Lettie laughed. 'I'm not so sure I'd go that far.' She finished her tea and stood up. 'I'd better get on with things. As it is I'm going to be working until quite late this evening.'

'Tell me what you're planning to do next and I'll come and help you with it.'

* * *

They were back in the yard after he had finished shearing the animals and he had helped Lettie lead them to the nearest paddock, when she took his hand in hers and leant forward to kiss his cheek, just as a car pulled up and stopped in the yard. Brodie got out of his old Land Rover and Lettie saw him look her way, then glance down at her hand in Joe's. She immediately dropped Joe's hand and stepped forward. 'Brodie? What are you doing here?'

'I, um... Hi, Joe.' He looked from Joe to her and seemed very awkward. 'That is, I was checking to see if you had everything in hand. I mean, here on the farm.'

She realised Brodie was taken aback to see her with Joe and knew he was reading more into the situation than he should. 'Would you like to join us? Have a cup of tea?'

Brodie shook his head, still holding onto his car door. 'No. Thanks. Unless you need me to help you with anything,' he added as an afterthought.

'No. But thanks all the same. Joe's here for the alpacas but has stayed on to help me. He's worked on a farm in the past so knows what's needed. Oh, and I've got the workers Dad took on before he left harvesting the last of the Jersey Royals, so at least they're taken care of.'

'No worries, mate,' Joe said. 'We'll be fine.'

Lettie saw Brodie studying Joe's face, unsure what he was trying to work out.

'Fine. If you're all OK here then I'll leave you to it. Do call me if you need anything though won't you?'

'I will do. Thanks.' Lettie gave him a wave and watched him drive away. 'Well, that was a little odd.'

'You think so?'

Surprised by his question she looked at him. 'Why? Don't you?'

'No, Lettie. I don't think it was odd at all.' He handed her his mug. 'Shall we get on with the next job then?'

'Yes,' she said setting both mugs onto the wall. 'We better had.'

25

BRODIE

Six weeks to go

Each time the phone rang in reception, or a notification pinged on his phone, Brodie tensed wondering if Lettie had changed her mind and needed him to do something for her. He looked at the sweet dog snoozing in a basket he had placed for him next to Bethan's chair behind reception and didn't relish the thought that he might not still be there at the end of the day. After his impromptu visit to Hollyhock Farm two weeks before and seeing Joe and Lettie so comfortable with each other it reminded him how awkward he sometimes felt in her company He really didn't need his day to get any worse. Why had he thought it a good idea to go there in the first place?

'Stop staring at him,' Bethan whispered bending to feed a treat to Thistle. 'I know you're worried he'll be claimed but I'll check them out thoroughly before we return him. I won't let this little guy go to just anyone.'

Brodie loved Bethan's dedication to the animals that passed through the practice. 'I know you won't.'

'And,' she added looking up at him a serious expression on her face, 'if his owners do come for him then we'll just have to focus on the fact that he's happy and has been reunited with them, won't we?'

Brodie lowered his voice so none of the people waiting in front of reception could hear him. 'I'm not sure why you're talking to me like you're my primary school teacher?' He grinned to let her know he was only teasing, not that Bethan would be bothered either way.

She nudged him with her elbow. 'We could always go for a drink later to take your mind of everything,' she suggested giving him a cheeky wink.

Thrown by her suggestion, Brodie swallowed. 'Um, er, right.'

'Never mind that now,' she said, beaming at him. 'Mrs Bellows is here with Tigger.' She gave him a pained look before turning her attention and addressing the woman on the other side of the reception desk with the pet carrier on her lap and a hissing tabby inside it. 'Mrs Bellows, Brodie is free to see you now.'

He had been hoping to make himself a quick coffee before seeing the next patient and wondered why Bethan seemed to have forgotten he usually took a few minutes to have one to refresh himself each day at this time. Had she forgotten because she was thinking about their drink in the pub? The thought worried him.

'If you'll follow me please, Mrs Bellows.' He held his left arm out in the direction of his surgery and waited for her to accompany him. He already knew from experience that Tigger was a vicious spit-cat, not that Mrs Bellows thought so. 'Thanks, Bethan,' he said, narrowing his eyes at her before giving Mrs Bellows his most charming smile. He closed the surgery door behind Mrs Bellows and waited for her to lift the carrier onto the examination table. 'What's the matter with Tigger today?'

* * *

'Vicious, bloody cat,' he grumbled, his mood not helped by the pain the animal had inflicted.

'Come here and let me look at that,' Bethan said opening an antiseptic wipe and carefully cleaning the deep scratch across the back of Brodie's hand twenty minutes later. 'I've been feeling guilty.'

'What about?' he asked, intrigued by her admission. Bethan always seemed very honest so it didn't surprise him that she wanted to open up about something that was troubling her.

'I saw your face when I mentioned going out for a drink.' She looked into his eyes for a few seconds. 'It was only a suggestion and I wouldn't want to make you feel uncomfortable.'

He liked Bethan but he had feelings for Lettie. Deep feelings. What right did he have to be put out about Lettie seeing Joe? he mused, still unable to get the image of the two of them holding hands from his mind. She was a free agent and hadn't he made a promise to himself not to get involved with anyone who was a client? If anyone was in the wrong it was him. He had been the one to instigate their kiss when he knew there couldn't be a future for them. At least while she ran the farm.

'Brodie?'

Embarrassed to have been so rude, he gave Bethan an apologetic smile. What had she been saying? Recalling her comment and wanting to make things up to her he shrugged. 'You couldn't possibly make me feel uncomfortable, Bethan,' he said hoping to reassure her.

'So you want to go out for that drink then?'

'Yes, of course I do.' What was he thinking? If he had been unsure about Bethan's feelings towards him before, he now suspected that she liked him. Would he be leading her on and giving her false expectations by going out with her? He hoped not, but didn't think that now was the time to change his mind. Not without upsetting her. 'Just let me know when you're free and we can go one night after we close up here, if you like.'

Her smile told him all he needed to know and Brodie felt his guilt deepen. 'Great. I'll do that.' He winced as the wipe stung his cut hand. 'Sorry. I know this is a bit sore.' She lifted his hand to get a closer look. 'It does look rather deep,' she said peering down at the long furrow through his skin. 'Maybe Tigger picked up that you weren't all that fond of him?'

'Very funny. Damned cat.' He wished the morning's surgery was over, but had noticed there were still three people and their pets waiting to see him. 'Is it going to be like this all day?'

Bethan nodded. 'It is. Though I'm not sure all of the pets have much wrong with them.'

He struggled to understand what she meant. 'Then why would they bring them in here and waste their time and money seeing me?'

Bethan stopped what she was doing and looked at him. 'And here was me thinking you were a man of the world, Brodie Murray.'

Insulted to think that she assumed he wasn't, he frowned. 'I am.'

She took a plaster and stuck it onto his cleaned cut. 'They'll stop soon enough, I'm sure.'

He didn't like the idea of not having any patients and said so.

'Oh, I'm sure you'll still have enough work to keep you going,' she assured him. 'Just that you'll have patients needing treatment, that's all.'

'That's a relief.' He looked at his hand. 'You've done a good job, thank you, Nurse.'

'My pleasure.' She gave him a lingering smile and Brodie was sure she was trying to send him some sort of message.

'Thanks, Bethan.'

'How about tomorrow night for our drink?'

'That would be nice.'

'Right, I'll tidy this lot up and go and make us both a coffee. I'll bring yours in after your next patient has left.' She raised a finger. 'I almost forgot. I have to pop out for a doctor's appointment. Nothing worrying,' she added. 'Just an annual check so that I can have a repeat prescription.'

'That's a relief. Will Tina be coming to stand in for you?' he asked hopefully. He had spent a week soon after his arrival covering both the reception and his surgery when Bethan had been on holiday and didn't fancy repeating the experience any time soon.

'She will.'

Typical Bethan to be so efficient. 'Thank you.'

* * *

Later that afternoon, Brodie saw the final patient out into the reception when Bethan returned.

'You'll never guess who I've just seen coming out of Hollyhock Farm,' she said quietly over the reception desk so that only Brodie and Tina could hear her.

'Who?' Tina asked, eyes wide.

'That delicious firefighter Joe. I wonder what he was doing there?'

'I don't think it's any of our business,' Brodie said feeling as if he'd been punched in his gut. Didn't the man have a job to go to? He knew Lettie would have been busy, so maybe Joe was helping her. He imagined he would be and was glad to think Lettie had extra help with her work but wished he could be the one helping her.

He turned to Tina. 'Thanks for covering Bethan today,' he said grateful for her understanding.

'It was no problem at all. I appreciate the extra money.' Tina pointed the biro she was holding in Thistle's direction. 'I'm happy to see this adorable dog is still here. He seems very much at home now.'

'Lettie was the one to rescue him,' Brodie said. 'I was happy to take him in.' He remembered the posts Lettie was going to ask Tina to arrange for his details to be posted on social media and asked Tina if she had spoken to her.

'No yet,' Tina said, thoughtfully. 'But she's probably forgotten with all that she has to do now that her parents have gone away.'

'Of course. I'm just eager to try and put something out so that the owners don't worry unnecessarily about him.'

'I thought as much. Bethan and I had a chat and I've now set something in place.' Tina indicated the computer screen. 'I've taken a photo of him.' She turned the screen so Brodie could get a better look.

Seeing the photos reminded him that Lettie had also taken photos but must have forgotten about them with all she had to focus on at the farm.

'And I've posted it up on various local platforms, so it shouldn't be too long until someone recognises him and alerts either us or his owners where Thistle is being kept.'

'Right. Thank you.' As much as Brodie hated to think of Thistle's owners worrying about him, he wasn't looking forward to giving him back, but knew that was very selfish of him.

He said goodnight to Tina who had agreed to lock up for him and leave the key through his cottage letter box. He walked with Thistle back to the cottage and changed into his shorts to go surfing. His eyesight was lousy without his glasses but he never wore them surfing, so placed them on his bookcase. He realised he would be hungry after spending a couple of hours in the sea and needed something for supper. Brodie was tempted to take a chance on the village shop still being open when he finished, but decided not to risk it. He was always forgetting the time when he was on his board and was already slightly hungry and knew he had nothing in the house to feed either himself or the dog.

He walked to the shop, quickly choosing something, before hurrying home to pop it in the fridge and fetch his surfboard, eager to get down to the beach while the surf was good.

26

LETTIE

Lettie waved goodbye to Joe as he left to go home and shower before starting his shift, hoping he hadn't overdone things when he had his own job to get to. It had been kind of him to come and help with the watering in the polytunnels and then going with her to deliver the goats' milk to several of their clients. Seeing that she had little food in the house she decided to take a stroll to the village before getting too settled. She quickly showered and taking her purse and a shopping bag walked the ten-minute distance there.

'Lettie, hey wait a sec.'

Hearing Tina's voice, she turned to her. 'Hi there, you're looking happy.'

'I am, very.'

Intrigued, Lettie gave her friend a quizzical look. 'Well, are you going to tell me why, or keep me guessing?'

Tina gave her a thoughtful look. 'It's the job at the practice.'

Supposing she was enjoying it, Lettie thought it best to ask to be certain.

'I'm loving it. In fact, I'd work there full-time if I didn't have

Noah at home to look after.' She lowered her voice as a couple of women passed them. 'That vet of yours is such a cutie.'

Lettie doubted Brodie would be impressed with that description of himself. 'I'm not so sure that's how I would describe him.' She grinned at the thought of him hearing them.

'How would you describe him then?'

Now she was on the spot. Lettie gave Tina's question some thought. 'I suppose I'd say he's, um...'

'Hot?'

Lettie sighed recalling his unexpected appearance at the farm a couple of weeks ago and wondering what he had made of it. 'I wouldn't have used that word exactly, but I have to agree with you.'

'You do still like him then?' Tina whispered looking, Lettie thought, very pleased with herself. 'I knew he was your type. Mind you, I gather you've been seeing quite a bit of that cute firefighter. Are you going to tell me what's going on?' Tina folded her arms and waited impatiently.

Lettie raised a finger to her mouth to quieten Tina in case anyone overheard their conversation. 'It's a bit complicated,' she said unsure how else to explain their situation. Suspecting her friend might conjure up a plan to orchestrate her and Brodie going out on a date, she decided to put her straight. 'I'm not really sure, to be honest with you. I have been to his cottage for supper.'

'Whose? Brodie's?' Lettie nodded. Tina gasped, clearly delighted with this unexpected development. 'When?'

'A couple of weeks ago.'

'That's so exciting. How?'

Confused, Lettie frowned. 'What do you mean how?'

Tina nudged her. 'How did you wrangle an invitation to dinner?'

'I didn't wrangle anything.' Lettie shook her head, not wishing

Tina to get carried away. 'It wasn't a big deal and it just happened. You know how it is...'

'I've been with Kyle so long that I can barely remember how these things are.'

Lettie didn't like being questioned and being made to think more deeply about her situation with both men. Not when she was battling having so much to contend with running the farm. 'It was very relaxed and unplanned. Nothing exciting.'

'Go on.'

Lettie told her about Thistle and what had happened, amused to see her best friend's delight.

'Did you kiss him?' Tina whispered, barely managing to contain her excitement.

'Yes,' she admitted, aware that Tina knew her well enough to sense if she was fibbing. 'But don't get excited, it was only twice.'

Tina clasped her hands together and went to say something, stopping when something caught her attention. She lowered her head slightly and discreetly pointed in the direction of the shop. 'He's there.'

'Who?'

'Your vet.'

'He's not my vet,' Lettie hissed, wishing Tina would stop referring to him in that way.

'Will you shut up and talk to him? I want to watch and see how he reacts to you.'

Lettie had no intention of behaving like a teenager just for her friend's entertainment. 'No, I won't. Anyway I need to get to the shop before it closes. I'll catch up with you sometime soon.'

'Spoilsport.'

Lettie began walking to the shop entrance. She smiled at Brodie as he walked in her direction. 'Hi.'

He looked her way. 'Hi.'

She expected him to at least stop and speak to her but instead he gave a polite smile like one she imagined he might give to a client and hurried on his way, presumably back to his cottage. Embarrassed to have been pretty much ignored, Lettie cast a glance behind her to see if Tina was still there, mortified to discover that her friend had witnessed everything and was looking bemused.

Not wishing to feel more embarrassed than she already was, Lettie forced a smile before heading into the shop.

Why had he acted as if they barely knew each other? Had she been foolish to assume that after their enjoyable evening together they were at least friends now? It was very confusing and, she had to admit, hurtful. Clearly any messages she had picked up and interpreted as meaning he might be even slightly attracted to her must have been wrong. What a fool she had been to even let herself think there could be something between them.

She shook away the thought of him and forced herself to focus on finding something for supper. Then, turning the corner at the end of an aisle, Lettie came face to face with Joe.

'Hello there,' he said beaming at her and looking as delighted to see her as she wished Brodie had been. 'Fancy seeing you here.'

Unable to help herself, Lettie was amused. 'What, in a food shop?' She noticed his basket filled with food.

He grinned. 'Good point.' He raised the basket. 'My turn to cook for the crew tomorrow night. Thought I'd make us a beef curry.'

Lettie felt even hungrier at the thought of how that might taste. 'Lucky crew.'

'You haven't tasted my cooking yet, so I wouldn't assume they'll enjoy this all that much.' He stared at her, smiling. 'I enjoyed today.'

'Me too. Thanks again for all your help.'

'It's no problem at all. I'm glad to be useful. Hey, if you're looking for supper, why don't we go to the pub and eat something together?'

She didn't see why she shouldn't. It was late and every part of her body ached. The effort of making food, even something heated up in the microwave, had disappeared. And now that Brodie had shown how uninterested he was in her for the second time in her life after they had kissed, she needed something to take her mind off him and her humiliation. Brodie Murray just wasn't worth her time and she had no intention of wasting any of it mooning after him. Not after wasting so many years over him years before.

'But what about your shopping?'

He cocked his head to one side. 'I can buy it tomorrow. Give me a sec and I'll put all this back and then we can go and eat.'

She liked the idea. 'The pub does do good food,' she said pretending she needed to contemplate his suggestion.

'It does, and I met Tina outside. She was just telling me that it's curry night there tonight. I love a tasty curry.'

She hadn't realised he knew Tina and said so.

'I don't really know her, but I do know her husband Kyle slightly. I met her for the first time at the antique market in St Aubin a few months ago.'

'She's one of my oldest friends,' Lettie said reminded how small the island was and how different it was living here where most people knew each other as opposed to the anonymity she mostly felt living in London. She decided liked the idea of a curry and didn't want to miss out on the opportunity to enjoy one. 'You're on then. What time do they start serving, do you know?'

He checked his watch. 'In about ten minutes. We could go and have a drink while we wait and at least we should get a good table.'

'Let's go then,' she said feeling much better than she had when she'd entered the shop.

Just as she had expected it would be, supper at the pub was not only delicious but also enormous fun. Joe's jokes were silly but funny and she managed to put Brodie's blanking of her to the back of her mind for most of the evening.

He looked thoughtful and was staring at her plate just when the bar staff took them from their table. 'What is it?'

Joe watched the plate as it was taken away. 'I wish I'd chosen the chicken curry like you did. How was it?'

'I'm sure you can have it next time,' she said. 'Anyway, yours looked tasty enough.'

'There'll be a next time?'

She couldn't miss the glint in his eyes. 'Maybe, if I ever have enough energy after another day's work. To answer your question the chicken curry was wonderful.'

'Will you join me when I come here again? They serve a pretty mean cottage pie.'

She saw the unmistakable mischievous look on his face and shook her head, smiling. 'So that's it.'

'What?' He laughed when she didn't immediately answer.

'You just want a dinner companion, don't you?'

He looked up towards the ceiling, and his hand went to his chest as he pretended to be hurt by her insinuation. 'I've no idea what gave you that idea.'

She drank some of her cider. 'Are you saying I'm wrong?'

'Yes.' He dropped the act. 'And stop avoiding the question. Will you join me here again?'

How could she say no, especially after all he had done to help her at the farm? Anyway, she mused, why would she want to? It might be Brodie who made her heart flutter, but Joe was great fun and adorable. As long as he didn't get the wrong idea about them seeing each other, it would be fun to spend more time with him. 'I'd love to.'

'Good, that's tomorrow's supper sorted then.'

It was her turn to sit open-mouthed. 'Tomorrow? I was thinking more like sometime next week.'

'What?' He laughed. 'Are you telling me you're busy elsewhere tomorrow night?'

'Yes, the way I feel right now I'll probably be collapsed on my sofa after another exhausting day on the farm.' She shook her head. 'Anyway, I usually spend my evenings with Spud.'

'I love your dog.'

She sighed, happy to hear him say so.

'But I'm sure Spud will be perfectly fine by himself for another evening. Another drink before we go?'

Why not, she thought. 'Just the one then,' she said standing. 'And as it's my round I'll buy it.'

He tried to argue but she wasn't having any of it. She also intended paying for their meal when they were at the bar. She realised that even if they were in a relationship she would do the same. Somehow though it mattered more now she had decided there was to be nothing romantic between them.

27

BRODIE

Brodie took Thistle down to the beach for a walk just after dawn. He would have loved to let him run free but didn't trust Thistle's recall and the last thing he needed was to lose the dog. Thistle seemed friendly with the other dogs they came across and although he tried to pull away a couple of times to go and play with them he soon settled down.

He arrived at the practice carrying two coffees and a croissant for himself and one for Bethan that he had bought at the village bakery. The pastries were still warm from the ovens and he was looking forward to enjoying his with his coffee. He had fed Thistle before leaving the cottage and watched as the dog had a sniff of the reception before settling down in his bed next to Bethan's empty chair.

He enjoyed being in the surgery before anyone arrived, relishing the peace and quiet but happy to think that very soon the place would be busy. Maybe he should call his sister and ask her about doing up his cottage now while he wouldn't be disturbed. He loved Maddie but she could be hard work and for a moment he hesitated, wishing instead to sit quietly and enjoy his breakfast. No.

He needed to call her and then he couldn't change his mind about involving her in the redecorating. He picked up the phone and pressed Maddie's number. He listened to the sound of the ringing but she didn't answer and he decided to try her again later.

By lunchtime Brodie was struggling to hide his impatience with a man who had brought in his dog. He had been trying to explain the reasons why the Labrador was very overweight and make suggestions about how to change the dog's diet but wasn't getting very far.

Brodie's stomach rumbled and he was desperate for his lunch break. So far the day had been less than satisfactory with his sister not returning a second call followed by a morning of difficult patients. He hadn't seen or spoken to Lettie since his impromptu arrival at the farm when she was spending time with Joe. His mood dipped further and he reminded himself that he had no right in that regard. Not wishing Lettie to get the wrong idea about his awkwardly timed appearance at the farm he decided to take Thistle to visit her so that she could see how well he was looking and give her an update on his situation.

She must have heard his vehicle's noisy engine because she walked out from the barn, peering in his direction. Brodie raised his hand in a wave expecting her to reciprocate, taken aback when she didn't. Instead, she turned around and disappeared back into the barn.

Maybe coming here had not been a good idea. Then it occurred to him that she might be troubled about something. One of the animals? He glanced at the footwell in front of the passenger seat, relieved that he had thought to bring his medical bag. Not that he went many places without it in case its contents were needed.

He parked the car and hearing barks from Spud he turned to Thistle. 'I think you should stay in the car for now. I'm not sure how welcoming her dog might be and we don't want you getting bitten.'

He picked up his bag and got out of the car trying to ignore Thistle's whining as he hurried after Lettie into the barn.

'Lettie?'

As soon as he rounded a corner past some old stalls that looked as if they might have originally been used for Gareth Torel's dairy herd before he sold it, he spotted her. She was sweeping as if she was taking her fury out on the broom and told the dog to sit, probably because she suspected he was bringing Thistle into the barn with him.

'Lettie, hi.'

Instead of seeming happy to see him, Lettie's dour expression didn't alter. He was surprised when she ignored him and continued to sweep. She was clearly upset about something. Brodie struggled to think what he could have done to upset her. He walked over to her and placed his case onto the floor.

'You seem upset,' he said carefully.

She didn't look at him but continued sweeping furiously. 'Do I?'

'Have I done or said anything I shouldn't?' he asked, unsure what it could have been, or even when he might have offended her. They had seemed perfectly fine the other evening. Was it because he had interrupted her time with Joe? 'If it's because I came when Joe was here...'

Lettie stopped what she was doing and, straightening up, she rested her hands on the top of the broom handle and glared at him. 'No, it isn't that.'

He wasn't sure why but it occurred to him that he should probably explain why he was there now.

'I wanted to come and tell you that we still haven't been contacted by Thistle's owner and thought you might like to see him again.' When she didn't react, he added, 'I've, er, kept him in the car because I wasn't sure whether your dog would appreciate having a strange dog in his yard.'

She still didn't speak and Brodie wished now that he hadn't come. Why was she staring at him as if he had done something dreadful? 'Look, if I've done something to offend you.'

'Why ever would you think that, Brodie?'

She almost spat his name. 'I… that is, you seem angry.'

'I don't want to be,' she said scowling. 'But I am.'

He wasn't sure whether to speak again because each time he did he seemed to antagonise her further, but how else was he going to find out what was wrong. 'Is it something I've done?'

She gave an irritated sigh. 'It is.'

They stared at each other for a moment.

'Sorry, you're going to have to enlighten me,' he said confused and starting to become annoyed with her.

'I thought we had a lovely time together at your cottage that evening,' she said finally.

'So did I.' This was getting weird.

'Right, so we agree on that, then?'

Was she a little mad? 'We do.'

'Then I'd like to understand why you chose to ignore me then when you saw me at the shop last night.'

When the hell had he seen her? He shook his head and shrugged. 'I don't recall seeing you.'

She narrowed her eyes. 'You didn't go to the village shop yesterday evening then?'

Village shop? He thought back but didn't recall seeing her there. Then he remembered thinking he had heard someone saying his name. 'You called out to me?'

'Sort of,' she said sulkily.

'Lettie, I'm so sorry,' he said, mortified to have blanked her. 'I didn't realise it was you otherwise I would have stopped to chat.'

'I should know by now that I'm pretty forgettable as far as you're concerned,' she said so quietly he only just heard her.

'What's that supposed to mean?' He reached out to touch her arm, but she flinched away from him.

'It's nothing,' she snapped. 'Anyway I'm not sure why I'm making a big deal of it.'

She was hurt and he wasn't surprised. He would have been too if she had done the same thing to him. He couldn't understand why he hadn't seen her, then it dawned on him. 'I was on my way to go surfing.'

She began sweeping again. 'I've no idea what that's got to do with anything.'

'You don't understand.'

'Obviously not.'

'I had taken off my glasses.' Relieved, he added, 'I never wear them when I surf. I must have taken off the ones I was wearing, my better ones, when I changed. I have another pair in the car for driving, just so I don't forget them.' He wasn't sure why he added the last sentence but supposed he didn't like her to think he was irresponsible to try and drive without being able to see properly.

He realised she was looking at him with a thoughtful expression on her face.

'You're short-sighted?'

'Very.' He risked an apologetic smile. 'I had a lovely time with you the other night, Lettie, and I would never just ignore you. I'm sorry I hurt your feelings.'

Her cheeks reddened. 'It's fine. I probably shouldn't have over-reacted like that.'

Relieved they were friends again he risked stepping forward. 'Can I make it up to you over a walk on the beach with our dogs, maybe tonight?'

'I'm afraid I already have plans.'

He wondered if her plans were with Joe, but knew he had no right to ask. 'Maybe another time.'

She rested the broom against the side of a stall. 'You mentioned Thistle was with you. Shall we go and see him?'

'I think we better had,' he said relieved she had calmed down. He laughed hearing the dog's whining that had now intensified into a loud bark.

28

LETTIE

Lettie gave Spud a cuddle and took hold of his collar so that he wouldn't charge at poor Thistle when he was let out of Brodie's car. She led the way out of the barn trying to hide her delight that Brodie hadn't intended blanking her at all. Now that she thought of it, he did look slightly different but it hadn't occurred to her that it was because he wasn't wearing glasses.

She stopped to let Brodie go ahead to let Thistle out of his vehicle, watching as he attached a lead to the dog's collar, which she noticed seemed to be a new one.

'I like the pale blue,' she said. 'The colour suits him.'

'I'd like to take credit for it,' Brodie said as Thistle jumped down. 'But it was Bethan who fitted him with one.'

'She's chosen well.'

Brodie pointed at Spud. 'Do you think we should let them check each other out?'

Lettie grinned. 'Yes, let's see what they think of each other.' He stroked Spud's black and white furry head. 'Gently now, Spud. Be nice.'

She held on to him, unsure what he would do and hoping the

greeting would go well as she waited for Brodie to lead Thistle to them.

They stood silently as each dog sniffed the other. Spud snarled once then seemed to calm slightly. 'I think he's showing Thistle who's top dog here.'

Yes, she thought. 'He probably is. Spud had always been an only dog and can be rather territorial.' She smiled, happy to see that Spud appeared to like Thistle. 'I think they're going to be friends.' She caught Brodie's eye.

'Like us,' he said smiling.

She was reluctant to agree. 'Yes, like us.' She would like to be so much more than just friends, but as she looked into his eyes she knew she would rather be something to him than nothing at all and would simply have to be satisfied with that. Although, going by her earlier reaction when he had upset her, she suspected she was going to have to make more of an effort to cover up her feelings for him.

'When shall we take these two to the nearest beach for a walk? I know Thistle loves running on the sand and I took him this morning.'

She enjoyed walking and the thought of going for a long walk with Brodie and the dogs appealed to her. 'I'm sure Spud will do too.'

He pushed his hands into his pockets and looked a little sheepish, she thought. 'It's a beautiful evening, but you said you're already doing something. I think the forecast is fine, so how about tomorrow evening then?'

'OK.'

'I'll look forward to it,' Brodie said whistling for Thistle to follow him. 'I'd better get back to the practice before Bethan needs to show in my next patient. I don't want to be late.'

'We'll both look forward to seeing you two tomorrow evening then.'

Lettie watched Brodie and Thistle leave and crouched down to give Spud a cuddle. 'Good boy. I think you and Thistle are going to be good friends.'

She pushed away the thought that it would only happen if the stray's owners didn't contact Brodie and claim him. As she returned to the barn, Lettie pictured how happy Brodie had been with Thistle and could tell he was already besotted with the dog. She didn't like to think how he would feel if he was claimed and he had to part with him. Even though Brodie was from here and had a family there was something very lonely about him. She wondered if maybe he had been hurt in the past, or if he simply enjoyed his own company most of the time.

29

BRODIE

Brodie found it difficult not to be distracted by thoughts of Lettie spending time with Joe. He wished he didn't think that getting involved with a client was such a bad idea, especially for someone trying to build up a new business. It occurred to him that Lettie was also working long hours and he doubted her busy life would allow her to spend much time with Joe. The thought cheered him slightly.

'Hmm, maybe.'

'Are you talking to yourself?' Bethan asked from the doorway. She held up the medication she had collected for one of the patients when he gave her a quizzical look.

'Sorry, I hadn't realised you were there.' He hoped he hadn't spoken Lettie's name out loud.

'You said maybe,' she said, a cheeky smile on her face. 'Could you have been contemplating the details of our date?'

Taken aback, Brodie struggled to reply. 'Date? Oh, you mean going for a drink?'

'Is that a yes?' She grinned turning to leave the room and glancing over her shoulder at him.

Remembering he'd already agreed to go with her, he nodded. 'It is.'

'Great. Shall we meet at eight?'

Brodie nodded. 'Eight is fine.'

'No problem.' She raised a finger. 'Ooh, I nearly forgot, Mrs, um, the one with the nasty tabby, is here to collect the food you wanted her to feed him. I couldn't recall which packet I should give her.'

'The weight-management one. The one with the blue writing on the cover, not the lavender writing.'

'Great.' She went to the door, stopping and turning to him. 'Your next patient has arrived, too.' She grimaced. 'With a very cross-looking Siamese cat.'

Brodie had come across the cat a couple of times before and gave a resigned sigh. 'Give me a couple of minutes to finish writing up these notes then send them through please.'

'Will do.' She left the room humming something to herself and Brodie immediately realised he should have put a stop to it, or at least let Bethan know that he saw her as a friend, rather than in a romantic way. He regretted agreeing to go out with her. Surely the only thing worse than becoming involved with a client was to do so with your most vital member of staff. Damn.

* * *

Later as his door closed behind another patient, Brodie's thoughts turned to Lettie. He was looking forward to walking their dogs together the following evening just like friends would do, he decided. He hoped the weather forecast that had shown squally showers would be passing the Channel Islands was wrong and wouldn't be bad enough to cancel their walk. Although, he doubted Lettie would be fazed by a bit of wind and rain – with her being a farmer's daughter.

His phone pinged and picking it up from his desk he turned it round to look at the screen. 'Maddie.' He read her message saying to let her know when he was free, about redecorating the cottage. Brodie decided he would do so as soon as he was finished for the day. He was amused to think of her reaction when she heard that he did want her help after all. Knowing his sister, she would be bracing herself for a row with him having come up with a list of reasons why it would be a sensible idea for him to let her get on with bringing the cottage up to date. He looked forward to seeing the surprise on her face when he spoke to her.

He replied with a message asking Maddie to call in at the cottage any time between five thirty and seven thirty that evening. It would give him time to see his sister, then go and meet Bethan. He went out to the reception to check on Thistle and picked up one of his toys that was somehow wedged behind the filing cabinet. His life was so different now after those dark months when everything had seemed so miserable after he and Tiffany split up.

Apart from a scrap between two dogs, the rest of the day passed with little incident. Even so, Brodie was happy to be back at the cottage and changed into his oldest jogging bottoms and T-shirt. He decided he had better tidy the place up and make sure the few dishes he had washed that morning were put neatly away in the cupboards. He fed Thistle who had just settled down in front of the fire when there was a loud knock on the door, causing the dog to leap to his feet and bark noisily.

'It's only my nosy sister,' Brodie soothed, stroking the dog's head and settling him back down. 'No need to worry.'

He went to the door and opened it. 'Tina?'

He stepped back, shocked to see her there and waved her inside. 'Is everything all right?'

'That depends,' she said carrying Noah through to the living room when he waved for her to go inside. She bent to stroke Thistle's head.

A sense of foreboding flooded through him. 'You've heard from his owners, haven't you?'

'I'm afraid I have.'

The thought of returning Thistle to his home upset him. 'Tell me everything,' he said, then remembered his date with Bethan. 'Sorry, I've just got to send a brief message to someone.' He tapped out an apologetic text telling her that Thistle's owners had been found and that they would need to reschedule their drink. Pressing send, he decided that when they discussed the matter he would have to let Bethan know that although he was happy to go for a drink as colleagues, he valued her too much as his practice nurse to want their professional and friendly relationship to change in any way.

30

LETTIE

Hearing her mobile ringing, Lettie opened her eyes realising as she raised her head from her arms that she must have fallen asleep at the kitchen table. She struggled to remember where she had left her phone. She yawned and reached out to grab her phone from the sideboard behind her just in time for the call to end.

Remembering that she had a date with Joe, Lettie was surprised to see the missed call had been from Brodie. 'Bugger.' She looked at the screen her heart racing slightly. What could he want? Not wishing to miss him completely, she quickly returned the call and hoped he was still available to chat to her.

'Hi, Lettie. Thanks for calling me back so quickly.'

Hearing the flat tone of his usually chirpy voice, Lettie sensed something had upset him. 'What's happened?'

'Tina popped round a short while ago to let me know that Thistle's owners have been located. I've called the woman, a Mrs Broadbent, and said I'll take him over to her now.'

There was something left unsaid and for a moment she wasn't sure what it was he wanted to ask her. 'Would you like me to come with you?' she asked before the thought had properly filtered through her brain.

He sighed, obviously relieved. 'Would you mind? I know it's getting late, but for some reason I was dreading going by myself. I know it's ridiculous.'

'No it isn't,' she argued. 'It's fine. I understand completely and can be at your place in ten minutes.'

'Why don't I come to you?' he suggested. 'Save you walking here and it'll give you a couple of minutes to sort out Spud and lock up.'

'Perfect. See you soon.'

She ended the call and remembering she was wearing her tattiest, holiest shorts and fleecy hood with a Jersey cow emblazoned across the front, ran upstairs to change into a pair of jeans and a T-shirt.

'That's better,' she said giving Spud a cuddle. He sensed she was going out and was lying in his bed near to the Aga, staring up at her with an accusatory look. 'I'm sorry. I promise I won't be long and then we can watch more telly from the sofa again.' She ruffled his fluffy head. 'How about a treat?'

His ears perked up at the suggestion.

She heard Brodie's vehicle arriving outside, and having given Spud his treat, left the house and locked the door behind her.

She hadn't had enough time to think about what this all must mean to Brodie but aware that he was finding parting with Thistle far more difficult than he had imagined, she got into the passenger seat and reached back to stroke the sweet dog's head. 'Hello, boy.'

Turning to face the front she strapped herself in as Brodie turned the Land Rover and drove back to the lane.

'How are you?' she asked, glad he had asked her to accompany him.

'Miserable.' He glanced at her with a half-smile. 'I know I should be happy for Thistle, and I am. I'm just upset that I have to return him so soon. Selfish of me, I know. And not very professional for a vet.'

'Rubbish. You're only human and you've become more attached to him than you expected, that's all.'

He sighed and she saw him look at Thistle briefly in his rear-view mirror. 'The lady who contacted Tina did sound very nice. In fact the reason I'm hurrying to return him is because she sounded very troubled by having lost him in the first place.'

'Oh dear.' Lettie didn't like anyone to be upset. 'We'll have to reassure her that he was fine and well looked after and none the worse for his experience in the wild, so to speak.'

He gave her a smile and nodded. 'Yes. I want to reassure her.' He glanced into his mirror again then back at the road. 'I'll be happy to see Thistle back with his owner again. He must have missed her as much as she missed him.'

'I suppose so.'

'Another good thing about living on this small island is that nothing tends to go missing for long.'

Lettie agreed. 'Yes, and there's always someone who knows someone else who can help.'

'True.'

'I wonder what Thistle's real name is,' Lettie said almost to herself.

'I'd like to know that, too. I was hoping she didn't mind us giving him a new name.' He indicated left before turning down another road.

'Where exactly are we headed?' she asked a little later. They'd been driving for longer than she had expected them to and Lettie was surprised that Thistle didn't live in one of the closer parishes.

'Trinity.'

'Trinity? But that's miles from St Ouen.'

He nodded. 'I know. The poor dog has come quite a way and I couldn't help wondering why.'

She was wondering the same thing. 'Maybe he tried to return to where he's taken for walks each day, or something.'

'Maybe.' He sighed. 'I guess we'll soon find out. It is a bit odd though, isn't it?'

'Yes, it is.'

Lettie thought back to when she had found Thistle. He had seemed hungry and somewhat distressed and was hiding in a bush. Surely there was more to why he had run off, if in fact that was what had happened. She was glad she could be with Brodie when he met the owner and find out for herself exactly what had gone on.

Brodie pulled up to the gateway of a bungalow. 'This is the address the woman gave me when I called her.' He parked the car and turned to Lettie. 'I suppose we should go and do this then.'

'I suppose we should,' she said miserably. She turned and reached out to stroke Thistle's soft nose. 'He doesn't seem all that excited to be here, does he?'

'I was thinking that, too.' He turned to her and reached back to stroke Thistle's head. 'Thankfully though he doesn't seem too worried about being here either, otherwise I'd leave him in the vehicle and go in first without him.'

She loved that Brodie was protective of this sweet stray. 'Come along then, let's do this.'

Brodie sighed. 'Yes, may as well get it over with.'

31

BRODIE

Brodie lifted Thistle down from the vehicle and clipped a lead onto his collar; the last thing he needed was for the dog to run away again just when they had arrived at his home. He might be returning Thistle to his rightful owner, but he had every intention of observing every one of Thistle's reactions to being back here. And he wanted to discover what it was that had caused this friendly dog to run away.

Lettie looked at him and pointed to the doorbell. 'Shall I?'

'Please.' For some reason it mattered that he wasn't the one doing it. He wanted to keep Thistle by his side for as long as possible. He reached down and stroked Thistle from his head to his tail. 'You all right, boy?'

The dog wasn't shaking or trembling and Brodie noticed with relief that his tail was wagging slowly. At least he wasn't scared to be here; that was something. If the dog showed any signs of fear or being uncomfortable he decided he would make an excuse to have to take him to the practice and keep him there until he had found out more about the owners.

The front door eventually opened and a very elderly lady clapped her hands together in delight when she saw Thistle.

'Derek, you're back.' She bent slightly and opened her arms and Thistle, or Derek as Brodie now knew his name to be, increased his wagging and pulled forward to get to her.

Brodie unclipped the lead, let the dog go and looked at Lettie. She was smiling and looking as relieved as he felt. As part of him felt. He realised the rest of him was sad that this was the last time he would have Thistle. No, he reminded himself, his name is Derek, with him.

'He seems very happy to see you,' Brodie said.

The old lady seemed to notice him and Lettie for the first time. 'I can see you have a few questions you'd like to ask me and if you want to come inside for a cup of tea, then I can answer them for you.'

Brodie hoped he hadn't shown his thoughts on his face but assumed that he must have done. He held out his arm for Lettie to go first. 'We'd like to see him settled, so that would be lovely. Thank you.'

As Lettie followed the lady into her neat little home, Brodie looked around. They passed a small kitchen where he noticed a clean and filled water bowl on the floor, then into the living room where a dog's bed with several blankets and a couple of toys lay to the side of an electric fireplace. The woman seemed to have catered well for Derek. Brodie watched as the dog came up to nuzzle him and he leant forward and cuddled the dog's head and shoulders, before the dog went to his bed, turned in a circle a couple of times and then lay down.

'He certainly seems settled here,' Lettie said thoughtfully giving Brodie a side-eyed look.

She was right. But if that was the case then why had the dog run away?

'Let me make that tea.'

Lettie exchanged glances with Brodie again and he gave a slight shake of his head. 'Tea isn't necessary, Mrs Broadbent,' she said. 'Why don't you tell us what you wish to and we can be on our way and leave you and Th—Derek in peace?'

The woman sat and folded her hands in her lap. 'Derek here isn't my dog.'

Brodie tensed. He had no intention of leaving this dog with an imposter. He sat up straighter and leant forward frowning. 'What exactly do you mean by that?' Was this supposedly sweet lady admitting to getting Thistle under false pretences?

'Please, don't get me wrong. I am supposed to have him here. I didn't fib when I said I was his owner.' Her lined face crumpled slightly as she squeezed her eyes closed for a moment and appeared to be gathering herself. Opening them she took a deep breath. 'I'm trying to work out how best to explain this.'

'It's fine,' Lettie said calmly, shooting a pointed look in Brodie's direction. 'Take your time. We're not in any rush, are we, Brodie?'

'No.' He took a steadying breath. 'We're happy to be here for as long as you need us to be.' He looked at Derek lying comfortably in his bed, his big eyes staring up at him, and wondered what the dog was thinking. *Don't worry, my little pal*, he thought, wishing the dog could hear what he was thinking, *I won't leave you here unless I'm certain it's the best thing for you.* Derek opened one eye briefly, looked at him as if to reassure Brodie that he believed him and then closed it again and began snoring softly.

'Do go on.' Brodie was looking forward to finding out exactly what the situation was with this woman.

'It's like this,' she began, her fingers knitted together. 'You might have noticed a matching bungalow next door.'

Brodie hadn't but he nodded, impatient to hear her explanation.

'The gentleman who lived there, Percy, moved in with his wife in the sixties when I moved in here with my late husband.' Brodie wondered where she could be going with this story but didn't show his confusion on his face. 'We were neighbours and good friends for almost sixty years and supported each other when our spouses died.' She stopped speaking for a few seconds and seemed to brace herself before being able to continue.

'Please carry on.' Lettie gave Brodie a sideways glance and he could tell she was as confused as him.

'Yes, do.' Brodie forced a friendly smile.

'His wife died sometime in the eighties and he moved to another parish, near where you found Derek, I believe. Then, when my husband died about ten years later, Percy and I bumped into each other in town one day and became close. We were companions.' She cleared her throat. 'You know, accompanying each other on short trips away, that sort of thing. Then he became ill late last year and begged me to take Derek on.' She took a handkerchief from her sleeve, blew her nose and looked at the sleeping dog. 'We both miss Percy. Don't get me wrong – I like the dog. He's very sweet and not much trouble, but I've never had dogs before, only cats. Not that I have any of them left now.'

She took a deep breath and flattened her hands and fingers on her skirt, gazing at them briefly before looking up at Brodie and then Lettie.

Lettie shuffled in her seat and Brodie wondered what she was about to say. 'I'm not sure though why Thi—er, Derek would be where we found him though.'

The older lady shrugged. 'I asked one of the neighbours' grown-up daughters if she wouldn't mind taking Derek for a walk with her dog while I was out at the hairdresser and she happily obliged. But when I got home, she was waiting for me in a terrible state. She said she had taken him to the beach but that as soon as she had removed his lead to let him have a bit of a play, he ran off, up the stairs to the car park and she couldn't find him after that.'

Brodie understood what must have happened. 'Was the beach near to where Percy and Derek lived?'

She nodded. 'I suppose it was closer to that area.' Her mouth dropped open. 'You think he was trying to get home?'

Brodie nodded. 'He was probably looking for Percy.'

Her lined face crumpled and she began crying quietly. Brodie turned to Lettie unsure what to do.

Lettie cocked her head towards the woman and mouthed for him to comfort her.

He stood and crossed the small distance between his chair and Mrs Broadbent, crouching down in front of her. 'Please, don't get upset. It's not your fault. It's a natural thing for the dog to have done.'

She wiped her eyes and looked up at him, sniffing. 'It is?'

'Yes,' Lettie agreed. 'I was the one who found Derek and I can assure you he was fine.' She pointed to the dog and smiled. 'Look at him. He's sleeping soundly in his bed and I think we can all see that there's no harm done by his little adventure.'

Mrs Broadbent blew her nose again and seemed to calm down a little. 'Thank you both. You're very kind.'

Brodie sat back down in his chair. She seemed reassured but there was something not quite settled about the whole incident, although he couldn't put his finger on what it might be. He went over what she had told them about Percy, then about not being used to dogs and it dawned on him what the problem might be.

'I was wondering if you knew how old Derek is?' He presumed the dog must be about seven years old, but thought he may as well ask the person most likely to know.

'I believe he's about seven or eight maybe?' She sighed. 'He's a rescue. Percy was kind like that. I think he's a greyhound cross, or something.'

'I had suspected as much,' Brodie said nodding.

'What, the dog's age, or breed?' She seemed very interested.

'Both.' He watched her as she spoke briefly to Lettie and it occurred to him that as relieved as she might be to have Derek returned to her she didn't appear to be as elated as most owners usually were when reunited with a beloved pet.

'May I ask you something?' Brodie hoped he was not about to overstep the mark. 'I hope you won't be offended if I ask how you cope with exercising the dog? He seems to have a lot of energy and I was wondering if it might be a little difficult for you.'

She dabbed at the end of her nose and gave him a quizzical look. 'I'm not offended at all. In fact, exercising him is the thing that concerns me the most. I'm not as steady on my legs as I was and find it a struggle to take him out much.'

'Is it going to be difficult having Derek back living with you?'

She looked aghast. 'I'm not the type of person to abandon a defenceless animal, Mr Murray.'

Horrified to have offended her so deeply, Brodie gasped. 'That's not what I meant.' He puffed out his cheeks, trying to think how best to rectify his mistake. 'You mentioned you're not used to looking after dogs.' She continued to stare at him, her eyes narrowed. 'What I'm trying to say, very badly, is that I've grown very attached to Derek in the short time he stayed with me and, if you were to consider him coming to live with me I would be very happy to take him on.' He raised his hand. 'But only if that's what you would like. If I've misread this situation I apologise.'

Her shoulders lowered and he noticed her relax slightly back into her chair. 'I see. Well…' She looked at Derek for a few seconds, seeming to consider his suggestion. 'I have felt a little overwhelmed having to look after him and especially now that he ran away.' She looked at Lettie. 'What do you think about all this? Would it be dreadful of me to agree to this young man taking Derek on when dear Percy entrusted him into my care?'

'Not at all,' Brodie was relieved but not surprised to hear Lettie reply. 'To be honest with you I haven't known Brodie all that long but he is well liked by the community. He's also a very good vet, so Derek couldn't be in better hands.' She put her hand up to the side of her mouth and whispered loud enough for Brodie to hear, 'And he does seem to already love this little guy.' She pointed to Derek snoring louder now on his bed.

Mrs Broadbent considered what to do, looked at Derek for a few seconds, then at Brodie. 'I'm happy for you to take him on. Would you mind if I visit him on occasion?'

'If you want me to bring him to see you all you need to do is call me at the practice and I'll happily drive him here.'

She smiled and patted her hands onto her knees. 'That's agreed then. You take this dear dog and care for him.' She stood. 'I'll show you out, if you don't mind. I'm feeling a little emotional and think I need some time alone.' She bent to stroke Derek, waking him from his sleep. 'I do feel guilty though.'

'Please don't.' Brodie stroked Derek. 'I promise you there's no need at all. He loved being at the practice when I was working and I'll walk him on the beach most days.'

Her face lit up. 'That's settled then.'

Derek stood and gave a good shake before standing next to Brodie and wagging his tail. He seemed to know exactly what had been agreed.

Brodie suspected seeing the empty dog's bed might not be the best thing for the older lady to find each morning. 'Would you like me to take his bed with me?' He noticed a few toys. 'And all his other paraphernalia?'

'That would be kind of you, thank you.'

He wanted to invite Lettie back to his cottage but she mentioned she was meeting Joe and he should be getting home in case Maddie arrived.

'I never imagined that happening, did you?' he asked as they drove down the lanes towards the farm.

She shook her head. 'No, but I believe it's the best outcome, for all three of you.'

'And you?' he teased, sensing she had fallen a little in love with Derek too.

'That goes without saying.' She laughed and took a mouthful of her drink. Swallowing, she frowned. 'There is one thing I can't work out though.'

Intrigued, he looked at her. 'What's that?'

'His name. Are we to call him Derek, or Thistle?'

'Good point.' Brodie studied the dog. 'I suppose his original name was Derek, so we should probably stick to that one.'

'I think you're probably right.'

At the mention of his name, Derek gave a soft growl.

Lettie laughed. 'I have a feeling he's trying to tell you it's supper time.'

32

LETTIE

Brodie pulled up in front of the farmhouse. 'I'd better get back to see my sister. I'd told her I'd be in for a few hours and don't want to upset her by not being there.'

Lettie was about to reply when her phone vibrated against her hip. 'Sorry, I'd better get this.'

It was a message from Joe.

> Sorry, can't make tonight. Am on call and on my way to a call-out. Will call you tomorrow to reschedule.
>
> Joe x

'Nothing wrong, I hope?'

She replied telling Joe not to worry and pushed her phone back into her pocket.

'No, nothing's wrong.'

'Well, I should be going. I'll meet you at the beach tomorrow night for our walk. Will you be able to make it at nine?'

She loved the late summer evenings. 'That'll be perfect.'

Lettie got out of the car and waited for Brodie to drive away before going into the house. Realising she would be spending the evening alone with only Spud – who tended to ignore her most of the time – as company, she smiled.

Her stomach rumbled noisily, reminding her she hadn't eaten since breakfast that morning. She rummaged around in one of the cupboards and found a tin of baked beans. 'Ooh, look, Spud,' she said holding up one of the eggs she had collected that morning. 'Isn't it a good thing we have an endless supply of these?'

Unimpressed with her conversation, Spud lowered his head and dozed off. Lettie laughed. 'You can be really dull company sometimes, do you know that?'

She recalled the fresh pasta and a tomato and basil sauce she had bought for her supper at the shop a few days earlier and decided to make the effort to cook something nourishing for herself, seeing as though she had the entire evening with little else to occupy her now that Joe couldn't make their date.

There was something about the warm welcome she always felt entering her mother's kitchen – a comforting feeling, which was what she needed at that moment. The heat from the Aga made the room cosy, but it was also the bright rug under the large, worn table and her mother's eclectic mix of crockery and family photos displayed on one of the walls. She missed her parents so much. They had been gone for weeks now and each day seemed more tiring than the last.

As her food was cooking, Lettie topped up Spud's water bowl, then stroked the dog's head and gave him his food.

Spud gave her jeans a cursory sniff before eating his food and returning to his bed, flopping back down to sleep once again.

As she ate her plain supper, Lettie's mind wandered back to her minimalist flat that she shared with Nessa near Vauxhall and smiled. She had almost forgotten what it felt like to have enough energy to feel compelled to go to a nightclub or bar and couldn't think when she had last visited a coffee house like those in which the pair of them had spent most Saturday mornings. She missed the choice of places to go, especially the endless choice of exhibitions.

Lettie yawned, deciding to leave the washing up until the morning. Her mother would be shocked to see her kitchen with dirty plates and pans in it, but Lettie simply didn't have the energy to do anything other than doze in front of the television for an hour while her food digested and then summoning up the energy to walk upstairs and go to bed.

As she lay in her bed, her curtains open and room flooded by moonlight, a wave of hopelessness washed over her. Who was she kidding thinking she had the tenacity to run this place? She had only worked for nearly eight weeks here, one month with her father and the rest alone, and it had nearly finished her. She was determined to see things through to the end. There was no way she could ever allow herself to let him or her mother down, but it was going to take more energy than she thought she had to keep going until they returned from their trip.

Lettie's eyes welled up and she cleared her throat, not wanting to give in to tears. 'You've got this, Lettie,' she murmured, wondering if hearing her voice saying the words might persuade her brain that it was possible to keep going. He uncle said she could always call on him but already he was checking up on his farm workers and making sure they were harvesting the potatoes properly and getting them to the harbour on time each day. She seemed to be doing so little, yet the physical work that she was carrying out was exhausting. How on earth had her father done this for decades? She felt a new respect for him and all that he had achieved.

Her eyes began to close and as she drifted off to sleep, her thoughts wandered off to her walk with Brodie and their dogs on the beach the following evening. She closed her eyes and turned on her side. She was going to need as much sleep as possible if she was to have the energy to do anything after finishing her work on the farm.

33

BRODIE

As Brodie drove up to his cottage he saw his sister get out of her car and stand, arms crossed, a large notebook in one hand, her right foot tapping impatiently for him to join her.

'You took your time,' she grumbled.

'Sorry,' he said curtly.

'Just unlock the flippin' door and let's get inside. It might be warm during the day but I'd forgotten it can get cold at night.'

He noticed she wasn't wearing a jacket and immediately felt bad for being so ungracious. It wasn't as if Maddie knew he was still smarting from Joe being the one to go out with Lettie rather than him.

'Er, Brodie?'

His thoughts disappeared as he heard his sister's sharp tone. 'Sorry.' He pulled his key from his pocket and let her and Derek into the cottage. Switching on the hall light, he followed them through to the living room.

'Er, since when did you have a dog?'

'He's a rescue. I've taken him on because the old lady who was looking after him couldn't cope with him any longer.'

'I didn't think there was enough space here for you, let alone any pets.'

'It's one dog and yes, there's enough room for him.' Deciding to divert her attention away from Derek, Brodie said, 'Look, you put on the kettle while I light the fire. The room will soon warm up.' He switched on the table lamps on either side of the sofa and plumped up the cushions, aware that his sister would probably return to their parents and tell their mother if the place was too untidy. Closing the curtains, Brodie surveyed the scene. Passable. He followed her to the kitchen and stood in the doorway. The room was too small to give two of them much room.

'You've had some ideas about this place then?'

She nodded as she took two cups from the cupboard. 'I have and I think you'll like them.'

He hoped so. He knew from experience that once Maddie had an idea fixed in her head it was almost impossible to persuade her she might be wrong, or that maybe there was a better alternative. 'I only want something simple,' he reminded her. 'Nothing flowery, or too, um...'

She turned, teaspoon in one hand. 'Too what?'

'Well, you know.'

'How could I know if you haven't told me?' The kettle finished boiling and she turned back to carry on making their drinks.

He saw the notepad on the worktop next to her and reached to take it.

'Leave that right there. I'll show everything to you when I'm good and ready.'

Brodie groaned. 'I'm not one of your fancy clients, Maddie,' he reminded her. 'All I want is to modernise this place a bit and brighten it up with a lick of paint and a few other bits.'

'A few other bits,' she repeated sarcastically adding a little milk to both their drinks and stirring. She turned and handed him one of the cups of tea and motioned for him to go to the living room before picking up what he now realised was a folder and not a notebook. 'Go. Sit and listen. I promise you're going to love what I've come up with.'

Brodie did as she instructed. He knew his sister well enough to understand that the sooner he heard what she had to say and hopefully agreed with it the sooner she would bugger off and leave him and Derek in peace. Derek? He looked around and saw the dog snoozing on the worn armchair underneath the window.

His sister must have followed his gaze. 'You know you shouldn't let that dog get too comfortable here, Brodie, and it shouldn't be allowed on the furniture when I can see it has a perfectly suitable bed on the floor.'

Here we go, he thought, swallowing a snappy retort that this was his house and his dog. Then he remembered she wouldn't know about Derek yet, so he explained exactly what had happened with the older lady.

Instead of his sister criticising his decision to take on the dog, she seemed delighted.

'You approve?' He wasn't sure why he had asked that question when it didn't make any difference to his decision to adopt Derek whether his sister was happy with the notion or not.

'Thrilled.'

'Seriously?' Usually she thought him impulsive, or boring. One of those extremes anyway.

'Yes. It means you're settling in nicely here and you're intending to stay.'

He took a careful sip of his hot tea. 'Of course I'm staying. I wouldn't have invested in the lease for the practice if I hadn't planned on doing so.'

'Calm down. I was only thinking how nice it'll be to have you here all the time. Anyhow, you're obviously lonely here, so this sweet dog will be company for you.'

'Why do you think I'm lonely?' He wasn't sure why he felt so indignant, but even if his sister hadn't meant her comment to be a criticism of him, he couldn't help feeling like he must be failing in some way. 'I've got a date, of sorts, with someone tomorrow evening, if you must know.' Why had he said that?

He could see the interest his words had sparked in his sister's eyes. 'I wasn't being mean,' she said, her voice softer. 'I just meant you've been busy with settling in at the practice since you arrived back on the island and can't have had much of a chance to catch up with old friends from years ago.'

'I see.' His feelings for his sister softening, Brodie reminded himself that although he and Maddie had always bickered, she could be sweet on occasion. Not very often, but this appeared to be one of those times and he was happy to hear her approval.

He gave her a conciliatory smile. 'Thanks, Madds. I don't mean to sound defensive and I'm glad you're happy I'm staying here. And that I have Derek here as my companion. He is a real character and I'm looking forward to training him a little and taking him for walks. He's already made a good impression on the staff and clients at the practice, you know?'

She smiled fondly at the snoozing dog. 'I'm sure he has.' She put her cup down on the table next to her and tapped the purple folder.

34

LETTIE

Four weeks to go

It had been another difficult day on the farm. The last of the Jersey Royals had been harvested and the equipment cleaned and put away. Lettie thanked the workers, and after treating them to an enormous cottage pie, she bid them farewell and called her uncle to thank him for letting his employees come to her farm to help her getting in the harvest.

'You've done an excellent job there, Lettie,' he said. 'I was disappointed at the beginning when you mentioned your intention to try and run Hollyhock Farm, but I'm glad your father gave you the opportunity. You have the makings of a farmer and you should be proud of yourself.'

'I'm not so sure about that,' she said close to tears. 'I've never been this tired and I'm sure I haven't done all that much really.'

'If you sat and wrote down all that you have done each day you'd probably be surprised.' He laughed. 'It is a bit daunting though for you, I imagine.'

She sighed. 'Most days I feel like an exhausted hamster on one of those wheels, constantly running to catch up with myself and getting nowhere.'

'Don't be so hard on yourself.'

They ended the call and Lettie leant back against the barn door. She knew her uncle meant well and was trying to bolster her confidence but she also knew that she couldn't keep this up. Her stamina might be building and her muscles were more toned than ever before, but she was drained. Realising the time, she hurried inside and showered ready for Brodie to collect her and Spud on his way to the beach.

Lettie sat next to him in his car, enjoying their friendly banter as he animatedly relayed stories about his day at the practice.

'Then Mrs Fitch told me that her husband was insisting they keep the largest of the pups from the litter, whereas she wanted to keep the runt. They apparently fell out.' He shook his head and laughed as he turned down a lane taking them to the beach.

'And, don't tell me...' Lettie giggled feeling slightly better now that she had stepped away from her responsibilities for a while. 'They ended up keeping both and together with the mum they now have three dogs.'

'Five.'

'Five?'

'Yup.' He slowed and waved the driver of a small car out of a difficult turning before continuing on their way. 'They already had a couple of dogs their daughter insisted on taking on when she moved back home a couple of years ago. She's since moved away and is working in Spain, leaving those dogs with her parents.'

Lettie tried imagining having so many pets somewhere that wasn't a farm. 'It sounds like they have a right menagerie going on there.' She heard the crashing waves before she saw them and closed her eyes to listen more intently to the sound that took her back to her childhood.

'Being back on the island I can't imagine how I managed to live away for so long,' she said almost to herself.

'I was thinking the same thing when I was out surfing the other day. How do we islanders ever really imagine we'll be able to settle anywhere far from the sea?'

'I suppose it's the yearning for something exciting and different to what we know.'

Brodie turned to look at her briefly. 'I know I couldn't wait to move to England and experience the thrill of the Underground, all the noise and hustle and bustle only to end up in Devon. I loved it there but it wasn't too unlike living in this place.'

Lettie wasn't so sure about the Underground being remotely thrilling. All it had ever been to her was a way to get from A to B without getting wet when it was raining. A necessity but not at all exciting. 'I did hanker after the nightlife in London before I moved there,' she admitted thinking back to when she was younger and how the urge to move to London had filled her every waking thought. 'And if I'm honest, I enjoyed having places to go for food whenever the mood took me, discovering shops and cosy pubs down back streets that were hundreds of years old, that sort of thing.'

'And now?'

She smiled. 'Now, if I want to go somewhere with a bit of history, I go to one of the older parish pubs, but I haven't done that yet apart from the other night. I haven't felt the need, or had the energy,' she said realising it for the first time. 'Although I did enjoy the few drinks I've had at The Plough recently.'

She noticed Brodie stiffen and realised he assumed she was referring to her evenings with Joe. Not sure where their relationship was going, or what it was, she didn't want Brodie to get the wrong idea about them.

'Of course, I saw you at the pub recently, didn't I?'

His voice was chilled as he turned off down towards the beach. Brodie parked the car and the two of them got out, taking each of their dogs with them down the cobbled slipway to the beach. Once they were on the sand, Brodie looked left, then right.

'Which way shall we go?'

She breathed in the cool salty air, looking first to the left at the longer expanse of beach, then to the right. Seeing a small group of people walking to their right, she pointed left, wanting to walk for as long as possible with him.

'There are fewer people that way. It'll be less distracting for these two.'

'Looks like rain is coming towards us across the Channel.' Brodie pointed out to sea where Lettie saw a steel grey band of clouds looming ominously between them and Guernsey.

She didn't like the look of the sky or the different look of the sea where the rain was falling. 'How long do you think we have before it reaches us?'

'Probably half an hour,' he replied thoughtfully. 'Maybe slightly less but enough time for a bit of a walk anyway.'

'We'd better get a move on then.'

They began walking, each lost in their own thoughts as the dogs trotted along in front of them, leading the way.

'Gosh, it's windier down here than I expected,' Lettie said trying to tuck a flyaway strand of hair behind her ear but giving up when it kept escaping and whipping in front of her nose.

'I meant to reply to your question.'

Lettie wasn't sure what question Brodie was referring to, then recalled her mentioning them seeing each other in the pub. 'I wasn't sure you heard me,' she fibbed, wanting to let him off the hook in case he didn't wish to continue with the subject.

'I did, then I was distracted by driving.' He turned to look at her slowing his pace. 'I remember seeing you and feeling envious that Joe was the one out with you.'

Surprised by his admission, Lettie forgot to make the next step and stood still, watching him take a couple more paces before realising she had stopped and turning back to her.

'You OK?'

'Er, yes. I hadn't expected you to say that.'

He gazed down at his feet for a moment before looking her in the eye. 'I probably shouldn't have admitted as much, but it's true.'

Lettie's breath caught in her throat. She'd never experienced such honesty from a man and was taken aback to hear someone she found as attractive as Brodie admitting he liked her. Her spirits soared and she struggled to contain her reaction.

'I see.' It was the best she could do if she wasn't going to show herself up.

Brodie reached out his hand waiting for her to take it. 'Do you mind me admitting my feelings towards you?' He looked away in the direction they were walking. 'I'd hate to think I'd spooked you by doing so.'

She took his hand and cleared her throat, trying to gather herself. 'No, I'm just surprised you feel that way.' She didn't add that after being kissed by him on two occasions in her life with neither occasion leading to anything romantic, she had presumed he wasn't interested in anything serious.

He pushed his glasses further up the bridge of his nose. 'Would you mind me asking how you feel about me?'

'I like you, Brodie,' she said honestly. She saw him smile, and added, 'Quite a lot.'

She lost her next thought as his hand gently squeezed hers and he stared down at her, an intensity in his beautiful dark blue eye that made her stomach flutter. He opened his mouth to speak but before he said anything, she felt a drop of rain on her nose. Then another immediately after. Brodie glanced up at the sky just as it began to pour.

'So much for half an hour,' she teased.

'Bugger, I think we should get the dogs back to the vehicle. This looks like it's going to be heavier than a shower.'

The wind had picked up too, she noticed. 'Good idea,' Lettie agreed, disappointed that their chat had been interrupted.

Back at the car, Brodie lifted the boot to shelter them as they quickly bundled the dogs inside. He grabbed two towels from the back seat and handed one to Lettie to dry her face and hair before using it to take the worst of the rain from Spud's fur.

As she dried Spud's head, she gave Brodie a surreptitious look and caught him watching her back. He smiled and she couldn't help reciprocating. 'This is more fun than I would have expected.'

He rubbed Derek's back. 'I was thinking the same thing.'

She finished with the towel and was holding it when he took it from her and pulled her gently into his arms. 'Would you mind if I kissed you?' he asked, brushing away several raindrops that had fallen onto his forehead from his wet fringe.

'You didn't dry your hair before doing Derek's fur did you?'

'I must have forgotten.'

His voice was gentle and Lettie sensed he wasn't thinking about anything other than the two of them standing in each other's arms.

'You didn't answer me.'

She tried to think what he might have asked her, then recalling his question about kissing her, she decided not to waste any more time talking and slipped her arms around his neck, pulled him gently down to her level and pressed her lips against his in a kiss. His immediate response thrilled her and Lettie had to focus on not getting too carried away. Brodie kissed so beautifully she doubted she would ever wish to kiss anyone else ever again.

An ear-splitting rumble of thunder shocked them out of their kiss and Lettie gasped at the same time Derek growled and began trembling.

'I think we need to get these two home, don't you?'

'I do.' She watched him cuddle Derek, and as she stroked Spud's head, looked up at the sky just when it lit up with an enormous crash of lightning. 'The sooner the better too by the looks of the storm that's about to hit us.'

They closed the boot and ran around to get into the vehicle.

Within minutes they arrived back at the farm. The storm was nearly overhead with thunder and lightning coming almost simultaneously. Derek cried out and began howling, then Spud joined in.

'I think you should come into the farmhouse with me,' Lettie suggested, deciding it was the best option. The rain hammered down onto the roof just as the sky lit up once more, followed by the loudest crack of thunder so far. 'We need to get Derek somewhere quieter than this car.'

'You're right.'

They leapt out of the vehicle and ran round to the back of the car. 'Hold on tightly to his collar,' Lettie shouted trying to be heard over the din of the storm. 'We don't want him running off again.'

She rummaged in her jeans pocket for her house keys, cursing to herself when she dropped them. Bending to pick them up, she had to let go of Spud's collar and he immediately jumped down from the vehicle and ran towards the barn.

'Here, take these and let yourselves inside.' She threw the keys to Brodie and ran after Spud calling out his name repeatedly.

Grateful that the barn door was ajar, she raced after Spud, relieved to reach him as he cowered in the corner. 'Hey,' she said crouching and cuddling the trembling dog to her. 'Why are you so frightened?' He was never usually bothered by storms. Maybe he had been frightened by Derek's terror. 'We're perfectly safe,' she soothed. 'Come along, let's go back to the house and I'll find you a treat.'

At the word treat, his black ears pricked up and his tail began wagging. She was relieved he had forgotten to be frightened. She didn't need her brilliant farm dog to find a belated fear of storms. She decided it might be best not to take hold of his collar and brazen out their run back to the farmhouse, hoping he didn't take fright again.

35

BRODIE

He was crouching down cuddling Derek and doing his best to soothe the poor dog when Spud raced into the house closely followed by Lettie. She stood in front of the sink dripping. 'It's still raining heavily outside, then?'

She grinned. 'Just a bit.'

'Spud OK?'

'He is now. I think he was frightened by Derek's fear and it made him panic. He's not usually bothered by storms and mostly sleeps through them.' She looked down at him now making circles in his bed before plonking himself down and closing his eyes. 'I think he's fine now though.'

'Good. I'd hate for him to be upset like this one.'

'If you want to try giving them both a treat, there's a choice in that cupboard over there.' She indicated a cupboard to the right of him. 'I'm just going upstairs to change quickly and will bring down more towels.' She stopped at the doorway and turned. 'Would you like me to find some of Zac's clothes for you to change into? The trousers might be a bit short on you, but at least they'll be drier than what you're wearing.'

He thought about her offer and nodded. 'That would be great. Thanks.'

He walked over to the cupboard and opened it. Spud was on his feet behind him almost instantly – clearly knew where his treats were kept. Brodie looked in each of the four tubs and discovered one containing gravy bones, and others with chews, bone-shaped biscuits and another small, rounded treat that he wasn't sure he'd seen before. He picked up two gravy bones for each dog, clipped the lids closed and shut the door.

'Here you go,' he said giving Spud the first treat before turning and trying to entice Derek to take one. He wasn't persuaded until he watched Spud wolf down his second treat, and then took both from Brodie's fingers in rapid succession. Relieved the dog's appetite hadn't completely vanished, he stood, filled the kettle and then plugged it in. From the little he knew about Lettie she seemed to like her tea and seeing her soaked only moments before he presumed that she would want one soon.

She was back within a few minutes, her hair towel-dried and tied back and an armful of towels and some clothes. He watched her place the clothes on the back of one of the kitchen chairs. 'The downstairs loo is the first on the left along the hall.' She looked down at Derek. 'He seems a bit calmer now, thankfully.'

'He is.' He stroked the dog's head, relieved to note that his trembling had subsided a lot. 'I think the treats helped. Two gravy bones each.'

He saw her smile and wanted to kiss her again.

'Are you all right?' she asked, looking unsure, and he hoped he hadn't been wearing a goofy expression on his face when he had been staring at her.

'Sorry, I was thinking.'

'I know, it's upsetting when an animal is frightened. It's the worst thing in the world – apart from them being injured, I mean.'

She had misunderstood him but not wishing to correct her, Brodie stood and picked up one of the towels and the spare clothes. 'Down the hall to the right, did you say?'

She laughed. 'No, to the left. But you can change in my father's study if you'd prefer. It's not as if he'll be back anytime soon to catch you in there.'

'I'll keep to the loo, I think.' Brodie glanced at Derek, now settling down next to Spud. 'I won't be long.'

'You've put the kettle on, I see,' she said taking two mugs from the hooks under the cupboard near her. 'I'll make us a hot drink while you change.'

When Brodie rejoined her in the kitchen he stopped at the sink to look out of the window at the sky, his attention diverted from Lettie at a loud roar and the sky lighting up. 'It doesn't look like this is going to abate any time soon.'

'No, it doesn't.' She pushed a mug of steaming coffee across the table towards him. 'At least the dogs seem to have settled down now and we're inside. I suppose we'll just have to sit it out here.'

He studied her face and hoped that what he saw in her eyes was happiness that he felt, knowing they had this unexpected time together. Alone. He felt his determination not to become involved with her wither away.

'I'm happy to do that.' He took a seat at the end of the table closest to her, yet so that he was facing her better than if he had sat on the chair next to her. He had noticed the dark circles under her eyes and the stiffness in her shoulders and wondered if the farm was getting too much for her. He decided to try and find out by asking a few indirect questions to encourage her to open up to him.

'Do you ever feel lonely here now that your family are all away?'

She gave his question some thought then shook her head. 'Not really. A little, I suppose, but more that I've missed my parents sometimes. I had expected to feel lonely but having Spud here and the chickens and goats means that I always have someone to talk to, cuddle and keep me company if I need them to.'

Brodie took a sip of his coffee, realising it was too hot to drink yet. He watched her, thinking he would rather she felt comfortable enough with him to go to him for any cuddles but doubted they were close enough for him to mention her doing so. He realised she was staring at him. 'What is it?' He hoped he didn't have any coffee on his lips and wiped a finger across them to make certain.

'I'm glad we chose today to take our walk.'

'Even though it was cut short so suddenly?'

She nodded. 'I'd much rather be with you right now than anyone else.'

His breath caught in his throat at her unexpected sentiment. 'You would?'

'Yes.'

He saw her cheeks flush slightly and, leaning forward, willed her to return his kiss – only just able to hide his delight when she instinctively did so. It was a brief kiss, but no less special for it. Brodie smiled. 'I'm so glad we met.'

'When?' She grinned, a mischievous smile on her lips and he knew she was about to tease him.

'I'm not sure what you mean.'

Lettie's eyes narrowed and she seemed uncertain about something. 'Well, are you glad we met when we were younger, at the school disco?'

'School disco?'

He studied her face as something in his memory stirred. Then it dawned on him where he remembered her from and his mouth dropped open. 'That was you?' He was confused. 'But it can't be. I only ever recall kissing someone called...' He searched his memory for the name. It was something unusual. 'Violet! That's right, her name was Violet.' He winced. 'Sorry, I know it sounds bad but I don't remember us kissing back then.'

Lettie threw her head back and laughed, confusing him. 'That was me though.'

He didn't understand. 'It can't have been. I told you her name was...'

'Violet. Yes, you said. And,' she said blushing, 'that's actually my name.'

What? Brodie frowned. 'Sorry, you've lost me.'

'Vi-oh-let? Lettie?'

'Ah, I see.' He realised his mouth was hanging open so closed it. He recalled only too well how much he'd fancied Violet Torel and agonised over his missed opportunity for years. 'That was you? But you must wonder why I never called you when I said I would.'

A cloud passed over her face. 'Something like that.' She stared at him thoughtfully. 'Do you remember why that was?'

He sensed she had been disappointed, although couldn't help being glad he had made an impression on her, albeit the wrong one. 'What a young fool I must have been. I owe you a date.'

She laughed. 'Yes, you do.'

He took her hand in his. 'I'm so sorry, Lettie. I wanted to call you, I really did.'

'And you didn't because...?'

He thought back to that tall, athletic boy he had been and the crippling shyness he had taken years to finally overcome. 'I was going to, but I was too shy. I know it probably sounds ridiculous, but I hadn't had a girlfriend before and I liked you so much. The thought of taking you out and disappointing you terrified me.'

She didn't look convinced. 'So you just did nothing?'

He shrugged. 'I know. Pathetic, isn't it. To think I had the opportunity to get to know you years ago and didn't do anything about it.

All I can say in my defence is that I was an awkward teenager with zero confidence.'

Her expression softened.

'Me too, so I'll forgive you.'

They stared at each, one hand holding their mug handles while holding each other's hand with the other. This girl was special. She was everything he had ever wanted in a partner: kind, intelligent, very pretty in a fresh-faced way that he loved. He adored that she enjoyed the company of her animals just as he did. He also admired her for having the guts to leave her old life behind to take on a farm with little experience.

He leant forward, wanting to try and make it up to her for letting her down all those years before. 'Lettie, I—'

A deafening crack of lightning made them both jump out of their seats, spilling their drinks as they leapt to their feet.

'Ouch.' Lettie winced shaking hot coffee from the back of her hand.

'Here.' He took her wrist and pulled her to the sink, holding her hand under the cold tap and turning on the water as they both then stood and stared outside.

'Do you think it hit something nearby?'

It certainly sounded like it, Brodie thought. He heard the tremble in her voice. 'I'm not sure. Lightning strikes hit the highest point. Are there any trees behind the house that might have been hit?'

'Many.' Lettie gasped. 'There's the metal weathervane on top of the bell tower over the large barn. It was used back in the day by my grandad calling farmworkers in from the field. Mum used it to call Zac, me and our cousins Adam and Damon in from playing in the woods when we should be in for supper.'

Bell tower? He hadn't noticed it. 'That's probably it.' He was anxious that the lightning strike might have caused some damage and didn't want Lettie to be the one to find it. The noise had been so loud the house had shaken.

'You stay here with the dogs while I go and check everything from the outside.'

'Please be careful.'

He leant forward and kissed her forehead. 'I will. You keep a lookout at the front and that hand under the running cold water.'

He left the room and ran down the hallway. Reaching a back door, he unlocked it and opened it, standing under a porch to survey the vicinity. The trees at the end of the garden and all around them seemed untouched, so he ran outside and when he was far enough away to look back and see most of the farmhouse roof he turned and looked up at it. No smoke, or any damage that he could see. It was a massive relief.

He was about to return to the house when something caught his eye to the left. It was smoke and coming from the side or front of the house. 'Fire?' He didn't waste time thinking but not wishing to leave Lettie and the dogs somewhere potentially dangerous ran back to the house and through to join her in the kitchen.

'You saw the smoke,' he said when he saw she was dragging her coat up over one arm as she pushed her right foot hurriedly into one of her boots.

'What are you doing?' Brodie took hold of her arm, not wishing her to do anything reckless.

'Didn't you see it? There's smoke out there and I think it's coming from the barn. The animals...' She burst into tears and tugged her arm from his hold. 'I have to get to them and let them out.'

Without waiting to hear more, Brodie ran outside closely followed by Lettie.

'No, Spud, you stay inside with Derek.'

He heard her shouting instructions to the dogs before slamming the front door. Brodie raced across the yard. His heel connected with a sharp stone reminding him that he was barefoot. Uncaring that his feet were bare, he kept going. He looked up to see the smoke was coming not from the bigger barn that he had assumed Lettie was referring to, but the smaller one next to it. Smoke was now billowing through what he assumed might be a hole in the roof.

His first thought was to get whatever animals might be in there to safety. He would worry about rounding them up later when any immediate danger to them had passed. He heard a noise behind him and realised Lettie was sobbing.

'Hurry, Brodie, please hurry. Fire service please,' he heard her say relieved that she was calling the emergency services.

He reached the door and yanked it open. 'What's in here?'

'Five, no six goats. Um, four elderly cows that Dad couldn't bear parting with,' she explained as she went to run past him. 'The alpacas are in the other barn, so they're fine.'

Brodie grabbed her arm. 'No. Please let me go in.'

'They're my animals.' She tried to shrug his hand from her.

'Lettie, like it or not, I'm stronger than you. Let me do this.'

'Fine.' She didn't look happy, but he was relieved she had seen sense.

Brodie counted the goats as they poured out of the building and waited a moment for the cows to follow. When they didn't, Brodie covered his mouth and nose with his sleeve and ran into the burning building. His eyes stung from the smoke and in one corner he saw the ominous orange glow of spreading flames. Where were they?

'Look to the left near the back,' he heard her shout from the doorway.

Hearing Lettie's instructions he changed course and reached the first cow within a few seconds. 'Come along,' he urged grabbing hold of the cow's horn and pulling the animal towards the door relieved when the other three followed. As soon as they saw Lettie just inside, the animals ran towards her.

'Well done,' Lettie sobbed flinging her arms around him as he tried desperately to take in fresh air. She let go and apologised. 'Are you all right?'

Unable to speak for a moment he raised a hand as he coughed.

'That was so brave of you.'

He didn't have the breath to argue with her. Bravery had nothing to do with him going into the barn; all he could think about was rescuing the trapped animals. And he had. The relief weakened his knees and he lowered himself to the ground to sit.

What was he doing? He pushed himself to his feet and looked around for a hosepipe. Seeing Lettie pulling one towards the barn he ran to turn on the tap then returned to her.

'Do you have another one?'

'Yes, but it's around the back.'

'That's fine, I'll turn it on to the rear of the building.'

'The fire service shouldn't be long,' she said just before the sound of several sirens emerged from the rain.

It was raining. The thought calmed him slightly. He couldn't bear to think that the fire might spread to the other barn and heaven forbid to the farmhouse itself.

The large red fire truck raced down the driveway and within moments several firefighters leapt out.

The first one raised a hand in acknowledgement. 'Joe?'

Brodie heard Lettie's question and turned to see Joe looking just like someone Tiffany might have mooned over in one of the romantic films she enjoyed watching. Joe raced over to her and hugged her before reassuring her and helping his workmates extinguish the fire in the barn, while two of them ran off to check the larger barn next door.

'Did you see Joe's here,' she said looking delighted, not taking her eyes off the man.

'I thought it was him,' he fibbed wishing Joe didn't look so heroic in all his kit. Brodie pushed away his shock, determined to show his gratitude for their speedy arrival.

'Brodie, hi.' Joe strode over to Brodie, his gloved hand outstretched. 'I gather from Lettie that you're the hero of the hour here.'

Brodie hid his surprise and shook his head. 'I only did what anyone else would do.'

'That's not true. What you did was brave, although could have been dangerous. I understand why you ran in to rescue the animals and I'm glad there were no casualties.'

Feeling awkward and not wishing to seem like a jealous boyfriend, Brodie excused himself, wanting to leave Lettie alone to speak to Joe. It was her farm after all and Joe was the expert when it came to firefighting.

Another clap of thunder reminded him of the dogs alone in the house. 'I'd better go and check on the dogs, but thanks for getting here so fast, Joe.'

'No problem at all, Brodie. It's what we aim to do.'

Several hours later with the fire extinguished Brodie kept himself busy checking on the animals who seemed a bit calmer but still anxious after their traumatic evening while Joe spoke to Lettie about the damage. He wasn't sure if he should leave her in peace, aware that she must be completely exhausted, but decided to wait and check how she was doing first.

With, the fire engines having left and the storm ended, Brodie helped Lettie finish settling the cows and goats into two of the small paddocks. 'How are you doing?' he asked gently.

Lettie kept her eyes on the goats in front of her and he suspected she was crying.

'Lettie? Are you OK?'

She sniffed. 'I don't think I can do this, Brodie,' she sobbed, her shoulders slumping as she gripped hold of the top of the five-bar gate.

Brodie walked up behind her and put his arms around her. 'You can.'

'You don't know that,' she said between sobs. 'It's all so overwhelming and much harder than I expected. And I'm so tired. All of the time.'

'You're already doing it, Lettie.' Taking her by the shoulder he turned her to face him, pulling her into a hug. 'And you're not alone. Don't forget that.'

'Aren't I?'

'No.' He thought of Joe and Zac. 'You've got me. And your brother. And there's Joe. Look how quickly he came here earlier.'

She sighed. 'It's his job to put out fires, Brodie.'

'I know, but I saw him talking to you afterwards and I know that he has your best interests at heart.' It was difficult to admit as much, but Joe clearly cared for her and as much as he loved Lettie the most important thing to him was that she knew others were there for her, whoever they might be.

'I'm glad you were here,' she sniffed. 'Thank you.'

'I'll be here for as long as you want me to be.'

She looked up at him. 'Do you promise?'

He nodded. 'I do. Now, I don't want any more talk about being alone. Everyone wants you to succeed and we're all here to help make sure that happens.'

She hugged him tightly. 'Thanks, Brodie, I needed to hear that.' She gave a shuddering sigh against his chest. 'I think I'm in some sort of shock because I feel almost numb.'

'That's not at all surprising,' he reassured her, aware how shocked he still felt after the dramatic evening.

'I think they'll be happier out here tonight,' she said closing the gate and standing with her arms folded across her chest. 'I checked the forecast and the storm has moved away now and it doesn't look as if there's more to come, thankfully.' She smiled at him. 'I don't know about you but I need a stiff drink after I've had a shower.'

'That sounds good to me.' Assuming this was his cue to leave, Brodie ruffled Derek's head. 'Come along, boy, let's leave Lettie and Spud to relax.'

'Oh, I didn't mean for you to go,' she said. 'You're welcome to shower here, if you like.'

He much preferred the thought of spending more of the evening with Lettie. 'I'd like that.'

They fed the dogs and she showed him the way to the bathroom. 'I'll fetch you more clothes and some towels.'

He stripped off and stepped into the shower, closing the curtain and turning on the warm water. It felt good to be clean again. He closed his eyes allowing the water to run over his head and body, surprised to hear Lettie's voice.

'May I join you?'

Surprised, but not wanting to miss another opportunity like he had done after the school disco or allowing himself time to overthink her question, he pulled back the curtain. 'I'd like that very much.'

36

LETTIE

Lettie didn't know where her courage had come from, nor did she care. She saw Brodie's dripping outstretched hand and took it, stepping into the shower to join him. She had no idea what had possessed her to ask him such a question and right now, as she looked at his handsome face, his sandy hair falling over his forehead, a look of longing in his dark eyes, and rivulets of water coursing down his muscular body, she didn't much care.

Brodie didn't speak, but took her into his arms and held her against him so that any doubts she might have about whether he was attracted to her vanished instantly. He kissed her. She was the breathless one now, she thought, in no doubt about him wanting her as her hands moved over his body and reached around behind him, one resting on his muscular back, the other on his rounded buttock.

She felt his hand on her bottom pushing all further thoughts aside as he began kissing her neck.

* * *

'Well, today didn't turn out remotely as I imagined it would,' Brodie said as they cuddled in front of the fire in her living room a couple of hours later. He kissed her again. 'I still can't get over what happened earlier.'

Confused and hoping he wasn't referring to her joining him in the shower, Lettie clasped her hands together. 'Sorry?'

He gave her an amused smile. 'I mean about the fire in the barn.'

She elbowed him, aware he had intended her to get the wrong end of the stick. 'I shouldn't have done that,' she said kissing his shoulder. 'Not when you've been such a hero.'

'I presume we're still referring to the fire now?'

She laughed. 'We are.'

'That's a shame.'

Brodie turned to her again. 'Do you know I don't think I've ever enjoyed a shower as much as that one.'

Delighted to hear him say so but determined to mistake his meaning, Lettie took her time before replying. 'Why, because of the excellent water pressure we have at this house?'

'Exactly that.' He laughed. 'No. The water pressure needs some work. My shower companion, on the other hand...'

'Yes?' She wondered what he might say next. 'What about her?'

He took her into his arms slowly, and lowered himself back onto the sofa. 'I was thinking that maybe we could see how well we fit together without water being involved.'

She liked that idea. Very much.

He put his arms behind his head. 'So, what do you say?'

She lay on top of him, relishing their closeness and kissed him. 'Is that the answer you were looking for?'

'Almost.'

* * *

The following morning Lettie opened her eyes to see Brodie resting his head on an elbow as he lay facing her. 'Have you been watching me for long?'

'Only a little while.' He kissed her nose. 'Good morning. Did you sleep well?'

She didn't bother hiding her self-satisfied smile. 'I certainly did. You?'

'Yup.'

She pushed herself up to lean back against the headboard and peered at her alarm clock. Six thirty. 'I should get up.'

'Me, too.'

'Shall I make us breakfast?'

Brodie took his glasses from the bedside table and slipped them on. 'I can go and fetch some eggs from the barn while you shower, if you like.'

'Sounds like a good plan.'

She watched him as he ate, unable to recall when she had ever been happier. Brodie looked up and, seeing her watching him, smiled. 'You not eating?'

'I am.'

'What are you thinking?'

She wondered if he loved her as much as she now realised she loved him. 'I was thinking how cute you look in your spectacles.'

He pulled a face. 'Spectacles? That's such an old-fashioned word, but I'm glad you think so. My sister always teased me that they made me look like an eccentric professor.'

'I'm not sure I've ever had a teacher who looks as cute as you do.'

'I'm pleased to hear it.'

She sighed happily and continued eating her scrambled eggs.

'I hope you're not going to try and do too much heavy stuff today, in the damaged barn I mean.'

She shook her head. 'No. Joe mentioned I should call my insurance company and leave everything until an inspector has been to visit.'

'Good idea. I've been thinking...'

About her, she hoped. 'About?'

'Maybe you could fetch seaweed instead.'

'Vraic, you mean?'

His fork stopped halfway to his mouth. 'Sorry, did you say vrak?'

Lettie giggled. 'I said vraic. Vraic is what my dad calls seaweed. You grew up here, didn't you ever hear it called that?'

He thought for a moment then shook his head. 'No, but probably because my dad is a dentist from Kent and not a farmer from Jersey, so we never spoke Jersey French.'

'It's called Jèrriais.' She wanted to know why he was thinking of seaweed. 'Why did you mention seaweed though?'

'I was remembering my uncle telling me how there's often a lot of seaweed washed up onto the beach after a big storm. Maybe it's something your father collects for his fields?'

'It could be but I've never seen him do it.' She wondered if she had simply never taken enough notice and felt guilty to think that might have been the case.

'I thought you might be able to gather some for your fields.'

'You weren't thinking about anything romantic then?' She narrowed her eyes.

He pulled an apologetic expression. 'You don't find talking about seaweed romantic?'

'Not really.' She finished the last mouthful of her food. 'Were you thinking about helping me collect it?'

'I wish I could, but I know I have patients already booked in for first thing and I'm not sure when high tide is. You're going to have to get whatever you need to off the beach before it's either gathered by any other farmers, or washed out to sea again. Hopefully,

I'll be able to help you when I have a break but I can't guarantee it.'

She liked the idea of gathering seaweed and that he was thinking about how to help her. 'It's fine. I'm happy to get it myself. If you finish your work while I'm still there, then feel free to offer a hand.'

'I'll do that.'

Lettie fetched her phone and checked the time high tide was due that day. 'Bugger, I only have about three hours before it'll get too high on the beach. I'm going to have to leave as soon as I've checked on the animals.'

'I'd better get Derek home and change into clothes that fit me a bit better than these.' He took their plates and cutlery to the sink.

She looked down at his bare ankles and laughed. 'Yes, I think you should. You don't want any of your staff or patients seeing you doing your walk of shame home.'

He washed and dried his hands and walked back to her, kissing her. 'I'm not ashamed of anything we've done together,' he whispered kissing her again.

Neither was she.

37

BRODIE

Three weeks to go

Brodie pulled into his parking space behind his cottage and let Derek out of the car. He unlocked the house and stepped inside only half aware of the sound of someone's voice nearby.

'And where have you been all night, you dirty stop-out?'

Maddie. He closed his eyes momentarily and resisted reminding her that he was an adult now and could do as he pleased. He would much rather have been left in peace to change and spend time before work going over everything that had happened between him and Lettie over the previous twenty-four hours. Instead he knew he would have to listen to his sister lecturing him on either the state of his decor or try to prise out of him where he had been and who with.

He let Derek into the living room and turned to Maddie, forcing a smile on his face. 'Why are you here so early?' He made a play of checking his watch. 'It's only, what, seven fifteen. You're not usually even up at this time.'

'I had to drop Dad off at the airport at six fifteen and thought I'd stop off here on my way home for a quick coffee and a catch-up.'

'Is something the matter with Dad?' His mind raced. 'Mum? Grandad?'

'Will you stop rambling.' Maddie pushed past him and made her way to the kitchen. 'I still need that coffee. I thought we could discuss more ideas for decorating this place.'

He didn't bother to stifle his groan. 'Really? Now? Can't it wait for another time?'

She turned after pressing on the kettle and leant against the worktop. 'No, Brodie, it can't. This place is a disgrace. You can't bring girlfriends back here.'

'Girlfriends?' His mind wandered back to Lettie and he sighed. Then, realising his sister was giving him a quizzical stare, went to retrieve two mugs from the cupboard. 'Here, use these.'

'Well, if not girlfriends, then other people.'

'What other people?'

'Me, or...' She shrugged. 'Mum, Dad, or Grandad. I don't know who. My point is this place is dreadful.' She waved an arm in a wide arc. 'I mean look at it. How can you stand living here?'

'We've been over this already. Why don't you make the coffee while I shower and change and then we can have a brief chat about your ideas. Brief, mind you. I have to get to the practice soon.'

He saw his sister's gaze take in his clothes and her confused look when she noticed his bare ankles. 'Whose clothes are you wearing? What's going on, Brodie?'

'Nothing.' He pointed to the cupboard near her shoulder. 'The coffee is in there. I'll be five minutes.'

He ran upstairs and hurriedly undressed, making a mental note to wash and return Zac's clothes to Lettie as soon as possible. As he soaped himself, Brodie remembered what it had been like in the shower with Lettie the previous evening. Now wasn't the time to go there. He stood letting the water run over his skin and rinse away the soap suds, unable to believe how lucky he felt that Lettie was attracted to him.

'What are you doing up there?'

At the sound of Maddie's irritated tone, Brodie turned off the shower and quickly dried and dressed before hurrying back downstairs. The sooner he let his sister have her say about her plans for the cottage the sooner he could go to work and have some peace.

'Well, it's about time,' Maddie said indicating for him to sit next to her on the sofa. 'That's your coffee. I'm not sure if it's strong enough, but we don't have time to quibble. Now, about the decorations.'

He tried to take in everything she was saying but only heard the odd word and something about sage paint, seagrass flooring somewhere and taking all the paintings in the cottage to the auction along with the bedroom and most of the living room furniture.

'We can replace it all with something more befitting your lifestyle,' he heard her say. 'You don't want people to think you don't have pride in the way you live, now, do you?'

Tired of his sister's bossiness, Brodie took a sip of his coffee. 'I don't really mind what they think about this place, as long as they trust my veterinary skills.'

Maddie gave an irritated groan. 'You're impossible, do you know that?'

'I should do,' he said becoming amused by her bossiness. 'You've told me often enough.'

'Shall we just agree that I know best where decor is concerned and that you leave all this to me?'

Desperate to end their conversation and go to the practice, he agreed. He showed her to the door, calling for Derek to join him, relieved Maddie seemed satisfied and was about to go. Then recalling how free she could be when it came to spending money ran over to her car.

'I'll agree to let you have a free hand with the decorations, but I have a budget and if you go over that amount then you can cover it. Right?' It was the only way to ensure Maddie didn't get carried away buying things.

She scowled at him when he told her the pitiful amount that he had to spend on the place. 'I've no idea how you expect me to do much more than paint walls for that figure.'

'That suits me fine then because that's really all I want. Are we agreed?'

She rolled her eyes and sighed heavily. 'I suppose I have no choice in the matter.'

'Not unless you want to pay for it yourself.'

'Er, I'm doing the consultancy work for nothing don't forget.'

He patted her arm. 'I know and I'm grateful to you. And,' he added, 'I promise I'll give you a glowing review when it's all done.'

'And tell your patients how brilliant I am.'

'Yes.'

38

LETTIE

After seeing to the animals, Lettie decided to go back to bed for an hour. She had no chance of lasting the day without a little more sleep so set the alarm on her phone and closed her eyes. She was woken by her phone ringing. She reached out and picked it up from her bedside table, squinting at the brightness of the screen. She had only been asleep for twenty minutes.

'Uncle Leonard? Is everything all right?'

'I'm calling you to ask the same thing.'

She heard the panic in his voice and realised he must have heard about the fire the night before. 'Everything is fine,' she said then explained what had happened and how quickly the fire service had arrived to put out the flames. 'No casualties, thanks to Brodie the vet's quick thinking.'

He sighed heavily. 'That's a relief. I never would have forgiven myself if anything had happened to you or any of the animals.'

She wasn't sure why he felt responsible for them but assumed it was because he was her uncle and that he had her best interests at heart. 'I understand you're only trying to protect me, Uncle Leonard. I also know that it must be very odd for you, well, my parents too that I've wanted to become involved with the farm when I've never shown any inclination to do so before now.'

'I understand that your father's decision to change his lifestyle must have been a massive shock to you and Zac, and I wanted you to know that you must feel free to call me if you need me for anything. Will you do that?'

Touched by his concern, Lettie promised that she would.

'I'm sure you've already discovered that farming is very different to the life you've been living in London.'

Lettie pictured her beautiful clothes and hectic life that until recently she thought she was destined to follow. 'I know, but things hadn't gone so well over there,' she admitted, frowning when she thought of Scott and all the aggro he had caused her. 'And although I've never considered farming, growing up on a farm and watching Dad, Mum and you and Auntie Sue's lives going on around me, it's not as if I'm completely unaware of what this life is like.'

He mumbled something to himself. 'True. But watching someone doing something and carrying out the work yourself are two very different things, as last night must have shown you. Not that it is the usual sort of thing that happens obviously. I just wanted to remind you that I'm here to help you while your dad is away.'

It was reassuring to hear him say so, Lettie thought feeling slightly better. 'Thank you – I appreciate that.'

'I suppose I should let you get on,' he said. 'What have you got planned today?'

Lettie told him about harvesting seaweed on the beach.

'Good idea.' He went quiet for a few seconds and she wondered if he was thinking or whether she should say something to fill the silence. 'I tell you what, I'm busy for the next few hours here with the herd but I'll pop over to the farm mid-morning and help you put the seaweed onto the field. How does that sound?'

It sounded great. 'Wonderful. Thanks, Uncle Leonard. I'll see you later then.'

Lettie looked out of the window, glad to see how quiet it was after the storm. It had been a little frightening worrying about how the high winds were battering her crops, especially after the horror of the smaller barn being struck by lightning. She shivered at the memory, then smiled recalling how amazing Brodie had been during the emergency. She thought of Brodie and her stomach did a little somersault.

Her thoughts morphed into what might have happened if Brodie hadn't been there. No. She wasn't going to let herself go there. He had been there and he had been amazing. Now he had left and if she wasn't going to become an anxious mess she would need to find something to take her mind off the dramas the night before.

'Seaweed.' She quickly checked high tide again to remind herself when it would be best to go and collect a mound of it. She had a few hours.

Showered and dressed and after wasting twenty minutes attaching her dad's trailer to the back of his pickup truck, she eventually drove onto the beach. She wasn't the first one there but that didn't surprise her. She knew well enough how early some farm-workers began their day, especially at times like these when there was a time limit to a job that needed to be done.

Hearing a tractor engine, she looked up to see a large vehicle with a huge trailer and mechanical digger coming down the nearby slipway. 'Bugger.' She needed to hurry if she wasn't going to let them take all the seaweed before she had a chance to collect enough for herself. She wouldn't need as much as them as she only had to cover two small fields.

She heard amused voices and saw two men talking to each other and looking her way. So what if she didn't have their fancy equipment. Maybe she should have thought about hiring someone to do this sort of thing for her, but it hadn't occurred to her. Another lesson learnt, she realised.

Determined not to let her error or lack of equipment stop her, Lettie slung another fork-load of vraic onto the back of the trailer and wiped the sweat from her forehead with her sleeve on the back of her right forearm. It was almost 9 a.m. and she had already been here for an hour and still the trailer was only half filled.

'Urgh, why did I think this was ever going to be easy?'

No point in moaning to herself, she decided. She needed this for her small field of Jersey Royals. The tide was starting to come in and she was proud of herself for putting in this effort to make the most of the island's natural resources for her land. It was a relief that the storm had happened on a Thursday because if it had happened the following night she wouldn't be able to harvest this valuable commodity because it was illegal to collect the dead seaweed that had been washed up on the beach over the weekend.

After a while, she noticed the trailer was almost two-thirds full. Hell, this was taking forever. Next time she was going to have to ask someone to come and help her. Her uncle might even have his own equipment to come and do this for her in the future. It was something she would definitely ask him about.

She heard a male voice calling her name and looked up to see a dark-haired man with messy hair striding towards her carrying something. She peered at him then realised who it was.

'Joe?'

'I thought it was you,' he said grinning from her to the trailer and back to the fork in her hand. 'You've not loaded all this by hand, have you?'

'Why, don't you think me capable?' She smiled to show she was only teasing, then realising how knackered she must appear, groaned. 'Actually, I hadn't considered how long it would take me or how heavy this work would be.'

'The wet sand that gets caught up in it makes is even heavier than it already is. Here, this coffee and bacon roll are for you. I'll put mine in your tractor while I have a go at doing this and you eat your breakfast and catch your breath.'

She had no intention of arguing with such a welcome offer, and although she had already eaten that morning, it was several hours before and the physical work loading the trailer had made her hungry and thirsty.

'Thanks, that's really thoughtful of you.' She rested the fork against the vehicle and took one of the cups and a bag containing a bacon roll from him and watched him take his to the tractor cabin. Lettie leant against the side of the trailer and breathed in the delicious-smelling coffee. 'This is wonderful, thank you.'

'No problem at all.' He began forking the seaweed into the trailer. 'How are you after last night?'

'Last night?' she asked mortified.

Joe stopped what he was doing and turned to her, then seeing the look on her face smiled. 'I was referring to the fire, at the barn?'

Embarrassed that her reaction had said more about her relationship with Brodie than she was happy to share, she cleared her throat. 'Oh that. It was a bit of a shock. Thank you for all you and your colleagues did though with getting the fire under control so quickly.'

'It wasn't too difficult. You must have noticed the fire immediately and called us soon after because it hadn't really got hold too badly.'

'It was an enormous relief to see you all, and I appreciated you checking that I was all right before you left.' She took a bite of her roll then drank some coffee. 'Delicious.'

'I had hoped to ask you out for another meal but I couldn't

miss the way our local vet was looking at you at the farm last night.' Lettie opened her mouth unsure what to say to his comment. 'And I also saw the way you looked at him, so imagine that you two are quite close.' He indicated the breakfast. 'This might not be very exciting but at least this way I get to share a meal with you.' He gave her a cheeky wink. 'And breakfast at that.'

Lettie laughed, relieved Joe was keeping things light between them. 'This is very welcome, as are you.' She ate more and then, determined to change the subject away from her and Brodie, admitted her error in thinking the seaweed collecting would be easier. 'My expectations were a little ambitious.'

'You've done well.' He forked another load onto the growing heap, then stopped to look at her. 'I admire your determination. What you're doing is very impressive.'

Baffled, Lettie laughed. 'I can assure you there's nothing impressive about me or what I do. I'm just trying my best to hang in there right now.' She thought of the near disaster the previous evening.

'Anyway, what are you doing down here at this time of day?'

'I stopped at the café at the top of the slipway to buy a coffee and bacon roll and while I was waiting for them got chatting to one of the lads who is with those guys.' He indicated the men who had been amused by her efforts earlier. 'He was saying how there was a young woman doing the collecting by herself without any machinery and—' he stopped shovelling and smiled at her '—I instinctively knew it would be you, so had to come down and see for myself.'

'And you were thoughtful enough to bring me food and something warm to drink, unlike that lot who just found what I was doing amusing.'

Joe looked over at them now busily working the machinery before one drove off a tractor with a full load behind him, passing a second returning with an empty trailer. 'They're as impressed with you as I am.'

Lettie laughed loudly. 'I doubt that very much.'

'It's true,' he said with little certainty.

She was a bit full after her scrambled eggs not long before, but gratefully finished her food and drink then went to take the fork from him. 'Your turn to eat now, although yours is probably cold,' she added guiltily.

'It's fine. I'm always eating cold food.' He cocked his head in the direction of the seaweed. 'Anyway I'm almost finished. This will only take a couple more minutes, and then you can sit with me while I eat mine. Deal?'

A deal too good to miss, she decided. 'Yes, and one I'm happy to accept without argument.'

Unable to sit on the damp sand, the pair of them leant against the trailer as Joe wiped his hands on one of the wipes Lettie had brought to clean her hands. 'You're very organised.' He smiled.

'Not really. If I was I'd have planned better than to simply bring something to clean my hands.'

'It's fine. You've done it now and that's all that matters. Would you like me to come and help spread it onto your field for you?'

She shook her head, not wishing to take up any more of his day. 'No, that's fine, but thanks for offering.'

Once he had eaten, he looked at her. 'So what is the story with you and the vet?'

He didn't sound as if he was digging only curious, but still the question made her feel awkward and Lettie knew she was going to have to admit she had feelings for Brodie. 'We have become close,' she said aware that it was an understatement. 'It's been nice.' Lettie wasn't sure what to say really and, preferring to keep her private life to herself, didn't want to divulge much more than that. 'He's very busy with his practice and I've only got a few months to prove my worth to my father where the farm is concerned so neither of us have much free time.'

'I can imagine.' Something seemed to occur to him. 'I'm glad you're enjoying your time back on the island, Lettie.' His eyes twinkled mischievously. 'If I'm honest I'd rather you were spending your free time with me, but Brodie seems like a good bloke and I'm happy you're both getting on well.' He stood. 'Right, I'd better get a move on. Let me take your cup and paper bag to the bin on my way off the beach.' He indicated her trailer full of seaweed. 'And don't forget, if you change your mind about needing help spreading that lot just give me a call.'

'Thanks again, Joe,' she said grateful to him for his kindness. 'I'm very grateful for your help and—' she laughed '—for that delicious and unexpected breakfast.'

'It was my pleasure, Lettie. Hopefully I'll see you again soon.'

She waited for him to take their rubbish from the cabin and then, after giving her a quick wave, he ran along the sand towards the slipway and off the beach. She checked her watch and realised it was almost nine thirty, time to get back to the farm and get on with the rest of her day.

39

BRODIE

Brodie drove up the long driveway to Hollyhock Farm, slowing when he spotted Lettie in one of the fields. There was someone else with her. It looked like one of the workers. As he pulled his Land Rover over to the side onto the grass verge he realised it was her uncle. Brodie was relieved to see he was helping her make lighter work of the heavy job. He opened the door and let Derek jump out. 'Come along, let's go and offer Lettie some help.'

They were spreading the seaweed Lettie must have collected that morning but neither of them hadn't noticed him yet. He let Derek go to her, hoping it would be less of a fright to see the dog than if he called out to her. He saw her still, then slam the fork into the ground and open her arms to greet Derek.

'He found you then.' Brodie quickened his pace and joined them. 'Hello, Mr Torel.'

'Ah, you're the vet, aren't you?' Brodie nodded. 'My niece has been telling me all about the fire last night and how you rescued my brother's animals and I wanted to add my thanks to hers. It was a brave thing to do and we're all very grateful.' He smiled. 'Have you come to help us?'

'I have.'

Lettie beamed up at him, her arms around Derek's neck as she cuddled the happy dog. She stood. 'Good to see you. Finished work already?'

He raised his arm and showed her his watch, pointing at the face. 'It's 6 p.m.' Brodie took in the trailer that still seemed about one-third full. 'You've not been doing this since this morning, I hope?'

Lettie shook her head. 'No. It was so heavy when it was wet that after a couple of hours I thought I'd leave it to dry out a bit before carrying on. Then Uncle Leonard arrived and we did an hour unloading and spreading it, before he went back to his farm while I had to meet the insurance assessor for the barn. Then he came back, helped me rearrange the inside of the other barn so that I could accommodate the animals properly in there.' She wrapped her arms around herself. 'I still can't believe what happened last night.' Looking up at him, she added, 'It frightens me to think what might have happened if you weren't here.'

His arms ached to hug her. He stepped forward and wanted to comfort her but didn't want to annoy her uncle by being too familiar, so thought better of it. 'Don't think that way. I was here and everything is OK.'

'Yes,' her uncle agreed. 'Everything turned out fine in the end, so there's no need to upset yourself about it.' He looked at his watch and passed his fork to Brodie. 'Well, I should be getting back to my herd and will leave the pair of you to finish up here.'

'Thanks so much for helping me today, Uncle Leonard, it really was very kind of you especially when I know how busy you are at your own farm.'

'Nonsense,' he said kissing the top of her head. 'What are family for if not to help each other out.'

When he had gone, Brodie pushed the prongs of the fork into

the soil and opened his arms to hug Lettie. 'You really must try not to worry about last night.'

She stepped forward into his arms and Brodie felt her warm breath against his chest. 'I'm exhausted from all this physical work,' she said quietly and sensed it took a lot for her to admit as much. 'I don't know how I would have managed to do this alone after loading the seaweed onto the trailer earlier, and Joe helped a lot with that.'

'Joe?' He hoped his surprise wasn't obvious.

'Yes, he came down to the beach and brought me breakfast, which was kind.' She looked up at him and smiled wearily. 'Even though I had already eaten before I left, but it was thoughtful of him. Then while I ate he continued loading the seaweed for me.'

Brodie was glad to know she had been helped, even it was by Joe.

'I don't know, Brodie. I seem to wake up tired. Everything aches, all the time. I feel like I'm in my seventies rather than my twenties. I'm not sure I'm suited to getting up at dawn and working until dusk. Maybe I'm just not cut out for this way of life.'

'Don't be so hard on yourself.'

'It's true though,' she argued. 'I'm beginning to think that Dad might be right, especially with what happened last night and how close the farm came to being burnt down.'

Concerned to hear her sounding so defeated, Brodie took her by the shoulders, held her away from him and looked her in the eye. 'Now you listen to me. What happened last night could have happened to your father, or anyone else. And as far as what I did, I know you would have been able to get those animals out of the barn too.'

She puffed out her cheeks and shook her head. 'That's the point though, Brodie. I wouldn't have had the strength to pull those cows outside. They're too heavy for me.' She let out a sob. 'If you hadn't been here, they would have died. I know they would. They were too frightened to come out on their own accord.'

He wasn't sure if she was right but didn't argue. Enfolding her in his arms again he hugged her tightly and kissed the top of her head, soothing her as best he could. 'Try not to torture yourself about it. Everything worked out fine and that's all that matters, isn't it?'

'I suppose so,' she eventually agreed.

'Tell you what, why don't you go inside and make us a cuppa while I finish spreading this lot for you. You seem a bit overwhelmed today, but that's not surprising after the day you've had.'

She looked up at him for a moment before relenting. 'I am actually. All right. I'll do that. Thanks, Brodie.'

'No need to thank me, just get that kettle on.' He picked up the fork and began spreading the seaweed, waiting until she had walked several metres away before stopping and watching her leading Derek back to the farmhouse. Her shoulders were slumped and she looked as if she was carrying far too much worry. He needed to find a way to help her out with the farm. Time was ticking and it wouldn't be long until her cousin returned and she would find out whether or not she could keep running the farm. He could tell how much it meant to her and didn't want anything to get in the way of her dreams for the place.

He wondered if there was a way to help her. He began working again while he gave the issue some thought. Maybe he could contact her brother, Zac?

Or, he mused, maybe he should go and visit her uncle. Almost as soon as the thought had popped into his head, Brodie pushed it away. Lettie would not want him to go behind her back even if he was trying to help her.

He cleared the trailer and loaded the fork into the back of it, then drove the pickup and trailer back to the yard wishing there was something he think of to help her long term.

40

LETTIE

Two weeks to go

Lettie couldn't believe another week had flown by. One week seemed to merge into the other. She went to check on the cows, glad to see them happily grazing on one of the fields that were lying fallow between using them for crops. She passed the field following Spud, who kept stopping to sniff scents along their way. She was relieved how well they all seemed to be coming along. Her father had planted most of them, so she didn't really feel like she had much to do with their success, but she had kept them watered and helped with the last bit of harvesting of the potatoes the previous month. She had also looked after the animals well and had managed to get the knack of milking the goats.

Mostly it had been the warm summer weather that had ensured everything was ticking along well, she decided, grateful that there hadn't been a heatwave like there had been the previous two summers. The massive storm they had experienced had flattened one field of sweet potatoes and damaged one of the polytunnels, ruining the crop of tomatoes that her father had planted before going away, but at least the radishes and carrots looked almost ready for harvesting and seemed to have come through everything pretty much unscathed. More than anything she was relieved that other than their initial fright when the barn caught fire, all the animals seemed unfazed by their close encounter with disaster.

She and Brodie had continued taking their dogs for beach walks whenever she mustered the energy and he didn't finish at the practice too late. There was still the familiar flutter in her stomach when she thought of him and she realised the more she saw him the further she was falling in love with him. Lettie had never been one for casual relationships and although Brodie hadn't professed his love for her, she sensed by the way he made excuses to phone her, or pop round to the farm when she wasn't expecting him, usually with little gifts like the custard horn cake he had produced the previous day, that his feelings for her were deepening at a similar rate as hers were for him. She hoped so at least.

As they walked through one of the fields checking the crops were being properly watered, Lettie mused that it was a relief too that Spud and Derek got along well. She thought of Spud and his bossy way, always having to be the kingpin and dear, sweet Derek who was settling into life with Brodie very quickly. If she did stay on working at the farm and her and Brodie's relationship continued to flourish then it would make life a lot easier if the dogs didn't have an issue with each other.

She left the field she was in, taking hold of the end of the gate. 'Come along, Spud.'

The dog stopped sniffing whatever had caught his attention to the side of the crops and looked at her, his ears pricked. 'Hurry up, we haven't finished yet.'

He loped towards her and as soon as he was also out through the gate, she closed it. 'Back to the barns now.' He ran ahead of her, understanding where they were going, and it occurred to her how much lonelier it would have been not to have a dog as company. She had never lived alone before and was grateful to have Spud with her, especially at night when the old house made some unnerving creaks and other unexplainable sounds that a house of over two hundred years in age would be expected to make.

As she neared the back door, she noticed it was ajar. Lettie tensed. She would only leave the door open if she was staying within the yard where she wouldn't miss someone coming or going. She would never do such a thing when she intended going further away and for a long time as she had done when inspecting the crops. Her parents weren't due back for another two weeks and Zac was away working somewhere. Her heart raced as she tried to think who it might be.

'Spud, here!' She clicked her fingers and he immediately came to stand next to her. 'Wait,' she whispered, leaning forward at the sound of two male voices laughing. 'Hang on a second.' She pushed the door open and marched inside. 'Zac?'

'Hi, sis,' he said as she entered the kitchen, oblivious to the panic he had caused. He pulled a face. 'You don't look very pleased to see me.'

'I didn't realise you were coming back so soon.' She noticed Brodie for the first time. He, unlike her brother, looked rather shame-faced. 'Brodie?' She looked from one to the other of them unsure why they would be there. 'Did I forget you were coming?'

Had she been supposed to collect her brother from the airport and, forgetting, Zac had to call on Brodie to fetch him instead? Her anger turned to embarrassment. 'Did I miss something?'

She saw her brother and Brodie swap secretive looks. 'Guys? What are you up to?'

'Why should we be up to anything?' Zac protested, his arms outstretched.

She glanced at Brodie and cocked her head in his direction.

'Clearly Brodie isn't as devious as you, so I'll ask him. Well, Brodie? Am I missing something?'

His gaze shifted from her to his hands, then back to Lettie. 'It's not really for me to say.'

More confused than before, Lettie frowned. 'What isn't?'

Zac motioned for her to join them and sit at the table. 'I told Brodie I was concerned that Dad and Mum are due home in a couple of weeks and wanted to be sure you had the best chance of winning Dad over. I was hoping he might reassure me or come up with suggestions about how we could help you.'

She decided to ignore the fact he clearly assumed she wasn't up to the task and, trying to remember it was his childhood home too, she told him, 'I wish it was that simple. But I'm not sure I've had nearly enough time to prove myself to Dad, and, if I'm honest, to myself that I have what it takes to do this permanently.' She waited for Brodie to answer, intrigued to hear his thoughts.

'I know it's been overwhelming for you at times, Lettie, and it's not surprising. But you've done amazingly to keep all this going with little experience, don't you think, Zac?'

'I agree. You've worked tirelessly here, Letts, and I'm sure Dad will be impressed. I know Mum will be. You've certainly put in the hours from what I've seen.'

Brodie seemed uncomfortable to be included in the conversation, but she knew he had her best interests at heart and didn't mind Zac asking for his opinion. She pulled out a chair and sat, giving him a reassuring smile. 'Thank you both for that vote of confidence. I've done my best.' But was her best good enough? 'Although, I'm not sure how I can increase my chances in any way, Zac.'

'Hey.' Zac put a milky-looking mug of tea in front of her. 'When your boyfriend saw me at the airport just after dropping off his dad and offered me a lift to save me paying for a taxi, I thought he'd be the perfect person to ask for advice.'

Boyfriend? Lettie forced her eyes in her brother's direction, not wanting to look at Brodie who she sensed had been thrown by her brother's referral of him in that way.

She went to correct Zac then, concerned that Brodie might take any correction as evidence she wasn't interested in him, decided against it.

'Thank you, Zac. I appreciate you wanting the best for me and I am grateful to you.' She braved a look at Brodie, hoping he'd had enough time to recover his equilibrium. 'And to you, but I'm not sure what any of us can do. I honestly don't think I can work any harder or for longer hours than I am already doing and if that's not enough I'll simply have to accept it. I just don't have the energy to do more. Anyway,' she said wanting to sound more positive. 'I'm doing my best to try and enjoy every moment while I can. I know I'm lucky to have been given this opportunity. And, if I do decide this life is for me and Dad disagrees, then I could always set up my own smallholding.'

'How would you finance it though, sis?'

'I have absolutely no idea.'

41

BRODIE

Brodie was learning more each day how independent Lettie was at heart and had to admit to himself how much he liked that about her. She was a challenge in so many ways. He watched her as she began brainstorming a few ideas with her brother.

'Maybe you could have a word with Tina,' Brodie suggested, wanting to be helpful. Lettie and Zac turned to him, their curiosity obvious. 'I just thought that she seems to know everyone and might have a few connections she could give to you.'

Lettie looked confused. 'Connections? We already deliver to small grocery stores and help top up stocks on farm shops or supply them with produce they don't grow themselves.'

'I was thinking more about local restaurants, or smaller hotels. You could offer to supply them directly with seasonal produce. It would save them taking time if you deliver several times a week. Diners are wanting more seasonal food now, I seem to recall reading in one of the newspapers. I think it makes us feel a bit virtuous to know that we're following tradition some of the time – and that we're being environmentally responsible.'

'That's a good point,' Zac agreed.

'If your father saw you had increased the income in some way for the business, or had plans to take it forward that way, then maybe he might be more encouraged to keep you on.'

'Brilliant idea,' Zac cheered. 'I can chat to a few friends and see if any of them know of catering outlets who might want new genuine locally produced stock. I know everyone here seems to want to buy local.'

Lettie seemed to like their ideas. 'I don't think it's just here. People are far more concerned now about the distance their food has travelled before reaching them. That's a great start guys, thank you.' She beamed at each of them.

Zac leant back in his chair and crossed one ankle over his other knee. 'It's a shame you don't have longer to put all these ideas into place.'

'Maybe not,' Brodie said thoughtfully, hoping to keep the tone of the conversation upbeat. 'However, if you put some kind of plan in place and have it ready to present to your father, then he'll be able to see how much background work and planning you've been doing and it might go a long way to persuading him that you're the right person to keep running this place.'

She puffed out her cheeks. 'I hope you're both right. Dad can be a stubborn man when he wants to be and I know he trusts Uncle Leonard to continue with his life's work.'

She rubbed her eyes and he noticed how drained she seemed. 'You seem tired. We can leave this for now if you'd rather do that.'

She shook her head. 'No, it's fine. I'm picturing Dad and Mum enjoying afternoon tea on the ship, then an evening dancing in the ballroom. There's no chance either of them will change their minds about wanting to continue running this place,' she said sadly. 'Mum showed me the cruise company's website online before they went away.' She sounded more and more dispirited. 'I have a feeling Dad might have already made up his mind to get rid of everything apart from the house and immediate outbuildings.'

Brodie could tell she hoped she was wrong to trust her instincts in this case. 'Maybe, but they could be open to persuasion when it comes to the next step for the farm, and there's little point in wasting your energy worrying about that yet.'

'Yeah, sis. Don't assume you've lost. Not until you've spoken to Dad about it.'

'You're both right.' Lettie smiled at each of them. 'I had no idea quite how much running this place would mean to me when I first suggested I take over. It seems nuts now when I think how I always had to be practically forced to help out here growing up.'

'I'm the same,' Zac said pulling a face. 'Now I can't help feeling sorry for Dad and Mum. How disappointing must it have been when neither of us showed any interest in wanting to work here?'

Lettie looked thoroughly miserable. 'I know. I feel guilty every time I think about it. I love this place so much and have only been doing this for a couple of months. Imagine what it must have been like to dedicate yourself to this place and your children only having ambitions to leave the island at the first opportunity.'

Brodie watched the pair of them and sympathised. 'Try not to be too hard on yourselves.'

Zac didn't seem comforted by his words. 'With all due respect, Brodie, you haven't let your family down.'

'You don't know that, Zac.'

'You're a vet for heaven's sake. They must be very proud of you and all you've achieved.'

Brodie could see how his life choices hadn't impacted on his family in the same way that Lettie and Zac's clearly did, but, like his older sister Maddie, he had still chosen a different path to the traditional one the rest of his family followed. 'They are, very. But in my case my father, uncle, grandfather and great-grandfather were all dentists and naturally they expected me to follow them.'

'At least you're still in the medical profession,' Lettie said.

Brodie had never thought of that and now she had pointed it out he wondered why it hadn't occurred to him. 'I suppose so.'

She shrugged. 'The nearest I got to following anyone in my family career-wise was going in to fashion like my mum, although in a different area of it, and Zac didn't follow anything remotely connected to our family.'

Brodie thought back to how her mother and father had seemed with her when he had met them a few months before. 'I've seen your parents with you though, don't forget. I could tell they were very proud of the pair of you and I think that you mustn't lose sight of that when you worry about what might have been with the farm.'

'True,' Zac agreed finally before turning to Lettie. 'This bloke of yours has a point.'

Her cheeks coloured again and she glared at her brother. 'Zac, will you stop with the insinuations? It's childish and annoying.'

Brodie tried not to show his hurt. Was she embarrassed for her brother to know about them? He hoped not.

Zac reached out and rested a hand on Lettie's arm. 'Don't be so sensitive, Letts.'

She shrugged him off and, pushing her chair back, stood. 'Thanks for coming and trying to help, Brodie. I'm going to have to get back to work now.'

Brodie didn't want her to leave without knowing how she felt about the situation. He hated to think that rather than helping Lettie, he had worried her. 'Do you want to walk the dogs on the beach later, as usual?'

She pushed her chair close to the table and gave his question some thought, then nodded. 'Yes, I do. Shall we meet there at eight? Or would you rather come here first?'

He didn't mind, he was simply happy to know she wasn't put off seeing him by her brother's teasing.

'I can pick you and Spud up, if you like.'

'Great.' She smiled before pushing her feet into her boots. 'We'll look forward to seeing you both then.'

'Can I come?' Zac asked.

Before Brodie said that he could, Lettie shook her head. 'No. You've been annoying, as always and can go on your own walk to the beach.' She flounced outside.

Zac laughed. 'You see, mate? This is what you're letting yourself in for getting involved with my sister.'

'Zac,' Lettie shouted from the yard. 'Shut up.'

'She loves me really,' Zac said rolling his eyes and making Brodie laugh.

'I wouldn't be so sure of that,' Lettie bellowed.

Brodie stood. 'I suppose I should be going but I might see you later if you're here when I collect Lettie and Spud.'

'If I'm not here, I'll be at the pub.'

He was about to answer when Lettie marched back into the kitchen. 'You can forget about that too. Put your boots on, Zac. It's time you came and did something helpful around here.'

Zac's appalled expression made Brodie laugh. 'I'd go while you still can,' Zac whispered.

42

LETTIE

Two days to go

Lettie leant back in her father's chair at his untidy desk in the small room that passed for his study, unable to believe that they would be home so soon. Although she felt as if she had been working at the farm for far longer than three months, now their arrival was imminent she couldn't shift her nerves at the thought of her father's reaction to all she had done.

She checked through the spreadsheet she had spent days putting together detailing her ideas, the names of people who had agreed to become involved or help in some way, her stock, perceived times it would take her to grow or harvest a crop, and finally how much she expected to earn from the business each month.

She arched her back and yawned. It was almost seven thirty in the evening and it had been a long day. A long few weeks, she mused, spent either working on this plan or working on the farm. She hadn't even had time to take Spud to meet Brodie and Derek for their evening walks on the beach, but reasoned that Spud spent most of the day out with her on the farm following her around so didn't need to be exercised with a walk, even though they both enjoyed meeting up with the others on the sandy beach.

The plan needed to be perfect but she had been looking at it for so long now, checking and rechecking the figures and the order of each different idea that it was all becoming a bit of a blur and she had no idea how to improve it further. Would it be enough to persuade her father should he still had misgivings about her taking over Hollyhock Farm?

Her mobile pinged, bringing her fretting to an end. She picked up her phone and looked at the screen, cheered up when she saw it was a text from Brodie.

Fancy supper at mine?

Her stomach rumbled in reply. She did. Her brother had popped in earlier but had left to meet friends in town for a meal and a few drinks. She needed reassurance from Brodie and the thought of not having to cook for herself was appealing.

Yes, please. What time do you want me and where?

I have food for you and Spud, so I'll hope to see you at eight-ish. x

She noticed the kiss and immediately her mood leapt.

Great. See you soon. X

She saved her work and closed the laptop. Then, remembering the time, left the study and ran upstairs to take a quick shower and change into a clean pair of jeans and a T-shirt. As she washed her hair, she pictured her shower with Brodie several weeks before. A warm glow spread through her. He really was gorgeous. She began humming and, not wanting to delay getting to see him again, quickly rinsed her hair and washed her body. After towel-drying her hair she decided to leave the curls to dry naturally.

She parked outside Brodie's cottage, anticipation of what the evening might bring bubbling inside her. Seeing the curtains move back and Brodie's handsome face briefly at the living room window, Lettie felt a warm glow sweep through her.

He was outside in seconds. 'Well, hello there, you two?' He opened her car door. 'It's good to see you again.' He stepped forward, waiting for her and Spud to get out. 'I've missed you.'

Spud nuzzled his leg. 'Both of us?' Lettie asked.

'Yes, both of you.' Brodie leant forward and kissed Lettie on the lips. 'But you most of all.'

'I've missed you too,' she admitted. 'It's been odd not seeing you when I've got so used to spending at least some time with you every day, but I've needed to focus on the farm in readiness for Dad's return.'

'It's fine, I understand how busy things can get. The bookings have been increasing by the week at the practice.' He frowned. 'If it carries on this way I'm going to have to consider advertising for another vet to help me out.'

They walked back into the cottage, following Spud when he pushed past them to find Derek.

'How's your spreadsheet coming along?' he asked when they reached the living room.

'I'm getting there slowly. I'd like you to have a look at it sometime tomorrow if you wouldn't mind. Just to be certain I've included everything we discussed and I haven't forgotten any of Zac's suggestions.'

'I'd be happy to look at it,' he said taking her in his arms. 'If you email it to me we can go through it tonight.'

She shook her head slowly. 'No. I'd rather make the most of enjoying the meal you've prepared for me.'

'You don't know what it is yet.'

'I'll wait for you to surprise me.' She stood at the kitchen door while he put on an oven glove and checked how the food was coming along. 'I hope we won't have to wait too long to eat, I'm ravenous.'

'Good. There's a lot here. I think I got a bit carried away.' He indicated a small fold-up table leaning against the living room wall and two fold-up chairs. 'We can either sit there, or have it on trays on our laps.'

'Trays are fine.'

'I've opened a bottle of wine, too. So if you want to pour us a glass each and take a seat on the sofa, I'll bring your food through shortly.'

She did as he asked and as soon as she was sitting on the worn but comfortable sofa Lettie took a drink of her wine. 'This is delicious.'

'Thanks. I grabbed the nicest one I could find at the supermarket and hoped for the best.'

She realised the room looked a little different. The old faded, discoloured wallpaper had been stripped from the walls and several holes and small hairline cracks had been filled. 'Your sister's begun your redecoration work, I see.'

'She has.' He pulled a face and she suspected Maddie was trying Brodie's patience. 'Make the most of this furniture because someone is coming to collect it in the morning and take away the carpet from throughout the cottage.'

He carried through two trays, handing one to her before sitting next to her and resting the other on his knee. '*Bon appétit.*'

She raised her glass and saw there were two piles of boxes against one wall. 'Thank you for this. I imagine it's the last thing you needed to do when you should probably be packing stuff away.'

'I've been putting stuff into boxes for days now. Most of it isn't mine but was left here by Old Man Winter. I did ask him what he wanted me to do with it and he said he didn't care one way or another.'

Lettie suspected that the reply hadn't been helpful to Brodie. 'What will you do with it all then?'

He ate a mouthful of his food and thought as he chewed and swallowed. 'Well, Tina has offered to hold a small market in the parish hall next Saturday and most of it is going to hopefully be sold there. Anything that doesn't go will be donated to an animal charity and whatever I make will also be donated to the same cause.'

'Sounds perfect.' And generous she thought but didn't add.

'My sister wanted everything gone by now but I don't have anywhere to store it.' He rolled his eyes. 'I think she forgets that I also work full-time and am on call most evenings too.'

Lettie was beginning to think that having a laid-back brother like Zac was probably lucky. She couldn't imagine having to cope with a bossy, insistent sister who constantly thought she knew better. She took a mouthful of what she now realised was a chicken stew. 'This is delicious by the way. Thank you. I had no idea you were such an excellent cook.'

'It's one of the two dishes I feel confident enough to make for guests.'

'Tell you what, why don't you bring the boxes and any furniture you're getting rid of to the farm. I can keep them in the smaller barn until the market is held.'

'Are you sure?'

'I'm glad to be able to help.' She was happy to have come up with a helpful solution for him. 'I have loads of space and I'm sure Dad won't mind it being stored there when he gets back. It's not as if the decorating will take too long, is it?'

Brodie shook his head. 'No, and as I said I'll be donating anything that doesn't sell at the market.'

'How are you coping with your sister working on the cottage? Did you like her ideas?'

Brodie frowned briefly. 'I'm grateful to her for doing it, I suppose, because I might have simply become used to the place as it is and not bothered.' There was a glint of amusement in his eyes. 'I am concerned that this is going to be very different to anything I might have chosen though, and Maddie can be determined when she sets her mind to something.'

Lettie studied his face and had a thought. 'I have a feeling you can be pretty determined yourself when you want to be.'

He threw his head back and laughed. 'You know, you're not wrong there. It's probably why Maddie and I fell out so much when we were growing up.'

'And, if you don't like what she's doing, tell her. As soon as you see something isn't to your taste. She'll probably not like it but it's far less frustrating to find something out at the beginning rather than when you've completed the job.'

His amusement vanished and he turned to look at her. 'Are you still talking about Maddie, or how you feel about the farm and your cousin coming home soon?'

She realised he was right to question her. 'I was meaning your sister, but I think you're right about the farm. I'm anxious about what I'll do when Damon returns and I'm not sure if I'll be able to cope with living at Hollyhock Farm when someone else is running the place. It think it'll probably hurt too much seeing that happening. And, what will I do work wise?'

Brodie's expression changed slightly and for a second Lettie thought she saw a spark of hope but wasn't sure why. 'Is it because you don't want to leave the island?'

It was, but she realised for the first time that more than anything she didn't want to leave Brodie. 'Yes,' she admitted. She moved her hand to his and waited for him to take it. 'More than anything, I like what we have going on here and I'm not ready for it to end.'

He lowered his knife and fork and moved his table away from him, turning to her fully. 'I'm happy to hear you say that, Lettie, because I'm also liking what we have between us. I'd hate for you to leave Jersey and return to the mainland.'

Her heart fluttered and she placed the fork she was still holding in her left hand onto her plate and pushed her table back from her to give her space to turn her body towards him, unsure what to say.

He pulled her into his arms and kissed her.

Lettie melted into his kiss and couldn't bear to think that this attraction between them would ever end. 'I can't help wondering what I'll do if I don't end up running the farm? I've lived away from home for too long to want to live with my parents again, and I don't have a job I can go to, or any savings,' she added with embarrassment. 'I really am very disorganised and unprepared,' she added quietly.

She calmed slightly as Brodie looked deep into her eyes, eager to hear what he had to say when he opened his mouth to speak.

There was a loud banging on the front door, making Lettie jump. Derek instantly woke, Spud barked and both raced to the front door nearly knocking over her table, which was only saved from tipping over by Brodie's quick reaction catching and steadying it.

'That sounds urgent,' she said resenting the interruption.

'It does.' He stood. 'I won't be long.'

Spud came back to her side and she stroked his furry back as she waited for Brodie to deal with whoever was at his door. Hearing hissed voices, then footsteps, Lettie stared at the doorway waiting to see who it was, when Brodie led his sister into the room, his teeth gritted.

'Sorry, Lettie. The urgency was my sister, Maddie.'

'Hello, Lettie.' Maddie peered around Brodie's shoulder and grinned.

'Hello.'

Maddie looked at the tables and half-eaten food before grimacing and turning her attention back to Lettie. 'I hope I haven't interrupted anything.'

'Never mind that.' Brodie scowled. 'I'm trying to work out why choosing between two paint colours needs to be done right now.' He held up two tins Lettie hadn't noticed him carrying before looking over his shoulder at his amused sister. 'Why this couldn't have waited until the morning I've no idea.'

Lettie knew from experience how annoying a sibling could be and also how they knew which buttons to press to cause the biggest reaction. Clearly these two had their spats and she hoped she wasn't about to become involved in one of them.

Maddie groaned noisily. 'Oh, do stop whining, Brodie, for pity's sake,' she said walking over to Lettie before indicating their plates of half-eaten food. 'That looks tasty.'

'It is. Brodie's a great cook.'

'He is?' Maddie seemed baffled. 'When did you take any interest in cooking?'

Lettie realised she had said the wrong thing and wondered if there was a right thing to say that might not set these siblings off against each other.

Brodie held the two paint tins towards his sister. 'If I choose one of these colours will you leave us in peace?'

'Aren't you going to offer me a drink?'

'You're driving.'

Lettie could tell by the muscle working in his jaw that he was annoyed.

'I meant a tea, or coffee. Surely you must have those in your cupboards.' Maddie sighed. 'I can tell you're trying to get rid of me, little brother, but I've taken time out to see you and you could at least be hospitable. You're not the only person I'm trying to help with their home you know.'

Lettie saw Brodie's embarrassment at his sister's argument and didn't think she should be there while the two siblings were squabbling. The earlier romantic mood broken, she thought it might be a good idea to go home and try to get some much-needed sleep. She was anxious about her parents' return and decided it wouldn't hurt to go over her spreadsheet one more time, just in case she had forgotten something. She moved her table away from her and rose to her feet.

'Maybe I should leave you both in peace.'

Brodie turned to her anguish on his sweet face. 'Please don't go yet.'

She couldn't miss his disappointment but had made up her mind. 'I'll catch up with you tomorrow sometime,' she said and kissed him on the cheek. Then she turned to Maddie. 'It was nice meeting you.'

'Please don't go on my account,' Maddie said. 'I didn't mean to interrupt your evening. Look, I'm only going to be a couple of minutes, then I'll leave you both in peace.'

'I don't mind.' She did really but thought it the right thing to do.

'I do.' Brodie's voice was firm. 'Please. Stay.' His voice softened. 'We haven't finished our meal yet and you wouldn't want all my cheffing efforts to go to waste now would you?'

Lettie saw surprise in his sister's face and relented. 'No, I wouldn't want that to happen. Fine, I'll stay then.'

43

BRODIE

Brodie's irritation with his sister shot up. Maddie knew better than most how hurt he'd been after his previous relationship ended and that he wouldn't want anything to disrupt his growing closeness to Lettie. Not caring which paint was on his walls, he held one towards his sister. 'You can return this one to the supplier. I'll keep this tin here so you know which one to use on the walls.'

Maddie rolled her eyes and took the tin from his hands. 'Fine. Personally though I would have chosen the other colour, but it's your cottage and you the one having to live with it.'

Brodie clenched his teeth together to stop from snapping at her. Not wishing to give her any excuse to stay for a moment longer than necessary, he refrained from arguing and began leading her towards the front door.

'What are you playing at?' he whispered as soon as they were out of earshot from Lettie.

Her expression changed and she seemed a little shame-faced. 'I feel a bit mean now,' she admitted. 'But sometimes I can't help myself.'

'Didn't you see her car outside?'

'Yes, which is why I was tempted to come in.'

'Really?'

Maddie stared at him thoughtfully for a second. 'You're so secretive when it comes to relationships, and I just wanted to meet her properly.' She lowered her voice further. 'You were so hurt by Tiffany and I was concerned about you. Is that so bad of me?'

He could tell she was feeling guilty but wasn't ready to let her off the hook. 'You embarrassed me and I imagine Lettie too.' Seeing her amusement vanish, he relented. 'I'm sure Lettie and I will laugh over it once we've had a chance to talk.' He stepped back. 'Now, if you'll bugger off I'd like to get back to my food.'

'And your girlfriend,' she teased.

'Goodnight, Maddie,' he said determined not to be riled by her. 'I'll see you tomorrow if you need to ask me anything else about the decorations.'

'Spoilsport.'

He went inside and closed the door behind him.

'I'm so sorry about that,' he said relieved to find Lettie finishing her food. 'My sister can be a little bit...'

Lettie smiled. 'Annoying?'

'Yes.'

'It's fine. Zac can wind me up too, so I know how that feels only too well.'

He let out a relieved sigh. 'Good. Well, not good, but at least you understand.'

'I do.' She patted the sofa next to her. 'Why don't you sit down and eat the rest of your food and we can forget that Maddie ever interrupted us.'

He smiled at her, thinking how incredibly lucky he was to have found someone as calm and kind as Lettie. Seeing her relaxing in his living room, a plate of food in front of her and their dogs settled on the rug in front of the fireplace, Brodie realised he wanted this as his future. That he loved her. The realisation struck him hard.

'Are you all right?'

He closed his mouth, aware that he must look ridiculous. 'Fine, thanks.' He needed to tell her. Tonight. He scanned the messy room. This wasn't the place he wanted Lettie to picture when she remembered tonight. Needing to think, he sat down and slowly began to finish his food. It tasted of nothing.

'Is something the matter?'

Brodie knew he had to take his courage in both hands and admit his feelings for her. If she didn't reciprocate them then he would have to deal with that, but nothing would be worse than her thinking he didn't want to see her any more.

It was a beautiful evening. He had an idea. 'Shall we go for a stroll on the beach?'

'Now?'

'Yes. It'll help our food digest. What do you say?'

'Do you want to go to the beach, Spud?' Lettie asked, laughing when both dogs immediately sprang to their feet and barked excitedly. 'I think that's a unanimous yes.'

Ten minutes later, they strolled hand in hand as the dogs ran back and forth with each other. The moon was full and its light cast a pearly glow on the slowly rolling waves.

'This was a perfect idea,' Lettie said, resting her head against his shoulder. 'We should do this more often.'

'I was thinking the same thing.'

Lettie stopped walking and looked up at him. 'Is something troubling you, Brodie? I'd like to think you know you can speak to me about anything.'

He smiled. 'So says the most independent woman I've ever met.' He leant down and kissed her lightly on the mouth.

'You seem very thoughtful though. Is there something wrong?'

He didn't want her to get the wrong impression about his reasons for their romantic stroll. 'Only that I like you, Lettie. A lot. In fact, I'm falling in love with you.'

'You are?' Her hand fell from his and she covered her mouth with it.

'Yes. I love you, Lettie Torel.' His stomach lurched when he saw her eyes widen. 'I know, you probably think it's far too soon. Damn, now I've gone and ruined what we had.' He took her hand in his. 'I understand if this is too fast for you. Or, that you don't feel the same way.' He felt his breath quicken. 'It's fine if you don't feel the same way, or if this isn't what you want from our, er, friendship.'

His anxiety increased the longer she was silent. 'Lettie? Please, say something. Anything.'

'Sorry. I'm trying to think.'

If she was needing to think about things then surely she didn't reciprocate his feelings. His heart ached at the thought.

'Let's walk to the water's edge,' he suggested, desperate to change the subject and try to rescue their evening somehow. He began walking, reaching the edge of the sea, his breath catching in his throat when he felt her hands slip around his waist and her head rest against his back. Unsure whether she was trying to reassure him or let him know she felt the same way, he rested his hands on top of hers He felt her warm breath on his back and then her head resting between his shoulder blades.

'Dare I let myself believe that you might feel the same way?' he asked slowly turning to face her.

She stared into his eyes for a moment, her face lit by the moonlight. 'I do.'

Her voice was barely more than a whisper. He rested his hands on each of her cheeks. 'You do?'

Lettie blushed. 'I said so didn't I?'

More relieved than he had ever felt before, Brodie pressed his lips against hers in a kiss before taking her tightly in his arms and showing her just how much he loved her.

44

LETTIE

As their kisses deepened, Lettie couldn't help thinking how nothing she had ever experienced before remotely matched the feelings being with Brodie gave her. Brodie loved her; he had said so and she couldn't be happier. So much for swearing off men after her catastrophic relationship with Scott.

She realised she hadn't said the words. 'I love you too, Brodie.'

Brodie kissed her again. Remembering the dogs, he took her hand in his. 'Hey, boys. This way.'

'Look at them,' Lettie said, enjoying the sensation of his hand around hers and watching his muscular back through his T-shirt before lowering her eyes to the shape of his bottom in his faded jeans as he walked slightly in front of her. She could barely believe he had told her he loved her. Brodie Murray loved her, and she couldn't be happier.

She slipped her arms around his waist and he stopped, turning to her and kissing her neck. The intensity of his kisses sent tingling sensations through her.

'I think the boys have had enough exercise for this evening.'

Lettie nudged him. 'Is that because you'd rather go back to your cottage now and show me just how much you love me?' she asked, amused to know she was right.

'How did you guess?'

Back at the cottage, the dogs were given a treat and settled back in the living room. Brodie led Lettie upstairs to his room, closing the door behind them. She didn't think she had ever been happier than she was at that moment.

He pulled his T-shirt over his head as she watched for a moment before taking off her own top, then unbuttoning her jeans. She kicked them off and stood facing him in just her bra and knickers.

Brodie pulled her into his arms and the next thing she knew they were somehow naked in his bed and making love.

Later, as she lay in his arms, her right hand resting on his muscular, tanned chest, Lettie couldn't help wondering where Brodie had learnt to be such an excellent lover. Not that she had much experience, she mused, but the sensations he had caused in her were on a level that she hadn't ever imagined possible.

'You OK?' he asked kissing the top of her head lightly.

'More than OK.' She hadn't meant to say that out loud and cringed inwardly.

'That makes me very happy.'

She couldn't mistake the smile in his voice and was glad now that she had been more honest than she had intended. She kissed his chest.

'Careful, unless you want a repeat performance.'

Surprised, Lettie moved her head back and looked up at him. 'Already?'

Brodie grinned at her and tilted his head to one side thoughtfully. 'Maybe give it a few more minutes.'

They laughed and Lettie wondered what she possibly could have done in her life to deserve becoming involved with someone as perfect as Brodie. Not only was he kind, clever and adored animals as much as she did, but he was handsome and very, very good in bed. She rested her head against his chest again and hoped that what they had would last.

'Would you be able to stay?'

Lettie wanted to more than anything, but although she had fed and put the animals safely away for the evening, the memory of the storm and the barn fire were still far too fresh in her mind to let her feel relaxed about staying away overnight.

'I would love to, but I don't think I should.'

He didn't respond immediately. 'Are you worried about the animals?'

She nodded and explained her concerns. Then an idea occurred to her. 'If you're happy coming to mine, you're welcome to stay with me at the farm. I'm sure Derek wouldn't mind. He seems happy enough there now he and Spud have become better friends.'

She felt the cooler air on her skin when he flung back the bedcovers. 'Hey, what are you doing?'

Brodie kissed her shoulder then sat up. 'If we're going to go to Hollyhock Farm then we need to do it soon. I'm getting far too comfortable lying here with you and if we leave it much longer I won't want either of us to go anywhere.'

Lettie realised she felt exactly the same and got up. 'Shall we go in my car?' she asked and she fastened her bra. 'I'll need to be up early anyway and don't mind dropping you off after I've seen to the animals.'

'Sounds like a good plan.'

'Then that's what we'll do.'

* * *

The following morning, Lettie got out of bed as quietly as she could. She watched Brodie sleeping soundly as she dressed and wished she didn't have to leave him just yet. She crept out of her bedroom and down the stairs, whispering for Spud to follow her. Derek pricked up one ear and opened his eyes, then deciding he wasn't ready to get up, closed them again and was snoring before she closed the front door behind her and Spud.

As she dealt with all the animals, she thought about her parents' return later that day and felt nervous. How ridiculous was she being – so anxious about seeing her father again?

As she opened the chicken coops and watched them chattering to each other as they scuttled in an untidy group out of the barn to the yard, Lettie groaned. It was all very well trying to tell herself not to worry, but working here, despite the terrible storm and worrying constantly whether she had done all she could to care for the farm had been the most rewarding time in her life. Could she seriously expect to do this permanently? Did she have what it took? She hoped so. She hoped her father thought so too.

She finished her chores and walked slowly back to the farmhouse. The memory of Brodie in her room cheered her up and she quickened her pace. She needed to make the most of this short time they had together before he needed to leave for work. Deciding to take a quick shower and get back into bed with him, Lettie ran the rest of the way to the house.

The unmistakable smell of breakfast being cooked reached her nose the moment she stepped into the hallway. Lettie hurried into the kitchen and stood at the doorway watching Brodie concentrating on frying several eggs. She hadn't expected him to be up yet, but enjoyed seeing him so comfortable in her kitchen. Well, her mother's kitchen, she reminded herself quickly.

'I expected you to still be in bed.' She could hear the disappointment in her voice but hoped it wasn't too noticeable to him.

He looked at her surprised to see her standing there. 'Damn. Were you intending on coming back to join me?' He seemed cross with himself.

'I hadn't thought of doing that actually.'

'Good.' He laughed holding up a spatula with a perfectly cooked fried egg on it and lowered it onto one of the plates next to the Aga. 'I would hate to think I'd messed up your plans.'

Lettie went to the sink and washed her hands thoroughly before sitting down at the table. Realising she could offer some help, she pointed to the kettle. 'Shall I make us coffee?'

He shook his head as he served the rest of the eggs, then bacon, mushroom, tomatoes onto their plates and placed them down onto the table. 'No, I've got it all in hand.' He indicated a rack of toast in the middle of the table that she hadn't yet noticed. 'You just sit there and enjoy this breakfast. I'm hoping it is the first of many I'll get to make for you.'

'I'm holding you to that.' She ate a mouthful of her food and gave a happy groan. 'This is very tasty. Thank you.'

'My pleasure.' He made them coffee and sat down next to her. 'I'm glad you like it.'

'You're spoiling me.' She nudged him. 'But carry on. I could get very used to this treatment.'

'That's what I was hoping for.' He ate a few mouthfuls. 'I hope you don't mind but I fed Derek some of Spud's food.'

'Of course.' She looked over at the two dogs now sleeping again, their backs resting against each other. 'It's such a relief they get on so well, isn't it?'

'It is. It makes life a lot easier when the two of us like each other so much.'

Lettie sighed playfully. 'I thought you said you loved me.'

He narrowed his eyes. 'Is this your way of getting me to repeat what I said to you last night?'

'Maybe.' Lettie laughed. 'But don't let that hold you back.'

He grinned and shook his head slowly before lowering his cutlery to his plate and twisting in his chair to face her better. 'Lettie Torel, I, Brodie Murray can confirm that I love you. Will that do?'

She pretended to think about it for a few seconds, then nodded. 'Yes, for now.'

He leant towards her and gave her a peck on her lips. 'We're going to have to get a move on. I can't be late to open up the practice.'

Lettie looked up at the clock. 'I hadn't realised it was this late.'

He rested a hand on her forearm. 'Hey, don't rush your food. I only meant we shouldn't forget the time and start chatting, like we do.'

'That's a relief. I'm enjoying this far too much to hurry it.'

He really was perfect, Lettie decided giving him a discreet look, her stomach flipping over as she watched him enjoying his own food. 'Me too.'

Brodie looked at her and smiled. 'I feel very lucky to have met you, Lettie.'

'Likewise.'

'I was sure you'd be more interested in Joe than me, especially after seeing the pair of you together that night in the pub.'

Lettie had almost forgotten that evening then recalled her own jealousy seeing Brodie with Cathy.

'He looks like many of those film stars and pop stars Maddie had on posters on her wall when we were younger. He seems self-assured too, unlike me, but clearly a nice chap.'

'Joe's just a friend,' she assured him. Joe might be devilishly handsome with his dark, Heathcliff-esque looks and his easy confidence but seeing him didn't make her heart flutter and stomach flip like it did when she saw Brodie. 'And he doesn't make me feel like you do.'

He kissed her lightly on the mouth. 'I'm so happy to hear you say that.'

'Good, because it's true.' She kissed him. 'He also knows that you and I have feelings for each other because he told me that day on the beach collecting seaweed how he had seen the way the two of us looked at each other the night before.'

'Oh, I see.'

45

BRODIE

The day has arrived

Brodie had to concentrate harder than usual at work to stop his mind from drifting off to the night before when he and Lettie made love and then how good it felt to be eating breakfast with her at Hollyhock Farm.

He waved his final patient from the room and leant against his desk, trying to picture his future with Lettie. If their relationship continued to get more serious and Lettie continued running the farm, would she want to stay there or might she agree to move into his cottage with him? He liked the idea, very much. The cottage was closer to the beach as well as being conveniently placed next to his surgery. He decided to agree to whatever it took for them to be together. Supporting Lettie's new career was something he was determined to do.

Brodie decided that he would take each step as he reached it. He wanted this relationship with Lettie to work. He had once asked his father how he knew his mother was the woman for him and couldn't understand it when his father told him that he knew as soon as he saw her. Brodie realised that it had been the same for him. He might not have known how important Lettie would be to him when they had met that night at the school disco all those years before, but he had definitely noticed her, even if he had been too embarrassed to do anything about it. This time round though, he had known instantly that she was special. He hadn't known quite how special she would be to his future. He knew now though.

The memory of her face as she stood by the kitchen door earlier that morning and the look of disappointment that he was already up made him smile. He wished he hadn't tried to impress her with his cooking. Who knew what might have happened between them if he had stayed in bed and waited for her to return. Then again, he mused, how presumptuous would that have seemed for her to come back to the house and find him lying in her bed as if he had every right to be there.

He looked at his watch and wondered if her parents had arrived home yet and if so, what Mr Torel's decision might be about the farm. He could still insist on selling the land if he didn't trust Lettie to make it work. Brodie hoped Gareth Torel would give her the opportunity to keep running Hollyhock Farm. She had clearly relished her time there and Brodie hoped her father was open to letting her at least try to run the place and prove herself for longer than the two months he had given her so far.

Wanting to show her he was thinking of her, Brodie took his phone from his jeans pocket and sent her a text.

Good luck this evening. I'll be thinking of you. Let me know how it goes with your dad. X

He waited for her to reply but after a few minutes decided to go back to his cottage and wash the dishes that he had left in the sink from the previous evening. Was it only last night that Lettie had come to his cottage for supper? So much had happened since then that it seemed much longer ago.

He recalled Maddie interrupting them and thought he should give her a call. She might be very annoying at times, but she did have his best interests at heart and was trying to help him make the cottage more of a home. It wasn't his sister's fault that she had lousy timing, he decided with a smile.

46

LETTIE

No time left

She glanced at the kitchen clock for the fifth time that hour. Lettie had received a text from her father earlier that morning letting her know they would get a taxi home so that she didn't need to fetch them. Surely Mum and Dad should be home by now? she thought trying to keep the concern from her mind. She may as well do something with the extra time and decided to go out and double-check that everything was just as it should be in the barns. She had already given the house a vacuum and a dust, cleaned her parents' en suite and made up their bed with fresh linen. They would be flying back from Southampton, so it was only a short flight, but they would probably be tired from all the travelling and packing up their stateroom on the ship after living onboard for the past few months.

She tried to imagine what it must have been like to cruise around the world. So many new places to discover and explore. She smiled to think of all the photos her mother would have taken and how long she would have to spend sitting as she was talked through each one. A warm feeling ran through her at the thought of giving her parents a hug and seeing them again. She had been so focused on working hard to prove herself and now her father's decision that she hadn't missed them nearly as much as she had expected she might.

The sound of a car engine interrupted her thoughts and she looked up to see dust flying behind a large taxi. How many extra suitcases had her mother needed to buy to carry everything she had bought for herself on the cruise? Lettie wondered.

She whistled for Spud to come to her and he dutifully did as she asked and sat patiently at her side, waiting for the taxi to draw into the yard and park up. The doors opened and her father then her mother stepped out.

'Lettie!' Her mother ran towards her and they hugged. It was good to have them back again, Lettie decided. She stepped back and looked her mother up and down. Her hair was in a different, more up-to-date style and she looked years younger. 'You look amazing, Mum.'

'I do, don't I?' Her mother patted her hair and gave Lettie a smile filled with confidence. 'It's been an incredible trip, Lettie. We've got so much to tell you. And the photos I've taken.'

'Hello, Letts.' Her father pulled her into a hug and kissed the top of her head. 'Do yourself a favour and have a good night's sleep before you agree to start looking through all the photos. There must be thousands of them.' He gave her mother a cheeky wink. 'Only joking.' He turned back to Lettie and lowered his voice. 'I'm not really. She never stopped taking the damn things.'

Lettie saw the taxi leave the yard and counted eight large suitcases. 'How on earth did you get all these back? You must have paid a fortune in excess luggage.'

'Shush, don't remind him.' Her mother widened her eyes and

grimaced. 'He hasn't stopped moaning about it from the time we disembarked.'

'Right, you two can grab some of these cases and help me carry them upstairs,' he said lifting the biggest two and marching into the house.

Lettie followed her mother, carrying a couple more.

'Phew, I'm glad that's done.' Lettie flopped back onto the unmade bed in the spare room where they had left the cases ready for her mother to unpack in the next couple of days. She waited for her father to leave the room and whispered, 'I've loved it here, Mum, and I'm going to tell Dad that I want to keep doing it.'

Her mother had her back to her but Lettie noticed her stiffen before she turned to her with a sympathetic expression on her tanned face. 'I'm so sorry, sweetheart. I know this is disappointing for you.' She pulled out the dressing table stool and sat down. 'The thing is, Lexi, we're not sure we're even going to be able to keep any of the farm now.'

'What? You're selling everything? Mum, you can't want to do that, can you?' Her parents had lived here their entire married lives and not once had she ever expected to hear something like this. 'But why?'

Her mother stood. 'Come with me. This isn't something I'm happy discussing behind your father's back. We'll go and find him and he can tell you his thoughts.'

Dread filled Lettie as she accompanied her mother back down-stairs, finally finding her father sitting at his desk in his small study opening mail that had come in during their absence. He glanced at the invoice in his hand then noticed them come in. 'Ah, you want to talk.'

It was a statement rather than a question, Lettie noticed. 'If you don't mind, Dad.'

He put down the piece of paper in his hand and rested his

elbows on his desk. 'Take a seat, both of you. I've not been looking forward to this, Letts, but your mother and I have been talking while we were away and have decided to put the farm on the market.'

Letting the land go was one thing, but selling the farmhouse itself made Lettie want to cry. 'Why though?'

'Because we loved our cruise so much and decided that we want to make the most of the time we have left to travel more.' He looked at her mother. 'Isn't that right?'

'It is.'

Lettie felt her mother's hand on her arm. 'I can't believe you're willing to part with Hollyhock Farm,' she said close to tears. 'Zac and I grew up here and we all have so many memories of the farm. I thought you both loved this place.'

'We do,' her father said. 'It's just that if we're to finance our travels then we have no option but to downsize. You'd always be welcome wherever our home is though – you know that.'

'But nowhere else will ever feel like this place, Dad. There must be another way,' Lettie argued racking her brain to try and conjure up a solution. She thought of the long hours she had put into the farm for the past few months and began to feel annoyed. 'Are you tell me that everything I've been doing here since May has been a waste of time then? And what about Uncle Leonard? Or were you still thinking of selling the land to him and the farmhouse separately?'

Her parents swapped glances and she could see they both felt guilty.

'We know it's a conversation we need to have with my brother. I think it was going to be a bit of a struggle to buy the land from us, so I can't imagine he'd be able to afford the house and maybe not the barns,' her father said.

Lettie thought of her own brother. 'Does Zac know anything

about selling the farmhouse yet?' She doubted he could do but wanted to point out that she wasn't the only one who would be affected by this plan to sell their family home.

'No, he doesn't.' Her father shifted uncomfortably in his chair. 'We'll call him this evening and explain everything.'

She wished they could explain things better to her. Lettie stood. 'I need time to mull this over. I'm going to go out for a bit. I'll see you later.'

It took all her efforts not to burst into angry tears in front of them but as soon as she was outside she got in her mother's car and drove from the farm. With little idea where to go, she headed to the beach, wanting to be alone to try and come to terms with this unexpected change in her future.

47

BRODIE

The water was perfect and Brodie enjoyed every second catching wave after wave with the other dozen or so surfers who were making the most of the late afternoon tide.

As he rode one particularly spectacular wave, he reached the shore and noticed a lone girl sitting up near the beach wall. She had her arms crossed and resting on her updrawn knees, her head down. Was she crying? He hoped she wasn't hurt.

Wanting to help if he could, Brodie jumped off his surfboard and picked it up. Then, looking over to her again, he realised it was Lettie. His heart pounded. Brodie ran up the beach with his board, stopping in front of her. As his shadow covered her, she sniffed and looked up at him, wiping her swollen eyes with the backs of her hands.

'It is you.' He dropped his board onto the sand and sat next to her, putting his arm around her shoulders. 'What's happened? Are you all right?' What a stupid question, he thought. Clearly she was anything but all right.

Lettie sniffed again and, after taking a tissue from her shorts pocket, blew her nose. 'Dad and Mum are selling Hollyhock Farm.'

He struggled to take in what she was saying. 'Why?'

He listened as she explained what had been said and pulled her closer to him as she burst into a fresh flood of tears. 'I'm so sorry, Lettie. I know how much you love that place.'

'Just when I was thinking there might be some hope for me to stay working there too,' she sniffed.

He waited for her crying to calm slightly. 'There must be some other way for them to raise money. I've been trying to think of ways you could help increase income at the farm.'

'Go on,' she said wiping away tears with the backs of her hands. 'Do you mean ways to diversify?'

'Yes.' He hoped she didn't think he was involving himself in her business.

'Well?'

He could see she was getting impatient. 'I read an article recently on agritourism and wondered if maybe you could do something like that.'

'I'm willing to try anything if it means we can keep Hollyhock Farm.' She frowned thoughtfully. 'Now you mention it, I've heard of others doing it. Some local farmers have been doing that sort of thing for a few years. It's basically finding other ways to make the farm bring in an income, isn't it?'

'Yes, the article I read mentioned retreats as one idea. My sister went to an artist's retreat a few months ago and that was at a farm in Devon.'

Lettie nodded, looking much happier he was relieved to see. 'There must be a whole range of events we could hold there throughout the year.' She thought for a moment. 'I remember going to a place here when I was small that had an animal petting area, not that I think there's much money in that but at least the animals we do already have at the farm might entice school trips and could be used as part of an educational project.'

Encouraged by her enthusiasm for the idea, Brodie added, 'You could plant a forest garden. If you have any fruit trees, maybe picking fruit is another thing visitors could come and either help with, or pick their own.'

'You're right. Hollyhock Farm has the barns and stunning views so maybe it could be used for wedding venues or other events.' She pushed a strand of hair from her face. 'We're far enough away from our neighbours to hold music festivals. Zac could look after the sound as that's his area of expertise and I know he'd want to be involved in some way.'

'I imagine they would bring in some money, too.'

'Thanks, Brodie. I'll think all this through and talk to Dad about it.'

Happy to see her looking calmer, he held her again. Feeling a drip of water on his arm, Brodie realised his wet hair was dripping onto her. He moved his arm back away from her and ran his other hand through is hair to try and get the worst of the sea out of it. 'Sorry, I didn't mean to wet you.'

'It's fine.' Her voice was quiet. She sighed deeply. 'Do you know what, Brodie?'

He wondered what she was about to tell him. 'No. Go on.'

'I know my dad well enough. If he's made up his mind to sell, then that's what he'll do.'

It seemed a shame for her to give up so easily, but Brodie knew how determined parents could be once they had decided something. 'Maybe, but there's no harm in you making a few suggestions to him don't you think?'

'I suppose not.'

'And even if he doesn't go for these ideas, you could always offer to keep running the farm for him until he finds a buyer. Who knows, they might want to continue as you have been and need you to hand over to them. Or—' his mind raced '—maybe someone just wanting to invest in a farm on the island could be the potential new owner of Hollyhock Farm. They might want you to stay on and run the place for them?'

She didn't reply straight away. Lettie shook her head slowly. 'No. I don't think that'll work for me, not if the farm isn't in my family.'

Brodie held her closer to him, hoping to comfort her. He wished he could think of a way forward for Lettie that would make her happy and hoped her father would surprise her and change his mind after all. He said as much to her.

She brightened slightly and looked up at him. 'It would be amazing if he did do that.' She stared out towards the sea. 'They're going to tell Zac.'

She needed cheering up. 'How about coming back to the cottage? I'll have a quick shower and then maybe we can go out for a bite to eat. Try to give yourself a break and forget about this for a couple of hours.' He winked at her. 'Your parents must be tired from travelling and maybe by then your father will have had a rethink.'

She smiled and nodded. 'Yes. I like that idea.' It was worth a try.

48

LETTIE

Although supper followed by a lovely kiss and a cuddle with Brodie was fun, as soon as she left him and was on her way home again her mind was filled with worries about what she might be able to do to save the farm.

She parked the car and went for a short walk, stopping and sitting down behind one of the dry-stone walls to call her brother.

'Hey, sis, I gather Mum and Dad told you the latest about the farm.'

'They have.'

'It sucks, doesn't it? What's happened to Dad recently? It's like he's a different person with all this travel stuff and wanting to sell. I just don't get it.'

Lettie knew it was her mum's influence when it came to the travelling but she doubted she was as happy as her father appeared at the thought of packing up almost thirty years of stuff from a five-bedroomed farmhouse. 'Nor do I. I've been chatting to Brodie trying to come up with some way of changing their minds.'

She heard him groan. 'I'll try to think of something too. I'd love to help put your mind at rest. I know how hard you've been working and as upsetting as this is for me it must be doubly so for you.'

'Thanks, Zac. I knew you'd understand.'

''Course I do, sis.'

She heard her father's voice in the distance. 'I'd better go. I'll keep you updated though if anything changes.'

'Great. And, Letts?'

'Yes?'

'Hang in there. This isn't a done deal yet. Don't lose hope.'

Lettie promised she wouldn't and ended the call. She shivered. It was a cooler evening than she had expected. She pushed her phone into her back pocket and walked slowly back to the farmhouse. It was almost dusk and the warm glow of the kitchen lights made her breath catch in her throat. She had to think of some way to dissuade her dad from making a terrible mistake. But how?

Her father didn't catch her eye and, happy not to speak to him about everything just yet, she went to stand by her mother who was stirring gravy in a pan on the Aga and lowered her voice. 'Do you need any help?'

Her mother stopped stirring. 'No, thank you, but why don't you go and talk to your father. I know this has upset you and Zac, but it's not an easy decision for us either, you know. And it's especially difficult for your father because the farm has been in his family for generations.'

She wondered where he had gone to and found him in the living room trying to find something to watch on the television.

'Dad.'

'Yes, love?'

She took a deep breath. 'I wanted to talk to you about agritourism.'

He settled on a programme and muted the sound before

addressing her. 'I've heard of it obviously but why do you think it's relevant to us here?'

'I know you and Mum are ready to sell but while you've been away I've drawn up a plan with ideas to diversify and make more of an income in a way that I would find sustainable and easier to cope with.'

'You mean you're wanting to find a way to persuade me that there are other ways to raise money with this farm than selling it?'

Lettie almost held her breath. Her father had always been a private man, keeping his thoughts to himself and rarely feeling the need to explain his motives about anything he did, but she couldn't tell if he was angry with her for taking it upon herself to do this.

'Sorry, Dad, I know you don't usually discuss the workings of the farm with us.'

Her father studied her face for a moment. 'You've been crying?'

She wasn't sure why he needed to ask such a question. 'Yes. Why? Did you imagine I wouldn't be upset?'

He patted the seat next to him. 'I'm sorry, sweetheart. I can see by your tan that you've spent most of your time outside in the fields. It's a lot for you to have coped with, especially when you had hardly any prior experience.'

'I've enjoyed it though, Dad.'

He put his arm around her shoulder. 'I'm glad to hear that, but I wish I'd have known you had some interest in the place years ago. I'd never have considered selling if I'd thought I could step aside and let you take over.' He groaned and rubbed his chin. 'I've been so busy making plans for your mother and I that I've forgotten about your feelings and that's thoughtless of me. Come here.'

She did as he asked, enjoying the familiarity of a bear hug from her dad.

'I naturally expected you to be unhappy about the decision to sell this place. I've seen for myself all the hard work and dedication you've given this place over the past few months and I appreciate everything. As does your mother. You've done a great job. But we must consider our future, and unfortunately, as I mentioned earlier, we need to fund it somehow.'

'But selling, Dad. It seems extreme.'

He sighed. 'I know. If I'm perfectly honest with you, now I've been back for a few hours and spent time with the animals and walking around the fields and by the stream, I've been reminded why I love this place so much.' He hesitated and after clearing his throat continued, 'I have to admit I'm struggling to picture someone else living here. The thought that everything here could be changed is difficult to accept.'

Could Zac be right? She hoped so with every fibre of her being.

Hope coursed through Lettie. 'Maybe.'

His mobile rang and he picked up the phone from the side table next to him. 'Zac.'

Lettie waited while her father spoke to her brother briefly before his eyes moved left as he gave her a knowing look. 'Yes, she said. So you've both been discussing options? I'll chat to you later.' He ended the call. 'Zac mentioned those ideas of yours.'

Aware that she couldn't put off sharing the suggestions she had discussed with Brodie earlier, Lettie nodded.

'Do you want to tell me about them?' He gave her an encouraging smile.

Lettie began to explain her thoughts and noticed that her father seemed more enthusiastic the longer they spoke.

'I'm not so sure about the music festival idea,' he said eventually.

'Why not?' she asked, curious.

'Think of the outlay paying for bands, and whatever else there is. Security. Clearing up afterwards. I've seen news reports about the mess people leave at some of these music festival sites and don't want that for this place. And what about the animals?'

'True, I wouldn't want them distressed.' Lettie thought hard, desperate to come up with a lucrative suggestion. 'I know, how about farm-stay experiences. Like people staying at an Airbnb, but on the farm where their food is prepared for them, and they can help with the animals if they want to.'

Her mother interrupted their discussion as she entered the room with a determined expression on her face. 'Gareth, I've been thinking.'

Lettie knew that tone. It was the one her mother used when she wouldn't accept any argument. 'What is it, Mum?'

'I've been for a walk down to the stream and it got me thinking.'

Gareth raised his hand. 'Let me guess. You've decided you're not ready to sell this place yet?'

'How did you know?'

Lettie enjoyed the look of surprise on her mother's face. 'Because Dad was pretty much saying something similar.' She laughed, hoping she was right.

'What shall we do then?' Lindy sat on the arm of her sofa next to her husband.

'I suppose we have just returned from a long trip away, so maybe while we're planning our next one we can give ourselves some breathing space. I'll go and see Leonard tomorrow and chat to him about things going forward. I can't imagine he'll be too upset to discover you're still interested in continuing at the farm. I think he'll understand me changing my mind about selling it to him.'

'You're keeping the land now?'

'Of course. If you're willing to keep going here then I'd only regret it if I didn't let you continue.' He raised a finger. 'At least for the time being. To be honest, if we did decide to eventually sell this place it would sell easier with land. More opportunities for a buyer.'

He had a point. 'But you're still intending to sell?'

She saw her parents look at each other before he turned back to her. 'I think we shouldn't be too hasty. Maybe we'll give it a year. It's going to be a while before we plan our next trip anyway and, in that time, maybe we can put one of yours and Zac's ideas into action – and Zac mentioned Brodie has ideas too that might be useful. We can see how it goes.'

It wasn't one hundred per cent the answer Lettie was hoping for, but it was far more positive than she had expected only the night before. 'I'll find a way to make this place work so that your retirement can be financed,' she said determined to succeed.

She kissed her father's cheek, feeling enormously relieved when she got up.

'Where are you going?' her mother asked.

'To tell Brodie the good news,' she said, excited. 'He's seen how upset I've been, and I know he'll be eager to find out what you've decided.' She sighed. 'I also want to thank him for being so supportive and helping me come up with ideas to hopefully change your mind.'

She ran out of the house thinking that if she had thought she loved Brodie before, she loved him more than ever now that he had helped secure her home and business for at least the next year. Who knew what she might come up with in that time.

She arrived at his cottage, realising he must have been waiting for her when he immediately ran outside to greet her.

'Well?' he asked holding her by the shoulders and staring into her eyes.

'He's changed his mind, for now at least. I have a year to see how it goes.'

He pulled her into his arms and hugged her tightly. 'That's brilliant, Lettie, I knew you could do it.'

'It's not the perfect ending, but it's a good start.'

He let go of her, and taking her face in his, smiled at her then leant forward and kissed her. 'It's a perfect start. I know you'll achieve great things in the coming year.'

'You really think so?' she asked, knowing he was telling the truth.

'I do.' He kissed her again. 'And you won't be alone. I'll be here for you whenever you need me.'

'I know you will.'

Lettie thought about how much had changed in her life in the past three months since her return to the island. She could never have envisaged how much this farm would mean to her, or that she and Brodie would finally get together and fall in love. She slipped her arms around his neck and kissed him. As his arms tightened around her and he kissed her back, her heart soared.

She had so much to be grateful for. She was still running Hollyhock Farm and she and Brodie were together. Finally. And she couldn't wait to find out what the next twelve months had in store for them.

ACKNOWLEDGEMENTS

I'd like to thank my amazing family for always being there for me.

Thank you to my wonderful editor, Rachel Faulkner-Wilcocks who has helped make this book a much better version than it might have been, also my copy-editor, Helena Newton for picking up any continuity errors and for her suggestions and to Sandra Ferguson for proofreading *Welcome to Hollyhock Farm*.

Thank you to the brilliant team at Boldwood Books, for another beautiful cover and for all that they do to support their authors, I'm delighted to be one of them.

My thanks also to Rachel Gilbey from Rachel's Random Resources and her excellent team for reviewing my books on the blog tour. I'm always grateful for their amazing quotes.

Finally, I'd like to thank you for choosing this book, I hope you have enjoyed my first book in this new series.

AUTHOR LETTER

Dear Reader,

It's always exciting, although a little nerve-wracking to write the first book in a new series. I've loved spending time at Hollyhock Farm and hope you enjoyed getting to know Lettie, Zac, Brodie, Joe, Bethan, Tina and Uncle Leonard, and of course, Spud and Derek, as well as all the other characters who will be making appearances in future books.

I grew up next-door to a farm here in Jersey and spent many happy hours wandering across the fields to go and play there with my sister, Kate when we were children. Although Hollyhock Farm is fictional, there are many beautiful farms here built with the traditional Jersey granite, which ranges from shades of pink to grey across the island, just like the farmhouse and barns in my book.

I've set the farm up the hill from St Ouen's bay, where I often walk my dogs. Like my vet, Brodie many surfers can be seen taking to the waves at the beach whenever the tide is right. My inspiration for the veterinary surgery came from various similar ones on the island, just like the small characterful cottage where Brodie lives. The pub is a cross between the Farmer's Inn in St Ouen's village and

The Priory at Devil's Hole, both of which are very different to each other, but have a traditional feel about them that I wanted to evoke in *Welcome to Hollyhock Farm*.

I hope you've enjoyed your first visit to Hollyhock Farm and look forward to hearing what you think about my new series and the characters.

Until next time, I wish you happy reading and warm wishes from sunny Jersey.

Georgina x

ABOUT THE AUTHOR

Georgina Troy writes bestselling uplifting romantic escapes and sets her novels on the island of Jersey, where she was born and has lived for most of her life.

Sign up to Georgina Troy's mailing list for news, competitions and updates on future books.

Visit Georgina's website: https://deborahcarr.org/my-books/georgina-troy-books/

Follow Georgina on social media here:

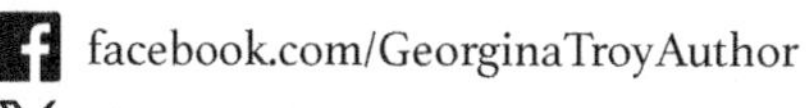
facebook.com/GeorginaTroyAuthor

x.com/GeorginaTroy

instagram.com/ajerseywriter

bookbub.com/authors/georgina-troy

ALSO BY GEORGINA TROY

The Sunshine Island Series

Finding Love on Sunshine Island

A Secret Escape to Sunshine Island

Chasing Dreams on Sunshine Island

The Golden Sands Bay Series

Summer Sundaes at Golden Sands Bay

Love Begins at Golden Sands Bay

Winter Whimsy at Golden Sands Bay

Sunny Days at Golden Sands Bay

Snow Angels at Golden Sands Bay

Sunflower Cliffs Series

New Beginnings by the Sunflower Cliffs

Secrets and Sunshine by the Sunflower Cliffs

Wedding Bells by the Sunflower Cliffs

Coming Home to the Sunflower Cliffs

Hollyhock Farm Series

Welcome to Hollyhock Farm

LOVE NOTES

LOVE IN EVERY CHAPTER